IDENTITY

IDENTITY: A SMOKE & MIRRORS BOOK - 3

Copyright © 2013, 2017 by H. D. Thomson

Previously published as Shrouded in Illusion in 2013 by Bella Media Management

Published by Bella Media Management.

CHAPTER ONE

"NO ONE MOVE! You! Get away from the door."

Skye Hunter snapped her head up from looking inside her purse and gaped at a tall, bald-headed man several yards away. In his tight-fisted hand, he pointed a gun at her chest.

She blinked. For a moment she didn't understand. Then panic crashed through her body, and her breath hitched painfully inside her throat.

My God. Tyler.

She whipped her gaze across the inside of the convenience store. Aisles of chips, dip, and candy, but no sign of her nine-year-old son.

They'd been separated but minutes. While he'd gone to get a hotdog, she'd run into the restroom. And now this sick nightmare.

The acrid taste of bile bubbled up her throat. Savagely, she swallowed it down. She needed her wits. For Tyler, for herself.

"Didn'cha hear him, bitch!" Another man, short and stocky, stood in front of the counter and several feet to the side of the other robber. Acne scars spattered most of his face, while his eyes, black, small and closely set, regarded her with rage.

"Okay, okay." She jerked her hands into the air. Her purse, its straps sliding along her arm, swung wildly and banged against her side. "Just don't shoot."

Great. They'd fled the violence in Boston only to encounter it here in Las Vegas.

Tension cut into every muscle and tendon across her back and shoulders. Skye stared past both men to the front door and freedom. Seeing no sign of Tyler through the glass panels, she inched away from the counter and register.

Another empty aisle without Tyler.

Where the hell is he?

"Are you an idiot?" the bald thug asked the clerk, a boy not much older than twenty. "Open the damn drawer."

"No."

In horror, Skye stared at the redheaded clerk as she eased further from the trio and the front door. The kid was crazy. These men weren't playing around. Agitation and fury radiated from both. Neither of them wore masks to hide their identities, screaming their recklessness, stupidity or savage intent.

"The cash, asshole. Now," the acne-faced thief growled, shoving his greasy, black hair from his face.

"I can't believe this shit." The kid shook his head. "Second time this week. If you think—"

"Shut up, you fuck!" The bald thug lashed out at a display rack with the flat of his hand, pitching packets of energy pills across the counter and onto the floor. "Give him the money. Now! Before one of us blows your mother-fucking head off!"

A new wave of panic rolled through Skye's body as she edged further away. Tyler had to be somewhere. He'd never run off voluntarily. She glanced past the surveillance camera to the far corner of the store and the convex mirror, which reflected the back section of the room.

There. Partially hidden behind the counter of the store's coffee bar in the back corner, a figure huddled on the floor. Tyler. Relief turned her limbs unsteady, but that relief mingled with a new fear. If she could see him in the mirror, the robbers could do the same.

"Where the hell do you think you're going?"

Skye jerked her gaze back to the acne-faced thug now glaring at her. She couldn't believe she'd dragged Tyler into this mess. "Nowhere."

"Don't give me that shit. I saw you."

"No. You've got it wrong." She lifted her arms higher. "I didn't—" Horror strangled the rest of the words from her throat. Two brainless thugs weren't going to end her life and that of her son in some sick parody of random violence. Not when she'd managed to elude far smarter killers.

The thug lifted his gun and aimed at Skye's head. Her peripheral vision faded as she stared at the gun. It gleamed silver-gray beneath the fluorescent light. From this angle, she could see the man's blunt, dirty fingers around the gun's handle. His index finger rested across the trigger, then flexed.

"Don't!" She dropped her hands and lurched to the side.

The thug pulled the trigger.

The gun jammed.

The thug tried again.

Again, nothing happened.

"Bitch!" The acne-faced thug hurled the gun at her and charged.

Tensing, Skye glanced at the display case of sunglasses and watched it tilt and crash in front of him. Unable to slow his momentum, he stumbled over the case. Plastic cracked. Metal twisted and bent. Hands outstretched, he fell, slamming his head and stomach into the case. Then he landed on the floor with a groan.

He didn't get up.

A gun blast ripped through the store. A bag of chips exploded by her head. Skye ducked. These guys weren't giving up. She scrambled wildly across the floor and glanced over her shoulder. As the bald robber fired at her and missed again, the clerk behind the counter bent down and came back up with a baseball bat.

The clerk swung. The metal bat smacked against the side of the bald robber's head with a sickening whack. The thug dropped to his knees and dove forward until his face slapped against the floor. He stayed down.

Skye gulped in a lungful of air, peered down the aisle to the security mirror and found Tyler still crouched behind the coffee bar. Thank God, he'd stayed hidden and hadn't tried to save her or the situation.

The clerk rubbed his palms against his shirt and glanced at the short robber sprawled on the floor by Skye's feet before meeting her gaze. "Are you all right?"

"Yeah. Their guns." Skye nodded in the direction where she'd seen the stocky man toss his. She wasn't going to put her prints on anything. "You might want to get them before either one comes to."

Not about to wait around for the police to arrive, Skye hurried to the counter where she'd seen Tyler in the surveillance mirror. With his arms wrapped around his drawn up knees, he huddled there on the floor. He wore a pair of beige shorts and a white t-shirt, neither of which showed signs of blood or tears.

Her baby was going to be okay. They both were.

A tide of relief washed over her, and with it, her legs started to shake beneath her weight. She caught the counter with one hand and took in a breath, forcing herself to calm down and focus. She couldn't afford to react now. Maybe later when she was alone with her son safely asleep for the night.

Fear glittered in his large, brown eyes. "Are they—are they gone?"

She offered her hand and whispered, "They're unconscious, but we need to get out of here now. They might wake up at any second."

Tyler jumped up and grabbed her hand. Silently, she guided him along the perimeter of the store and to the front entrance, avoiding both unconscious men.

"This security system's a piece of crap," the clerk said into a phone as she and her son reached the door. "I hit the button ages ago and still no cop. I could be dead for all anyone cares."

While the cashier, his attention focused on the two men sprawled across the floor, had his back to them, Skye eased open the front door with a shoulder and guided her son outside.

A hot July sun burned from above. Used to Boston's milder

weather, Skye found the intense heat of Vegas daunting as she urged Tyler to hurry across the sidewalk.

Skye and her son made it to her truck. Once inside with the doors locked and her son buckled in his seat, Skye backed out and guided the truck onto the street. The air-conditioner blasted cold air against her bare arms as they headed west and away from the robbery, but she didn't relax. The howl of a siren penetrated the truck's interior. The sound swelled, then slowly, surely, as Skye continued to put distance between themselves and the store, the siren's wail dimmed and melded with the other city noises.

She glanced over at Tyler, who wiped a tear from his cheek with a forearm and exhaled in one loud, ragged breath.

Guilt caught at her heart and twisted as she reached over and squeezed his arm. "We'll be okay."

"You always say that."

"Things will be different. You'll see."

She couldn't blame Tyler for not believing her. Why would he? Nothing had changed these last two years. They were still not okay. Still moving from city to city with no stability or security.

Now this latest trauma.

Somehow Tyler had kept his head and known when to keep quiet. But then, he'd had experience on his side. Few adults—never mind nine-year-old kids—had to deal with what he'd been handed these last couple of years. Thank God they'd gotten out of there alive. She didn't know what she would have done if Tyler—

No. She couldn't think that way. Instead, she'd focus on what she needed to do later in the week. Find the nerve to meet David Bishop and make that meeting look like a chance encounter. Thoughts about Bishop didn't make her feel better. The man was an enigma and could prove more dangerous than the thugs with a gun.

"I'm hungry," Tyler complained.

"Then how about we get that hotdog I promised you?"

"I don't want a hotdog anymore."

Skye nodded in complete understanding. "I've got a better

idea. Why don't we get something to eat at the Sphinx? Jamie will probably be working, and we can say 'hi.' Sound good?"

"Yeah."

"We'll have a hotdog another time."

But Skye didn't think they'd want a hotdog any time soon. She'd always known they were unhealthy, but until today, she'd never thought of them as downright lethal.

Twenty-minutes later, Skye turned down Las Vegas Boulevard toward The Pharaoh, one of the larger, more prestigious casinos along the Las Vegas strip. Over a month now, she'd stayed there in a room with Tyler and watched one of the hotel's star attractions, David Bishop. *Not the most ideal living conditions, but it beat the street.*

After parking, they entered the casino and headed for the Sphinx on the second floor. They arrived before the dinner rush and the hostess immediately led them to a booth in Jamie's section. Tyler liked the place because two huge, but fake sarcophaguses stood on either side of the entrance and hieroglyphics filled the metallic gold walls. And of course, Jamie worked there.

"Well, who do we have here?" Jamie, tanned, bleached blonde, sleek and sexy in black pants and a low cut white blouse, grinned down at them. She leaned over and tweaked Tyler's chin with a knuckle. "Hey, sweet cheeks. I see you're looking as cute as ever."

"Hi." Tyler rolled his eyes and flushed before he ducked behind his menu.

Skye hid a smile. On some things, her son acted very normal.

She opened her menu, looked at the items with little interest, then glanced up at Jamie. "How are your college classes going?"

"So far, so good."

"Getting all As then?"

Jamie shrugged a shoulder, her gray eyes darkening. "It's expensive and harder than I thought. Then I made the stupid mistake of taking summer school, which is worse when it comes to cramming in homework, exams..."

Skye gave Jamie's an encouraging smile. "It'll get easier. Just give yourself more time, and you'll see. It's tough going back to school while raising a boy. I remember. At least for the most part, I wasn't doing it alone as a single mother."

"But you are raising a child on your own now."

"Yes, well, so I am." Shifting in her seat, Skye cleared her throat and stared at her menu. "I guess we'll have pizza and ice water. Sound good to you, Ty?"

Above the menu, the top of Tyler's head nodded.

"Then pizza it is." Jamie flapped her order pad at them before moving to a couple down the aisle.

After their pizza arrived, Skye took a bite, chewed and forced herself to swallow. Tyler's appetite looked as dismal as her own, the way he picked the pepperoni off his slice and piled them into a short tower on one side of his plate.

"I know how frightened you must have been at the store."

"I don't want to talk about it."

"Fine." But Skye remembered other moments in their past when she hadn't been able to stop him from talking. My God, those days seemed more of a figment of someone else's life.

Several minutes later, Jamie came over and placed the bill on the table by Skye. "I see the pizza wasn't much of a hit. Want me to box it up?"

Skye thought of the small refrigerator in their hotel room, but then she eyed the pizza's congealed cheese. "Maybe next time."

"Can I pay the bill?"

Skye met Tyler's eager brown eyes, and then glanced around the restaurant with its open floor plan. The cash register, visible from their table, rested to the left of the restrooms, while the diners, tourists and little else, populated only a few tables. At least no one looked like some crazed wacko out to get them.

"Sure." Amazing how confident she sounded. "Just don't wander off."

Tyler rolled his eyes and scrambled from the table.

With a crease between her finely drawn brows, Jamie slipped into his vacant seat. "Hey, are you okay? I wanted to ask earlier, but Tyler was around."

"I'm fine." Skye didn't want to get into any detailed explanations. Yeah, she might look like the Grim Reaper from ducking a couple of bullets, but no one else needed to know it. She wanted her life to stay private—one of the reasons why she'd slipped from the store before the police arrived.

"Well, you don't look good. You couldn't get much whiter when you first walked in, and right now your color isn't much better." Jamie tapped a manicured nail against the table. "You know, if you're worried about being low on cash, that offer still stands. With your looks, Roger'll hire you on the spot. You could bring in some decent money. The tips are really good here, even better when the customers have had a couple of drinks."

"No thanks. I'm fine right now."

"Hey, if I could make a living off gambling, I'd be doing the same. I've met a few pros in my time, but they always seemed to have a cigar in one hand and a drink in the other."

"I've never liked cigars."

Jamie winked. "Oh, it depends on where you put them."

Skye lifted a brow.

Jamie laughed, a loud, full-bodied sound Skye suspected turned many a male head if her figure and face didn't do it on the first look.

When Jamie started to rise, Skye said, "Oh, while I've got you here, I wanted to ask you for a favor."

Jamie sank back down. "Shoot."

Skye tensed. 'Shoot' wasn't exactly a word she appreciated at the moment. "Can you watch Tyler later this week? I forget which night you're off."

"Crap, I have a hard enough time remembering myself with the way Roger changes the schedule all over the place. But if my mind hasn't completely gone down the toilet, I've got Thursday off." She stood and brushed the creases from her pants. "You know, I'm always happy to have Tyler come over. He's like my very own babysitter. With him around, I don't have to constantly entertain Houston and keep him away from the video games."

"Thanks. It means a lot." Far more than Skye was willing to admit aloud. When it came to having her son in a safe, secure environment, she'd lucked out at finding Jamie, a woman who dripped 'normal' in every aspect of her life—something Skye envied, craved and hoped to somehow achieve.

"You betcha," Jamie said and walked away to take care of a customer.

Skye sighed. Thursday might turn out to be *the* night she finally faced David Bishop—something she dreaded, yet desperately needed. The evening would also bring in some cash—just in time to pay for their room and keep Tyler and herself off the street for another month.

But she was too exhausted to think about that now, and because Tyler was equally exhausted, they went up to their room on the eighth floor and stayed there for the remainder of the evening. After she finished taking a quick shower, she stepped from the bathroom and into the adjoining room to find Tyler on her bed in a position much like a mummy inside one of the sarcophaguses he found so fascinating. The blue-white tint of the television cast an eerie glow across the room and Tyler's inscrutable features.

She frowned. "Is everything okay?"

"Can I sleep with you, tonight?"

She glanced at the two queen-sized beds. Merely feet separated the two. Then memories, violent and vivid, flooded Skye's mind. The gunshots, the anger, and rage from both robbers, the possibility of dying—all traumatic for an adult, never mind a nine-year-old boy.

"Of course."

"And can we keep the TV on?"

"I don't have a problem with that." She put her dirty clothes in a bag inside the hotel's bureau. "I wanted to tell you how proud I was of you and how you reacted."

"I didn't do anything."

"I know, but you were—"

"I don't want to talk about it."

Skye nodded abruptly, unable to shake off the savage prongs of guilt. Too many times she'd thrust Tyler into situations he had no business being a participant in, no matter how coincidental. "But you do know I'm here if—"

"I said—"

"Okay. Okay. I'll drop the subject." But one of these days, she wasn't going to be dismissed.

Skye slipped under the covers beside Tyler. With tentative fingers, she clasped his hand. Suddenly, he rolled toward her and wrapped his arms around her in a fierce hug. Skye cupped his head against her shoulder and held on. Beneath the television's blue-white glow, she lay silent, still, too afraid to move for fear he would turn away.

Skye's throat thickened and a band of emotion tightened around her chest as she inhaled his distinct scent of soap and vanilla. The baby powder days were long gone. Even the hugs and kisses seemed to be fading.

After a while, his hold slackened and his breathing slowed. When she feathered his bangs from his brow, his nose twitched and he snuggled deeper against her side. Knowing this closeness would disappear with tomorrow's dawn, she cherished the touch of his breath on her neck, the weight and warmth of his head against the crook of her shoulder. As her limbs grew languid with exhaustion, Skye realized what life was all about.

Love.

But at twenty-nine, she'd also learned love came with a price.

CHAPTER 2

PLACING THE FILE folder on the floor of the office, Peter Weaver crouched and opened the cabinet's bottom drawer and breathed a sigh of relief at finding such an archaic storage system. It made his task much easier. He gripped the penlight between his teeth. It illuminated three rows of cassette recordings in their plastic cases. Names inked in black ran across each spine. He skimmed a gloved finger along the second row and pulled out three cassettes.

Unexpected light appeared through the frosted glass window to the right of the office door and cast fresh shadows over the desk and chairs.

For one pulse beat, Peter froze. Quickly, he turned off his penlight and gripped the cassettes in a tight-fisted hand. He rose to his full six-foot height and heard footsteps echo against the tiled hallway. He hadn't expected any interruptions after ten tonight. This added a different spin on things. He didn't like complications.

The orders had been to get in, retrieve all available information on his mark, and get out undetected. Only when everything was evaluated would the decision be made on whether or not to kill the woman. But if a sudden obstacle developed, then Peter had been given the go-ahead to eliminate it.

He'd memorized the building from every angle. The two-story, simple rectangular structure on the outskirts of Boston consisted of offices of varying medical and dental practices. The elevators were on one side, and the stairwell rested at the other. This office stood on the top floor and in the middle of the building. The person walking this way sounded as if he or she were coming from the elevator.

The alarm system had been easy to breach, and the offices themselves were pathetic when it came to added security. After entering the building, he'd reactivated the alarm system and locked the office door behind him. That gave the person in the hall the misguided belief of being alone.

A shadow appeared behind the thick, opaque window. Peter moved around the desk, over to the wall and set the cassettes on the floor by his feet. He stood left of the door and flexed his gloved fingers.

The scrape of a key against metal and the whisper of the lock being eased back broke the silence. The door opened inward and shielded him from view. Someone flicked on the light switch. Peter didn't move as the door sighed shut, revealing a woman in beige slacks, a sleeveless brown shirt, and shoulder-length, straight brown hair. She turned toward the desk, which gave him her profile, and confirmed her identity as the woman in the photo he'd been given.

She hadn't noticed him against the wall. She turned again, this time exposing her back to him as she bent over her desk.

Perfect.

The carpet covered the sound of his step as he eased up behind her. Then he struck, whipping his forearm across her throat and under her chin. She jerked back against him. Her hand caught at a stack of files. Papers swept off the desk and into the air. He drove his other forearm into the back of her neck in a chokehold, while crushing her windpipe and rupturing her larynx with his other arm. He stepped back, throwing her off her feet and giving him added leverage.

She never had a chance to fight back or cry out. Her hands

fluttered midair, then dropped. Peter snapped her neck. He felt her body give, the energy within evaporating, leaving a husk of bone and muscle.

It took all of three seconds to complete the kill.

Peter dropped the woman to the carpeted floor in frustration. Now he had to dispose of a body. He'd killed a few people over the years, and they'd stayed buried, but only because he'd taken the time to do it right. As for evidence of foul play, he'd eliminate all signs of a struggle and dispose of the body in his favorite dumping ground. That's why he liked using his hands. They didn't leave a mess like a gun or a knife.

He stepped over the woman's body, cleaned the room of evidence, and pocketed the cassettes.

~~*~~

Thursday at the Pharaoh, Skye stood by the roulette wheel and watched the ball jump and kick over the numbers, pause, dive, then land on 15.

"We have a winner!"

The croupier slid the chips over the baize, and Skye added them to her growing stack. Several more people joined the table to watch. Even though it was inevitable, she didn't like it. A crowd drew more attention to her and interfered with her concentration. Skye took a deep, calming breath. She needed to slow down, lose once or twice, and focus on the end result.

Skye needed this money tonight. Her funds were running dangerously low. She didn't have a job, hadn't had one in six months. Being on the run kind of did that to a person. So she played craps and roulette, an easy way for her to make money— far more cash than she'd ever seen when she'd been a staff accountant.

A man moved up to her right. The heat of his body, the breadth of his shoulders and his six-foot-plus frame crowded into her space. Skye didn't glance over to acknowledge his presence or confirm his identity. She didn't need to. She already knew the man at her side. She'd studied him off and on all evening.

David Bishop.

Weeks before she'd done a thorough search on the internet and learned Bishop was a twenty-nine-year-old, single, white male, with no prior record. As a member of The Society of American Magicians, Bishop's career as an illusionist included numerous awards and referrals. Considered by many as one of the top illusionists during this decade, he'd performed at several Las Vegas casinos and national theme parks. He'd even performed on a prime-time television show. Her research showed an impressive career, but it didn't tell her a thing about the man.

But she did learn one important fact—every now and then Bishop liked to walk the floor and play a couple of games of poker or roulette after his evening show. She'd decided to try a 'chance' meeting with him on the floor, instead of the nearly impossible task of slipping past the casino's security to face him backstage or in his dressing room. Even if she did manage the confrontational approach, she was liable to look like some deranged or paranoid stalker.

Thank goodness, tonight seemed to be the night. Less than two hours ago, she'd spotted Bishop on the floor. Ever since, she'd had a devil of a time concentrating on the roulette wheel, knowing he walked, stood, breathed somewhere near. She'd watched his every visible move with a mixture of fascination and fear.

She wiped a hand against the silk of her dress. Talk about luck. She hadn't even had to work hard at her 'chance' meeting.

Skye glanced at his profile. Dressed in a long-sleeved black shirt and slacks that matched the color of his severely cropped hair, Bishop radiated energy and raw masculinity.

The man probably encountered any number of groupies because of his career. Throwing herself at him wouldn't hold his attention but a day or two, and even if it did, she didn't think she had the nerve to climb on a strange man for sex. Plus, putting herself out there like that dramatically increased her chance of rejection—something she'd never handled well. She'd had more than most in this life, thank-you-very-much. Being somewhat aloof and hard to get—now that sounded more her style.

But when it came down to it, she'd do almost anything to uncover the dark secrets behind his public persona.

Unexpectedly, he turned and looked over at her as he sat in the chair beside her. Skye met his eyes and swallowed. Her heartbeat stumbled, then fluttered violently.

With only feet separating them now, Skye realized how much she'd underestimated his appeal. Thick brows slashed over deep-set, smiling brown eyes. A straight, high-bridged nose, prominent cheekbones, and angular jaw added to a face filled with raw masculinity. Yet any woman would envy his tanned, unblemished complexion and thick lashes.

On stage, he possessed an undeniable magnetism, even a dangerous sexuality, but she'd assumed the show's music, lights and other stage elements enhanced his persona.

Talk about being dead wrong. On stage he was dangerous, but off it, he was absolutely lethal—especially when he smiled at her with that lop-sided grin of his, which crinkled the corners of his eyes and revealed straight, white teeth.

This wasn't good. Not good at all. She'd never expected to be this darn attracted to the man. Two minutes within arm's reach, and she was thinking things she didn't have any business thinking.

When he lifted a brow, Skye realized she'd been staring. At least she didn't have her mouth hanging open, but her face did grow hot with embarrassment. What a great first impression, Skye thought in disgust. Then she realized she needed to say something and quickly before she looked like a complete idiot.

"I saw your show earlier tonight. The way you work with candles is very romantic," she said with honesty. "And your two golden retrievers—the levitation is amazing."

His smile deepened, further blasting Skye's determination to remain detached. "It helps when I've got two partners who only bark back. They're also pretty agreeable to having their paws in the air."

"Have you had them long?" she asked, surprised at his sense of humor when he had such smoldering, serious features.

"Since they were pups."

Skye nodded. He had this deep, scratchy baritone voice that made her think of moonless nights and sweaty limbs. Not a good image right now.

Swallowing, she forced herself to focus, shut up, turn back to the table and place another bet. She didn't dare start asking questions too soon, because she feared once she started, she'd never stop. And if that happened, she'd scare off Bishop. Not something she wanted when he might be instrumental in keeping her alive.

~~*~~

David Bishop watched the woman circle the rim of her chips with a thumb. Her fingers, long, elegant but without polish or a wedding band, deftly moved a stack across the felt to the line dividing four and five.

He'd noticed her almost immediately after the show. Not because of her beauty. God knows, he'd associated with many a beautiful woman, but because of the way she moved, sat, held herself. Fluid yet controlled, sleek and sensual, and her legs... Wow. Completely illegal. Toned, slender, like cool marble. Her black, impossibly high-heeled sandals only emphasized their incredible length.

He'd also noticed she didn't have a companion of either sex with her. So far, it seemed like she wanted to keep it solo by the way she'd brushed off the last couple of men. Granted, they hadn't been much to look at. He at least had a full head of hair and didn't show signs of being in a nursing home anytime soon.

After the dealer swept this plays chips off the layout, she leaned forward to place a corner bet, which gave him a great view. Her sleek body, encased in a tight, little, black dress, elevated his interest—among other things. She brushed a thick strand of chestnut hair over a bare shoulder. He eyed the strapless bodice that clung to perfectly shaped breasts and wondered if the whisper of freckles dusting her pale peach shoulders and nose covered every part of her body.

She turned and caught him staring at her breasts. She lifted a brow and eyed him with a cool smile. "Like what you see?"

David didn't blush. He hadn't in over a decade, and he wasn't going to start now.

He raised an eyebrow. "Oh, yeah."

The room's lighting caressed her chestnut hair, which flowed past her shoulder in gentle curls, and turned several strands into dark copper. He wondered if her hair felt as silken as it looked and decided he wanted to find out.

When she met his gaze, the heat flaring in her hazel eyes caught him unaware, hitting him in the gut and momentarily cutting off his breath. David couldn't remember a time when a look twisted him in knots, and he didn't know if he liked it.

But then she blinked, and her expression turned unreadable, which made him doubt if he'd seen the hot emotion in her eyes as she swept her gaze over his body.

"Do I pass?" he asked.

"I'm sure some women find you easy on the eye."

"I've never had any complaints. At least not to my face," he replied, somewhat taken aback at her unenthusiastic appraisal. He usually didn't get a hands-off reaction from a woman. The opposite, in fact. There'd been a couple of times where he'd had to forcibly remove a hand or two from his body.

Oh, well. She might be worth the work, David decided as he leaned closer and smiled. "But I'm not interested in any woman's opinion. I'm interested in yours."

"Then if you must know—I'd say you pass. I don't find you ugly."

"Why..." What an ego deflator. "...thanks."

She smiled.

Finally a positive response.

"You're drop-dead gorgeous," she admitted, a distinct twinkle now brightening her hazel eyes, "and the problem is that you know it."

"And here I thought you were going to take pity on me and be nice."

"Nice? I have an idea your definition of nice doesn't compare to mine." Her smile turned sheepish as the roulette wheel stopped and the ball landed on black eight. "And as for pity, I might be the one who needs it soon."

David glanced over to where the croupier raked in her chips. "That didn't go well."

"I expect to lose every now and then. After all, when it comes to roulette, the odds are against me."

She shrugged, obviously not upset at dropping a couple hundred. In his opinion, the woman was far too detached and in control of her every movement and expression to be anything but a pro, but she wasn't a regular. He'd been performing at this casino for the last two months, and he'd have noticed her by now.

When he watched her lose two more times, David inwardly winced. Over a thousand in less than fifteen minutes and not one bead of sweat on her brow.

David wondered if she handled sex with the same cool, controlled way she gambled. Did that façade hide a wild side? Did a touch, a word, send her over the edge? Or did it take more?

She lost yet again. By God, if his dad had been watching, the man would have had a coronary.

She glanced his way. "Relax."

David hadn't realized he'd protested aloud. "I guess my background's showing. Can't seem to get rid of memories of being dirt poor as a kid."

She wrinkled her nose, drawing attention to her freckles. He really did like those freckles. Or maybe he just liked them on this particular woman.

"You don't have to worry," she assured. "I'm not throwing my savings away or stealing from my son's piggy bank."

"You have a son?" he asked in surprise.

"Yes."

The expression on her face didn't change, but David sensed an immediate tension and wariness radiating from her. Despite his curiosity, he decided to respect her privacy and veer off the subject of her son.

"You might not be throwing away your savings, but you're tossing enough around that if you keep it up, management's going to love you."

Hey, if she wanted to waste her money, that was her business. He wasn't interested in her bank account, but her body on the other hand...

She glanced up at him. This time he hadn't been ogling her breasts, but his thoughts hadn't been any better. Twice now she'd caught him. The woman must have a sixth sense when his mind hit the gutter.

"Possibly. But the evening's not over. I could go all night. It depends."

At the double-entendre, his gaze sharpened, but her angelic expression gave nothing away. Maybe he'd twisted her words into something he wanted to hear. Then again, her mind might have dove into the gutter alongside his. Wishful thinking perhaps...

"What's your favorite number?"

At her abrupt question, he frowned. "Seven."

"Then seven it is."

She placed her remaining chips on his lucky number.

David stiffened. "Are you sure you want to do that?"

"Don't worry. If I lose, I won't come after you."

David swallowed. Another innuendo. This one worse than the last. If he kept this up—

Jesus. There he went again—

"Watch," she urged in a whisper.

David did. The ball tumbled and clattered around the roulette wheel. As the wheel slowed, the ball landed on seven and quivered as if struggling against some invisible force. The wheel whispered to a stop and the ball stilled and remained on...seven.

Just like that. She'd recovered her losses and added a couple of thousand to her pot.

"That's amazing!" he exclaimed. And strange. The odds of something like that occurring were astronomical. "By God. Talk about luck!"

"You think it's luck?" She searched his face, her expression growing serious.

"What else could it be?"

"I thought you might know."

"What's that supposed to mean?"

At the sudden, unnerving intensity of her gaze, David tensed, feeling strangely vulnerable.

"Nothing. Absolutely nothing." She shook her head and looked disappointed as she collected her chips. "I'll see you around."

She planned on cashing in, and David hadn't even gotten her name. "Hey, don't go yet. How about a drink?"

"Not tonight."

She turned and didn't give him another glance.

"Hey, tell me your name," he called after her as he stood, acting completely out of character. He didn't chase after women. And he sure the hell didn't yell after them either.

She paused and glanced over her shoulder. Their gazes caught. "It's Skye Hunter."

Her name hit David as if someone slammed a fist into his face. He stood unmoving, unable to catch his breath, think or respond as he watched her turn back around and walk away. Sudden sweat filmed across his brow and sent a chill racing across his flesh. For a wild second, he thought he was going to pass out. He shivered and frantically searched his pockets. He pulled out a roll of antacid tablets and stuffed two down his throat.

Skye Hunter.

Just saying the name in his head launched his heart rate into overdrive. The crazy part of the whole thing—he didn't know why. He'd never heard it until she'd told him seconds before.

So then, why in God's name did her name bother him so much?

CHAPTER 3

AFTER SHE LEFT the main floor of the casino, Skye double-checked to see if Bishop followed before she turned into a marble entryway and slipped into the elevator to her room. All she wanted to do was get out of her clothes before picking Tyler up from Jamie's place. She was convinced the high heels she'd crammed her feet into hours before were some sick and vindictive torture device invented by the male species.

The elevator door sighed open, and she stepped into the hall and onto the eighth floor. No one followed her into the empty hall. Head bent, exhausted from her encounter with Bishop, she searched inside her purse for her hotel's card key.

She looked up several feet from her room. On the opposite side of her door, a figure edged out from a deep alcove where she knew a table and plant rested, almost as if he'd been lurking, waiting for her. She froze. Tension cut into her limbs and her heart pounded inside her chest.

Skye didn't move from her spot in the hall as she slipped her hand from inside her purse and asked, "How did you find me?"

"I do still have a couple of friends on the force. Even so, it took a while to figure out what alias you were going under. Mary Ann Summers from Gilligan's Island? Hell. I knew you liked the show, even collected some memorabilia. I just didn't figure out how much."

She stared at her ex-husband with a jumble of emotions she couldn't even begin to define.

"What? No smile of greeting?" Jay grinned and stepped closer.

The bastard was just as attractive as ever. If his tall, wiry physique didn't get a woman, his smile always did. It lit up his blue eyes and brought out his killer dimples. Sad part—he knew exactly how to screw over a woman with that smile and a few glib words.

"Why would I do that?"

"I guess it was worth a shot."

Her wits or her memory hadn't dulled since their last meeting. "You haven't told anyone we're in Vegas, have you?" She glanced down both ends of the hall. "I hope you didn't have anyone follow you here."

Jay frowned. Then a look of disgust washed over his face. "I thought we were through with all that paranoia crap. What with the damn psychiatrist to get your head on straight. You must have pulled one on her if she gave everyone the thumbs up."

"I'm not paranoid." Skye hoped she sounded confident as she glanced over at her door. Thank God Tyler was over at Jamie's apartment.

"Sure. Whatever you say."

At his condescending tone, Skye's gaze narrowed. "What's so important that you left Boston and tracked me here?"

When a couple appeared from an intersecting hallway and moved their way, they both stepped to the side for them to pass.

"Can we talk inside?" When she hesitated, he nodded to the couple further down the hall. "Unless you want anyone walking by to hear our business."

She forced herself to relax. Jay might have a vicious tongue, but he'd never grown violent. "Sure."

Skye opened her door and stepped aside, giving Jay enough room to pass without touching her, but not far enough away to miss the smell of stale alcohol. She snapped on the light by the door, and he followed her into the small sitting area where she turned on a floor lamp beside a leather, maroon chair.

The furnishings and non-descript wood coffee and end tables looked clean and adequate, nothing like the luxurious surroundings of some of the other suites in the hotel. She'd never see the interior of those rooms with her income. If not for the gambling, she'd be struggling to find a one-room apartment in a safe neighborhood.

But then, since their last encounter—verbal brawl might be the better term—Jay's financial situation hadn't been any better than her own, and like Skye, he'd taken a financial plunge as deep as the Grand Canyon. A vicious divorce tended to do that.

Both lights glared against Jay's face and amplified the damages of time she'd missed. Deep lines cut along the sides of his mouth, between his eyebrows and by his eyes. Eyes that now regarded her with an indefinable expression. "Where's Tyler?"

She straightened, her spine crackling from the base to the nape of her neck. "He's at the babysitter's."

"When can I see him?"

"You've got to be kidding." Skye fisted her hands at her sides. "You're not interested in seeing Tyler. The only reason you went after custody in the first place was that you knew how much he meant to me."

"Save the preaching. You're not exactly moral yourself."

"But I wasn't the one who started it all, making me look like an unfit mother. You threw every imaginable insult until I was forced to retaliate."

"Is that what you call it? Well, thanks to you, I lost my job, the respect of my co-workers and some of my friends."

"And I almost lost Tyler!" Skye dug her fingers deeper into her palms.

"It might have been better that way. That way he'd have had a chance at some normal life, because we all know you're not normal."

"At least I have a brain. I don't stick powder up my nose or deal it—" Skye forced herself to calm down, mortified at how the past still managed to shred her self-control, her confidence and her ability to act the mature adult. "Sorry. That was uncalled for. But be honest. You didn't come to see Tyler. Give me that at least."

The lines in his face deepened, and his shoulders dipped as if an added weight settled across them. "I need money."

Just as she suspected. Jay showing up had nothing to do with his son. "I don't have any to give."

"You must. Do you know how hard it is to start over again with worse than nothing? I was a cop for God's sake! Who's going to touch a cop who was fired for dealing drugs? Can you tell me that?"

"I'm sorry. But you're the one who made that choice."

Jay walked over to the television, drummed his fingers against its top and eyed her purse with suspicion. "I'm just asking for a bit. Enough to get me started in another town."

"I don't have it." She fought back the urge to clutch her purse to her side. Yeah, she could pay him after her winnings tonight, but she had no intention of supplying him with funds, especially when he might be using again.

"But you could get it. All I have to do is look around here and know you're doing the casinos instead of holding down a real job. You'd be crazy not to. Those slot machines must be like a free teller machine to you."

"I can't touch the slots. They have computer chips. Something too sophisticated for me."

"What about Tyler. He could—"

"No! Absolutely not."

"Then there's gotta be other ways. You're smart enough to figure something out."

"I can't help you."

"You're such a damned hypocrite." Jay glared at her.

He wasn't going to intimidate her. He didn't have the power or the authority to come after her this time. "I can't help you. I can barely help myself."

Another moment of silence. Then he shook his head, strode to the door, but paused. His gaze narrowed and his mouth twisted into a sneer. "You better figure out something, because I need some money."

He disappeared into the hall, but Skye quickly followed. "What's that supposed to mean?"

He didn't turn around to answer as he passed three women in the hall. Skye bit her lip and thought about following. Then she noticed the curious looks in the women's eyes. Not wanting to draw attention to herself, and mindful of how frantic she probably looked, she retreated back into her apartment.

After she closed and locked the door, though, she realized the real reason why she hadn't followed. She'd been too afraid of Jay's answer.

Fifteen minutes later, changed into a pair of jeans, tank top, and blessed running shoes, she ventured out of her room. After finding Jay nowhere on the floor, she hurried from the hotel and to her truck. For three miles, she glanced in her review mirror for signs of a tail. Seeing none, she backtracked and drove to Jamie's apartment.

Moments after Skye's knock, Jamie opened the door, waved her inside and whispered, "I let him fall asleep watching TV, if that's okay?"

"That's fine." She walked into Jamie's living room. The plants, comforter slung across the back of a chair, and fashion magazines splayed out across a coffee table gave the place the look of a home, unlike Skye's sterile hotel room. She hated how it magnified her own inadequacies as a mother and inability to give her son the stability only a home could give. "He didn't give you any trouble, did he?"

"God no. The kid's perfect. A little too serious, but we did get him laughing. We even got a game of Scrabble going."

The light from the kitchen illuminated the sofa where Tyler lay curled on his side. Seeing him safe, asleep and untroubled, Skye smiled, and the tension and anxiety eased from her muscles.

"Hey, Ty. It's time to go home."

Tyler groaned, stretched and lifted his arms in the air. "I don't want to get up."

"I don't think Miss Jamie wants you sleeping on her sofa when she wakes up tomorrow."

He groaned some more and lifted his hand. "I can't move. Help me up."

"You're getting a little too heavy to be—"

"So you're saying you're a little weakling?" He gave her a sleepy grin and waved his fingers in encouragement.

With a grudging smile, Skye shook her head, grabbed his hand and lifted. "Holy cow, Batman." She dug her heels into the carpet and pulled. "I lied. You're not heavy. You're heavier than heavy."

Tyler bounced to a stand. "You're just lucky I did most of the work."

"Yes, I'm lucky." She smiled, liking the happy flush to his cheeks and how hanging with Houston always lightened Tyler's mood.

At the door, Skye paused with her son. "Thanks for everything. Just let me know when I can return the favor."

"Oh, believe me. You'll be repaying me and then some. What with midterms and finals coming up."

"We'll probably stop by for dinner tomorrow if you're working." Skye followed Tyler outside.

"I'm always working," Jamie called after them. "That, or I'm studying."

When they exited the gate leading from the apartment complex and reached the parking lot, Tyler turned and started walking backward beside her. "First one to the car gets dibs on the shower."

"Hey!"

Tyler whipped around and raced down the sidewalk to their truck. Skye leaped into a run after him, gaining on him with each yard. Then suddenly, the distance between them lengthened as Tyler appeared to get a burst of power and Skye's body acquired an energy leak.

Her son slammed a hand against the hood. "I win!"

Skye stumbled to a halt, placed both palms against her thighs, and gasped for air. She was getting too old for this. "Only because you cheated."

"I didn't cheat."

The parking lot light illuminated Tyler's offended expression, and Skye couldn't help but laugh at the comical look. "I know. That's the sad part. I remember a time when I made a point of losing."

"You don't do that now, do you?"

"No, you won that one all on your own," she assured, wanting to erase Tyler's frown. "I think you'll be winning every time from here on out."

Tyler walked to the passenger side of the truck and said over the hood, "You know, the person who wins the shower also gets dibs on the TV."

Arching one brow, she shook her head ruefully. "Let me think about that one."

"It's only fair."

After unlocking both doors, she pulled herself up behind the wheel of the truck with a grunt and more of a struggle than she liked to admit. "Okay. You win that too. You're just lucky I'm so nice."

He jumped into the passenger seat from the other side. A big grin spread across his face as he buckled his belt. "I know."

Seeing his teeth flash in the darkness of the truck's cab, hearing the pleasure in his voice, Skye clutched the steering wheel. She prayed she'd get to see more of those smiles.

Thank God, he never saw Jay tonight.

Skye wanted to keep it that way. Jay didn't have empathy for anyone but himself, and he surely didn't have any paternal feelings for his own son. Tyler didn't deserve to experience that indifference. To her, having no parent around was better than being exposed to the apathy of one. Indifference ate away at a child's soul, chipped at his self-confidence and stifled his growth. All she had to remember were the homes she had lived in as a foster child.

Her ex-husband may have given her the best thing in her life, but unlike Tyler, Jay belonged to her past, and she intended to keep it that way.

But another part of her past haunted her thoughts, goaded her every action and had drawn her to Vegas. She'd been going on gut for months now, running from faceless strangers with dark, unfathomable motives, but now by mere chance, a name and face had appeared from her past. David Bishop. He might be the only person with the ability to answer her questions.

Otherwise, she didn't know what to do, because she couldn't last on survival mode much longer.

~~*~~

"I want you to get your ass over to Vegas," Ferguson demanded. "She showed up on the local news there."

Peter paused in the middle of his kitchen and gripped his cell phone harder. "Where in Vegas?"

"I don't know. One of the newscasts had a segment about dumbest robberies on tape. Her face came up on one of the surveillance tapes."

"You're joking? We're talking Las Vegas. Do you have any idea—"

"Just do it. All you need to do is focus on the roulette wheel. Eventually, you'll find her hanging around one of them." A long drawn out sigh came from the other end of the line. "Don't screw up."

"I won't." With his free hand, Peter pulled the dead rabbit from the kitchen's sink. The warm, limp body bowed over his hand as he carried it to a large, glass cage where he placed it gently inside.

"Well, just remember Andy. I took care of him two years ago when he made such a mess of things with Hunter."

At Ferguson's warning, Peter clenched his jaw. The guy was a prick. If Ferguson wanted to keep Peter in line by threats of him ending up dead like Andy, then the guy was doing it all wrong. Peter didn't scare easily. Not anymore. He'd lost it all—friends, family, his job and the respect of his coworkers. If Ferguson pushed him too far, he'd soon find out Peter would be the one calling the shots. Peter would sooner kill Ferguson before getting shit on.

"I don't screw up like Andy."

"Keep it that way. I want you to get the job done."

Peter shrugged a shoulder. "That's what I get paid for."

"Remember that. Andy didn't seem to 'get it.'" A pause of silence followed. "I've got another chance with Hunter, and this time everything's going to go my way. No mistakes. You understand?"

"Gotcha."

Peter disconnected the line and looked down into the aquarium-like cage. George, his red-tailed boa, had taken the rabbit's head into his mouth. Over the course of two hours, George would alternatively extend the opposite sides of his face and milk the animal's body down his esophagus until it disappeared between his extended jaws.

CHAPTER 4

WHAT'S SO DANG interesting behind me?" Gordon Bishop asked.

"Nothing." Seated at a booth by the window, David forced himself to look across the restaurant's dining table at his dad. "Have you decided what you want for breakfast?"

"I guess I'll have my usual." His dad sighed and placed his menu by the edge of the table.

David tried to focus on his menu, but his mind, incapable of merging letters into words, veered back to Skye Hunter. She sat alone, approximately twenty-feet down the aisle, against the wall and to the left of their booth. She was busy talking to the waitress. This morning she'd pulled back her thick chestnut hair into a ponytail. The black shirt with spaghetti straps emphasized the pale hue of her shoulders and arms. She looked fresh, vibrant and of all things—innocent.

But David wasn't fooled. The woman had to be following him. Why else would she show up here? This diner, miles from the strip, didn't attract tourists, so the odds of a chance meeting were improbable at the very least. He didn't trust anything about her.

Three days after meeting Skye Hunter, and still her name filled him with a mixture of anxiety and dread, though not as mind-numbing as his initial reaction. After thoroughly searching his past, David didn't have any justification behind his behavior.

"There you go again looking at God knows what." His dad grunted and peered over his shoulder.

"Hey," David said in a harsh whisper. "You're being obvious!"

To his relief, David found Skye still talking to the waitress, a stout woman with a shock of thick, white hair.

His dad turned back around and made a face at him. "And you're not?"

"I'm not making a big production of it."

Their waitress came for their orders, but when she left, David realized his dad didn't plan on dropping the subject.

"So who is she?" Gordon asked.

"How do you know I'm looking at a 'she'?"

"Because she's the only one worth looking at. And anyway, after twenty-eight years, I should know my own son by now."

"It's twenty-nine."

"You don't have to tell me something I already know! I just like to forget that one year when you were seventeen and a complete turd."

David groaned and suppressed the urge to rub his face in frustration. Sometimes he wondered who was the parent, the way his dad deliberately tried to provoke a reaction, however negative. But even at his most frustrated, David knew his dad wouldn't hesitate to sacrifice his life to save his son.

For years it had just been the two of them. His mother had decided raising a child didn't fit in with her life after all and took off out-of-state. Over the years, he'd seen her five or six times. Last year, he'd received a Christmas card from her, revealing she'd moved to Florida with her current husband.

Some might consider her mothering abilities appalling, but David stopped caring when he realized he didn't have anything in common with the woman. But he did wonder at the other, deeper scars she'd left behind.

His dad never remarried. Oh, there'd been girlfriends. He remembered very few when he was young, but when David reached his twenties, the women became a more prominent fixture. They never lasted longer than a couple of years, though.

Even today, women—he'd been told by the very same—found his dad at fifty-eight attractive with a tall, lanky frame and a thick head of hair that was more gray than brown. He'd lost a good percentage of muscle mass from a bout with colon cancer a few years back. Thank God, he'd made it through.

"Do you plan on asking her out?"

David blinked. It took him a second to realize what his dad was asking. "No! I mean, no."

"Why not? You've been gawking at her like you've never seen an attractive woman before. Which is odd in itself, because I know how spoiled you are when it comes to women. I swear your front door's like a dang airport terminal. I'm just glad I don't live with you. That way I don't have to see all that monkey business going on around me."

"Funny. Ha, ha." David pulled out a roll of antacid tablets from his jeans pocket and peeled back the wrapping.

"Then why have you been staring at her?"

"She's been following me."

The truth slipped out before David had the sense to keep silent.

"Following you, eh? Has it gotten so bad you've got them following you now?"

David frowned and shook his head, avoiding his father's sharp, brown-eyed gaze. "It's not like that. At least, I don't get the feeling she's some crazed stalker."

His dad swiveled around and looked over his shoulder.

"Stop staring!" David dug two tablets out of the roll, stuffed both in his mouth and chewed as he stared over at Skye. Thanks for small favors. Her attention seemed to be on the table in front of her and not on this booth.

When his dad twisted back around, he glanced over at the roll of tablets in David's hand and muttered something under his breath before saying, "I'll stop, if you stop shoveling those antacids down your throat. How many times have I told you that there's over-the-counter medicine that lasts twenty-four hours?

And if you'd just lay off the diet soda and the Mexican food then you—"

"Dad, I think we've been down this road before."

"Of course we have, and I wouldn't keep at it if you just listened to your old man..."

David gave his father a threatening look, which shut him up for all of two seconds.

"I think you should ask her over," his father urged.

"Hey—what—no. Are you crazy? You can't do that." He said the last in a low, panicked voice as he watched his dad turn and wave at Skye until he caught her attention.

Skye didn't appear shocked at having some strange, old man gesture at her to come over. But then, David didn't believe anyone read past her ambiguous expression unless she wanted them to.

"I just did 'that.'" His dad flashed him a smug smile. "You can't find out about someone from across a room. You've got to talk to them. Maybe if you just asked her why she's following you, you'll get a simple explanation. And anyway, she's easy on the eye, and it'll be nice to talk to a female for a change. I'm getting tired of talking to a bunch of men day in and day out."

"I don't like being manipulated and—" David stumbled to a halt.

Skye appeared at their table. He noticed the thick, black belt wrapped around a pair of low-slung jeans, an inch of bare midriff and a form-fitting black shirt. How wearing something so simple could look so damn sexy was beyond him. She had the type of lean, limber body that had his mind veering to thoughts of hot, wild sex. Up close, he'd forgotten how gorgeous she was, but having her two feet away amplified every feminine feature.

Geeze.

If only he wasn't so damn attracted to her.

His dad broke into a smile, deepening the lines already bracketing his mouth. "Hey? I'm Gordon, David's father. I thought I'd introduce myself and get you over here before David here embarrasses himself further by staring like some lovesick fool."

"Dad!" David rubbed a palm across his face in complete mortification.

Skye lifted a brow but looked amused.

"You're going to have to excuse my dad. He's made a career out of embarrassing me."

"Only because he makes it so easy," his dad added quickly, a definite twinkle in his eye. "Will you join us? Or have you ordered yet?"

"I'd love to, but I'm waiting for my food."

"We can have Jennifer bring it to our table."

The man wouldn't give up, David thought in disbelief as he met Skye's gaze. "Don't let my dad railroad you into doing something you don't want to."

"He's not." A muscle along her jaw flexed. "And no one makes me do anything I don't want."

By the determined glint in her eyes, David believed her. He couldn't remember seeing a woman with such determination, even ruthlessness in her face, no matter how brief. For some crazy reason seeing those emotions further stoked his interest. This woman wasn't some tame kitten. No. He had a good idea if he got too close and decided to cross her, he'd come away flayed.

"Move over, David, so she can sit down."

David glared at his dad before sliding across the seat to make room for Skye. The booth's cushion adjusted to her weight as she sank down beside him. The scent of her, a hint of lavender and something else—something equally feminine—drifted toward him. He watched Skye grip the edge of the table with long, delicate fingers.

A vision of those same fingers on his skin flashed in his mind, making him think of how they'd touch his body. Were they as dangerous as the look in her eyes? Would they claw or caress? Were they experienced or—

"I'm sorry, but I didn't catch your name," his father said, interrupting David's wild speculations.

"It's Skye. Skye Hunter."

"Well, Skye—Hell, you've got the most amazing freckles. I can't remember the last time I saw so many on a woman—"

"Dad!"

Gordon waved a hand at him. "Don't get your panties in a bundle. I meant it as a compliment. I love freckles on a woman. Always have."

"Why, thank you."

David heard the amusement in Skye's voice and the laugh that immediately followed, but rather than relaxing, he tensed. Damn, his father might be right when it came to his reaction to Skye. Her presence kicked up his pulse rate and tossed his composure down the toilet. And right now, his response didn't have anything to do with the feelings her name instigated or the mystery behind why she'd followed him here today, but everything to do with this sexual awareness she fueled inside him.

Jennifer came with their breakfast. Several minutes went by until his dad decided to be his usual blunt self. "David seems to think you've been following him."

David jerked his gaze to her face. He wanted to reprimand his dad at his lack of tact, but he wanted to gauge her reaction far more.

"Really?" She lifted one beautifully arched brow at David. Slowly, she reached for her coffee cup and took a sip. Only after she placed the cup down on the table, did she say, "How strange."

So cool, so controlled. It drove David nuts. She could deny all she wanted, but he knew she'd followed him here. "Then why show up at this restaurant?"

"Why would I follow you? And here, of all places? And even if I did, how would I do that? I would have to know where you lived. And even if I did know where you lived, what possible reason would I have to follow you? Yes, I found your show fascinating, but not nearly enough to shadow your every move. Being in the same restaurant is mere coincidence."

"You're lying."

Anger flashed in her hazel eyes, and she took a savage bite of her toast. Finally, he realized with satisfaction, he'd managed to chip at her composure. Turning toward her more fully, he placed an elbow along the back of the booth and searched for something else to get past her self-control.

"David, you're being rude."

He ignored his dad's comment and continued to stare at Skye. At his dad's well-placed kick to his shin under the table, David grunted.

"See David? She's not following you. How about we put it down to wishful thinking on your part."

Hearing the hard edge to his dad's voice and not wanting his other shin kicked, David shifted back against the booth. "Fine."

"So what do you think of Vegas? Do you live here or are you just visiting?" his dad asked Skye.

"We moved here over a month ago."

"Because of family?"

"In part." Skye nodded and took another sip of coffee.

"She has a son," David told his father. "Is he in school right now?"

"He's at the babysitter's. He doesn't start back to school until the fall."

"Well, if he's anything like mine, the little guy'll give you a run for your money."

David smothered a smile, amused at his dad's quick wit but not about to admit it. "A regular comedian you are."

His dad smirked. "I like to think so. I get even funnier after a full stomach." Gordon chewed a mouthful of scrambled eggs, then wiped his mouth with a napkin. "Do you want to hand me the ketchup? My hash browns need a little color."

From the other side of the table, the ketchup bottle slid across the table without the aid of anyone's hand. It stopped when it rested against his dad's palm.

Gordon curled his fingers around the plastic container and glared at David. "Nice trick. Just don't start elevating the table."

"I really must let you both go." Quickly, Skye rose to her feet and took her bill. "I have to get my son. It was nice meeting you Gordon, and David—" She smiled. A devilish expression crossed her features. "Let's just say it was interesting."

Like an idiot, David stared at her retreating back in silence.

She'd completely blind-sided him, and he had a good idea that's exactly what she'd intended.

"What's with the antics for God's sake?" his father asked, his words filled with a distinct bite.

David turned back around in his seat. "Antics?"

He leaned over the table and glowered at David. "Are you trying to impress Skye? I would have thought you'd have outgrown your parlor tricks!"

Tension stiffened the muscles along David's back and shoulders. "I don't get what you're saying?"

"The ketchup bottle. Moving it across the table like that! Do you have to try to impress every woman who comes around with your little magic moves?" Gordon grabbed the morning paper beside him, opened a section with loud, jerking movements, placed it on the corner of the table and scowled at it.

"Dad. Will you look at me?" He waited until his dad stared at him from across the table. "I didn't touch the ketchup."

Snorting in obvious disbelief, his dad snatched the bottle and waved it in the air. "We both know it wasn't me. So if it wasn't either of us, then who moved the ketchup? Houdini?"

"Not Houdini." David caught and held his father's gaze. "Skye Hunter."

CHAPTER 5

DAVID STARED OUT the diner's window as Skye hurried across the street. What the hell type of game was she playing? What was the meaning behind the ketchup? Magic? Or more? If something other than a trick, then that would mean the impossible.

He gripped the table's edge. She seemed bent on pushing him. But why?

His thoughts turned to their encounter at the casino, of her playing roulette, of her strange words regarding luck and the astronomical odds of landing on seven.

Numbers from the roulette wheel flashed in his mind's eye. Colors. Red. Black. The spinning wheel. A picture, blurred and shadowy, of another time, of another roulette wheel whispered from his past.

Frowning, he closed his eyes. The number twenty-two pushed into his consciousness and swirled into focus. Black backdrop with bone colored numbers. Sudden fear peppered his flesh.

His grip tightening on the edge of the table, he pushed past the fear and focused harder, searching beyond the image of the wheel and the ominous number he'd grown to hate and—

A vision of a grotesque face blind-sided him. Reptilian eyes peered down at him. Light glared off a bald, green-mottled head.

Fingers touching, probing. Then pain. Excruciating in intensity as it lanced into his skull.

He jerked in his seat, smacking his back against the leather cushion. The same sick image from that damn nightmare. Talons of fear dug a path up his spine, while his stomach clenched into a knot. The restaurant's air conditioner amplified the sudden chill that scurried across his skin.

Why the memory after all this time? Fear? He hadn't seen that face in his nightmares for years. And what did it have to do with Skye?

David scrambled to his feet. He needed answers from Skye. Shit. She was a walking menace. If she exposed his secret, he'd lose everything he'd built, his career, his home, his livelihood.

"Where are you going?" his dad asked, glancing up from his eggs.

"After her."

His dad stopped chewing. "Are you nuts?"

"Probably."

He wagged his fork at David. "I don't care how beautiful. You don't go chasing after some woman. She'll get the cops on you."

David grabbed his wallet from his back pocket, pulled out a twenty and tossed it on the table. "Sorry, but I've got to find out where she's going. Thanks for understanding."

His father rolled his eyes. "Like I have a choice. You know, it's a good thing I drove myself, or you'd have left me stranded." His dad's disgruntled voice followed him down the aisle.

David stepped outside and blinked against the glare of the sun. A car door groaned shut. He turned in time to see Skye slip behind the wheel of a beat up, god-awful looking pickup.

When she pulled out of her space and toward the parking lot's exit, he ducked across the street and into his silver, far too conspicuous Lexus SC430. He wanted to tail her undetected, knowing he'd get more answers this way than outright questioning her.

Adrenaline surged through his veins. He guided the sports car into traffic and remained a good two car lengths behind Skye. If she decided to take more than one look in the rearview mirror, she might notice the hardtop convertible. Well...he'd just have to make sure he kept his distance.

He'd never followed anyone, and after the first few turnoffs, he realized remaining undetected was a hell-of-a-lot harder than what the movies made out.

Skye's pickup veered into the left lane, jerked into a sharp left turn and crossed the path of oncoming traffic. She escaped being broadsided by an oncoming car and reached the neighboring street intact.

Shit!

David swerved to follow but slammed on his brakes, avoiding a collision from the opposite direction. In the rearview mirror, he saw a car behind him swing to the right. It nearly clipped his bumper before passing. David glimpsed a woman yelling obscenities at him.

Skye must have spotted him. And here he'd had this idiotic idea that he'd been so careful. Now, he'd never find out her intended destination.

When an opening in the traffic appeared, he gunned the engine and turned into the road she'd disappeared down. He didn't find any sign of her on the street, but at the next intersection, he glimpsed the tail end of her pickup. Relieved, he reversed quickly and followed with more caution. No. Followed wasn't the word. Guessed. He was playing some damn guessing game as to where she'd drive next.

David strangled the steering wheel with frustration. What he wouldn't do for a tracking device right now.

When Skye turned into a street congested with traffic, he tailed her with more caution and overworked the engine, the gas pedal and brake by veering the Lexus behind a semi, a van, then an SUV.

He raced through three more damn traffic lights and hit two crater-sized potholes before following Skye into a residential neighborhood. To ensure she didn't spot him, David hung back and drove down a parallel street. After a minute, he backtracked and found she'd parked in front of a clay-tiled, one-story house, similar to all the others in the subdivision. Seeing no movement by the truck or house, he drove slowly down the street, rifled through the glove compartment for a pen and paper and scrawled down the address.

As a white car crept past in the opposite lane, David debated about getting out and confronting Skye. Her secrets, the possibility of her influencing his life and future drove him nuts. His hands tightened against the wheel as he debated over the temptation to jump out after her and shake some answers from that delectable body of hers.

He decided against it. The information he got from following her would be a hell of a lot more reliable than anything coming from her mouth if he dragged a response from her. Also, by the way she parked on the side of the street instead of the garage, he suspected she didn't live there.

He pulled to a stop on the next cross street where he hoped to hell only the car's bumper and hood were visible from the house. He grabbed his roll of antacids and stuffed two in his mouth. Chewing, he stared down the street, waited and watched, while he kept the engine and air conditioner running.

Over an hour behind the wheel, he sat with no entertainment other than a cat sauntering across the street. Then finally, movement. David jerked from his slumped position.

Immediately, he recognized Skye by the fluid way she moved across the sidewalk to her car. From this distance, he couldn't tell if she was upset, pleased, or bored.

Who had she seen? And what had she talked about? Was it important or about him? Maybe she'd been hatching some scheme with the person inside. He rubbed his brow with the heel of his hand. He'd always been a bit of a game player, but never where he found himself the target.

Then David wondered why the hell he was sitting in his car on a strange street, stalking a woman as if she were some criminal. Had he gone insane?

But he hadn't started this. She'd followed him. She wanted something. But what? Money? Revenge? Some weird sex game? Or blackmail?

Despite the air conditioner, sweat broke out on his brow. Fear coated the inside of his mouth. If she knew the secrets behind his magic show and planned on blackmailing him, then— No. He pushed the supposition aside along with all his doubts and followed her truck onto the next street with more determination. Somehow he needed to get leverage against her.

Thoughts of the roulette wheel, but more the image of the green creature twisted his gut. An alien for God's sake. A nightmare he'd thought dead until Skye blasted into his life. Maybe there was a tie, but it all sounded too crazy.

He shadowed Skye to another neighborhood where she parked in a large apartment complex. As he pulled into the lot after her, she disappeared down a sidewalk between two of the buildings.

She'd acted completely unaware of him. Good. He might be getting better at tailing a person after all.

He pulled into a spot beside a van, thoroughly shielding his car from the main entrance, got out and moved carefully in the direction he'd seen her go. From a distance, he watched her climb the stairs to the second floor and enter the apartment furthest to the left. He waited a few minutes, took a deep breath and headed that way.

She couldn't escape this time—unless she planned on jumping over a balcony.

The apartment door opened and she and a boy stepped out onto the cement landing bordered by black wrought iron and walked toward the stairs.

"Shit!" David hurried back to his car. Sweat and annoyance slid down his spine as the sun burned against his skin and through his shirt.

So she hadn't lied about having a son, which didn't mean a thing. Just because someone had a child didn't automatically make him or her a model citizen. But the idea of her being a mother made him think of her as vulnerable, something he'd never considered until now.

Next, he followed her into the parking lot of the Pharaoh. *What the hell?* She couldn't gamble with a boy in tow.

David quickly discovered following by car was a whole hell-of-a-lot easier than by foot. Luck did help. Only mother and son entered the hotel's elevator, so when it paused on eight, he knew they'd gotten off on that floor. He dashed up the stairwell to the eighth floor, pushing his body until a fine coat of sweat clung to his skin and his blood quickened his already pounding pulse.

On the landing, he peered through the small rectangular window. Skye and the boy stood by a vending machine. Then as one, they turned in the opposite direction of the stairwell and walked down the hall. Several yards further, Skye used a room key. Then they both disappeared inside a room on the left.

Finally.

He'd wanted to catch her at her home. But a hotel room? And at The Pharaoh?

Unease pressed in on him. He suspected the only reason why he knew of her existence now was that she wanted it that way, which made him wonder how long she'd been following him. Weeks? Longer? The entire time he'd started his show in Vegas?

At their door, he knocked, waited, and stared at the peephole in the middle of the gold metal door. He didn't get an answer. Somehow that didn't surprise him.

"It's David Bishop. Open up." He raised his voice. "It's important."

When continued silence answered him from the other side, he knocked harder.

"Skye. I don't want to make a scene out here, but I will if you don't show your face."

The door eased open. Skye muttered something to someone in the background—he suspected her son. Then she slipped outside, and closed the door behind her.

Tension radiating from her slender body, she stared at him with narrowed, hazel eyes. "How did you find me?"

"I followed you."

She swore under her breath. "I thought I lost— Are you alone?"

"Yeah. Why?"

Shifting, she glanced up and down the hall. "That's my business."

"Well, I'm making it my business."

"I don't think so." She jammed a hand onto her hip. "Okay. You've got my attention. What is it you want?"

"I want to know what sick little game you're playing. Somehow you've included me in on it and I want none of it."

"I don't know what you're talking about."

David fisted his hands at his sides and forced down his growing anger.

Defiance flashing in her eyes, she stood with a hip thrust out and a wide band of naked skin between her tight t-shirt and jeans. The hall's lighting caressed her taut arms, flawless face and revealed a dusting of freckles on both.

Suddenly, her sleek, tight body made him wonder how she'd look naked in bed and astride—

Shit. She was too beautiful. This attraction he had for her was crazy, even dangerous when he didn't know what motivated her. He didn't like it and he didn't want it.

"Oh, come off it. You know exactly what I'm talking about with that parlor trick you pulled at the diner," David insisted, dismayed at how much he sounded like his dad. "Are you trying to impress me with your little magic trick?"

"Magic? Are you sure it's magic?"

David started to lift an arm to rub at the back of his neck but stopped himself, not wanting to reveal how much her words bothered him. "Magic, illusion, whatever you want to call the stunt. It can't be anything else."

"I guess you're entitled to your own opinion. But I think your show isn't just magic. I think it's much more than what you've made the public believe."

David stiffened. A breeze from the hall's air conditioner caught against his damp shirt and chilled his skin, while a bead of sweat slithered down the seam of his spine from running up eight flights of stairs.

By God. She knew.

David fought against the panic tightening around his chest

and throat. All this time, he'd wondered and worried why she'd singled him out. But how could she know his secret? Other than his father, no one knew how he did his show.

"Are you talking blackmail? Is that what you're getting at?"

"What if I am?"

Her lifted brow and cool smile made him want to physically shake an answer from her. No way in hell would he let her ruin everything he'd worked so hard to achieve.

A door opened down the hall. Frustrated at the interruption, David glared as a plump, silver-haired woman set a lunch tray on the floor then closed her door. "This isn't the place."

"At least that's something we both agree on. And you can forget my room. I'm not about to let my son witness anything you have to say."

He stepped toward her, felt the heat and hostility radiating from her and experienced the same boiling inside him. "Are you always this confident?"

She stared back. "Always."

"Really? Or is it all bravado?"

David took another step closer, pleased at how her eyes flared and that he sensed a sudden stillness settle around her. He reached over, lifted a strand of hair from her ponytail and let it glide through his fingers. With the back of his index finger, he then touched her cheek. She didn't flinch, didn't do one thing to give away what she was thinking.

He wanted to rattle her composure, push her over the edge. He'd never felt this out of *control*, particularly when he was with a woman who seemed to be the embodiment of control.

"You're adopted, aren't you?"

What the hell? He jerked his hand back as if she'd landed a fist to his face. "What type of question is that?"

"Are you?"

David swallowed, struggling to meld his splintered thoughts. At the muffled thud of footsteps on carpet, he tensed and turned to find a middle-aged man with a floral shirt. He nodded and waited until the man disappeared into his hotel room three doors down, which gave him added time to compose his thoughts. "If you want to know that, meet me after my show in the hotel lobby."

"I can't."

He arched a brow, not believing a word. Hell, he'd be crazy to.

Skye flushed. "My son. I have a hard time getting someone to watch him in the evenings."

He pulled his wallet from his back pocket and slid out a gold-embossed card from inside. "Here's my card with my address. I'll be home Friday afternoon. I want to know what you're after, and maybe if you give me enough answers, I'll tell you if I'm adopted or not."

"I don't think—"

"No. Somewhere public isn't going to work. They'll be too many interruptions. And if you're worried about being alone together, I promise you'll be perfectly safe. I'll even have my dad around if that'll make you feel better." When she still didn't answer, he threatened, "You don't want me showing up here on a regular basis. I don't think your son would like that."

Her hazel eyes narrowed, and it appeared as if she were about to retaliate with some scathing retort, but instead, she nodded and took the card. "Fine."

But she didn't look pleased. Tough. She was the one who started this. Yes, he'd used her son to get her to agree, something he wasn't particularly proud of, but it had gotten results. He'd do it again if it meant ridding himself of her games.

He backed away. "I'll see you then, and don't try backing out. I'll track you down."

Her chin hitched up and her hand closed into a fist, crumpling his card within her grasp. "Watch your step. You might get hurt."

Something thudded to the floor. David looked at the doorway to the next room. A linen covered trolley filled with plates, silverware and leftovers rested against the wall. I large steak knife had fallen to the floor. It had landed only a foot from where he stood, its silver tip pointed directly at him.

He jerked his gaze back to Skye. "Is that a threat?"

Her eyes widened in shock. "Not at all."

Suspecting her surprise an act, David nodded and backed

away. He almost asked aloud if she'd moved the knife, but he was too afraid of her answer. And anyway, a question like that was liable to raise more than eyebrows.

Before he turned and left, he noted her room number. He'd check with hotel security on Skye. His friend on staff owed him a favor, and David planned on taking him up on it.

This time, he took the elevator down instead of the stairs. When he reached the parking lot and aisle to his Lexus, a white car raced past, missing him by a bare two feet. Tires shrieked against asphalt as it swung into the next aisle, spitting up dust and bits of rock. Exhaust fumes hit him in the face. Glancing over his shoulder, he watched the car turn onto the street and vanish.

Frowning, David opened his car door but paused. He stared at the street where the car had disappeared. The sedan looked similar to the one he'd seen by the house Skye had visited earlier in the day. But by the time he realized it, the vehicle was gone along with its license plate.

~~*~~

Skye slumped against the closed door of the hotel room and inhaled a long, rattling breath. The air-conditioner clicked on and sent a faint breeze whispering against her flesh. She shuddered. Not from the room's chill temperature. No. It came down to Bishop. The fierceness in his eyes, the menace in his size not only intimidated her but made her question what she was doing messing with a man like him.

She should pat herself on the back for the way she'd held herself together in front of him. But because she'd ruthlessly reigned in her control, her legs now trembled like brittle cornstalks against a violent wind, while she swore a swarm of nasty flies whirled inside her stomach.

Tyler slipped from the chair in the corner of the room and walked over to her. "What's wrong?"

Straightening, she met the concern in her son's big, beautiful brown eyes and her chest tightened. She wished she could unwind the last two years, do things differently, be a hero in

Tyler's eyes, or at least someone he might come to respect later in his life. But she was none of those things.

Maybe one day...

She could always hope. She sighed. Hope. A four letter word. One that had kept her moving forward, acting on instinct, and fighting back with hunger and desperation. All for a future her son deeply deserved.

"Mom? Are you okay?"

Skye blinked and stepped away from the door. Okay? No. She was frightened. With Bishop showing up at her door, others would soon follow. Men far more deadly than Bishop. But she couldn't run like she'd done so many other times. At least not just yet. In Vegas, she needed a little more time. Bishop held too many clues to her past, though the man seemed clueless.

With a gentle hand, she squeezed Tyler's narrow shoulder. Maybe one day she'd also get some weight on his too frail frame. "I'm fine. I just had to talk to a very crabby man, that's all, and I'm trying not to let him bother me."

"Oh. Is he, you know, bad?"

Skye thought about lying. These last couple of years she'd been as truthful as possible to her son, while, at the same time, she'd tried to protect him from the worst. She realized now wasn't the time to try something different. "I'm not sure. It's too soon to tell."

CHAPTER 6

SKYE DREADED THIS meeting, or more importantly, she dreaded what she would uncover.

Rolling her shoulders to ease the tension locked around her muscles, she strode up the walkway to a red-tiled, one story home. Bougainvillea with their cascade of vivid pink flowers bracketed the window by the door, while the scent of hot, baked dirt drifted through the air.

Pausing, Skye glanced down both sides of the street for signs of Bishop or any suspicious looking car or person. Heat shimmered off the concrete and into the air, crowding her from all sides. No one walked their dog, mowed their lawn or stepped from their home in this middle-class neighborhood. The only person crazy enough to be out in this heat was herself.

The harsh shriek of a cicada pierced the silent afternoon. She flinched, then exhaled in a loud whoosh. Damn. One day she'd like to react like a normal person. Right now, though, nothing would shake off her growing anxiety.

Last week, her ex-husband reminded Skye of her vulnerability, fueling an already urgent need to unearth this crazy mystery buried in her subconscious. Jay might be the only one who would think to link her to a character from Gilligan's Island, but the people after her possessed their own resources and might

49

trace her whereabouts. She would be a fool to think her assumed identity infallible.

Skye jabbed the doorbell with a finger before she changed her mind. A moment later, Kathy Rodriguez, a tiny woman in jeans and a wispy blouse opened the door.

"Thanks for letting me see you again," Skye said, wrapping a hand around the strap of her purse. "Especially on such short notice."

"No problem." Kathy ushered her in with a slender hand. The bangles on her wrist flashed silver and snapped against each other. "I hope we can do better this time."

"Well, it means a lot." After Skye stepped inside the cool interior, the other woman closed the front door. "I'm hoping we can get through this block I seem to have on a part of my past. Bev did try."

Kathy laughed and shook her head. Short, dark brown hair cropped in jagged angles hugged an equally angular face, yet Kathy's smile and light brown, almost golden eyes held a gentleness and warmth Skye found impossible to resist.

Those characteristics reminded Skye of another woman long since dead, but whose memory would always linger. Unlike all the other foster parents, Glenda had loved Skye for herself, not the money that came with fostering a child. But that was fifteen years ago, and those two years were far too brief...

"Bless her heart," Kathy said as she led the way down the hall and into a living area where a coffee table made from a large tree trunk and lacquered to a glassy sheen sat between a sofa and chair in deep earth tones. "Hypnosis is not one of Bev's specialties, and she'll be the first to tell you that, but she's one of the best psychiatrists I know."

"Bev must have thought the same about you. She recommended you above anyone else in Vegas." Skye crossed the parquet floor and sank down in the chair while Kathy turned on her stereo system. Within seconds, the sound of a running stream flowed through the speakers.

Kathy turned away from the stereo to face Skye. A half-smile hovered on the other woman's lips. "We go back years. More than I even like to admit! She's a great lady, but you didn't come here for me to reminisce."

"No."

"Hopefully, this time we'll get past this block of yours, but I'm not promising miracles."

"At this point, anything will help." Skye shifted in the overstuffed chair and struggled to control the nervous flutter in the pit of her stomach.

Kathy walked over to the oak fireplace mantle and lit a votive candle beneath a glass sphere filled with a yellow, translucent liquid. She must have seen Skye's questioning look, because she explained, "With this session, I thought a little boost with an essential oil might help. Juniper's been proven to stimulate memory. I didn't have any on hand for your first visit, but hopefully it will help when we get you in a hypnotic state."

Skye wiped her damp hands against her jean-clad legs, then clutched the arms of her chair. "If I get agitated while I'm under, I don't want you to stop."

"I don't think I would feel comfortable—"

"Please. This not knowing is driving me crazy."

Kathy sighed heavily and bent down to light a thick, chocolate-colored candle in the center of the coffee table. "We'll see. That's all I'm going to promise."

Skye didn't like her answer, but really, what choice did she have? She didn't dare start going down a list of hypnotists on the internet for fear of word somehow getting out. Maybe a paranoid thought, but better irrational and alive than dead.

Opposite from Skye, Kathy sat down on the edge of the sofa. "I want you to look at the candle on the table. Concentrate on the light. With each exhalation, you'll find yourself relaxing further."

Skye forced her hands to loosen their grip on the leather armrests as she sank deeper into the cushions. Still, the flurry in her stomach continued.

"Now I want you to focus on the light's warmth," Kathy instructed in a throaty, yet soothing voice, and for several minutes their breathing permeated the room until she urged gently, "Feel yourself being completely absorbed by this pure, white light with each breath you take. Let it flow through your fingers, arms, legs, and torso and enter each and every pore of your body. Your limbs are growing languid with its soothing power."

Skye closed her eyes and nodded, forcing her mind to go blank. She inhaled slowly, taking in the scent of juniper and allowing herself to escape the constraints of time and place. Unease seeped from her stomach as serenity flowed through her mind and body.

"I want you to go back to that time, back to where you were before," Kathy instructed in that low, calming voice, "but when you do this, you will remain relaxed. As you remember, the events will be as if you are observing them from a distance and not as if you are a participant. Do you understand?"

"Yes."

After a moment, Kathy asked, "What do you see?"

Sounds and colors filtered into her mind's eye. From above her head, a fluorescent light inside an opaque box shone from the ceiling while walls on both sides of her came into focus. "A hallway."

"What else?"

"It's just a hallway. There's a door on either side of me, and the walls are sky blue."

"How about the doors? Can you open one and go inside."

"No."

"Why not?"

"I'm lying down on a bed of some type." An inexplicable tension tightened around Skye's shoulders and back. "I'm being rolled down the hall by someone."

"Are you in a hospital?"

"I'm not sure."

"Do you see anything else? What about the person who must be pushing you?"

Skye glanced around, but her head wouldn't move from its position on the bed. Next, she tried to move her arms and legs but remained somehow bound to the bed as if they were restrained. Alarm meshed with the tension grinding into her muscles.

"Skye. Pay attention. Who's there with you?"

Along with her peripheral vision, she became aware of a shadow. She sucked in a lungful of air. "There's a person nearby. But I don't know who."

"Relax. We have lots of time. Just concentrate on that person. It will come to you."

As Skye tried to focus on the person in shadow, an ominous feeling snatched at her insides. She didn't want to see who it was, because if she did—

"No." Skye struggled to close her eyes but an invisible force kept them pried open. The stench of evil clung to the shadowy figure as it inched closer.

"What is it?" Kathy asked.

Ever closer...

Raw panic caught against the back of her throat.

Shadows ebbed. Unexpected light flooded the figure.

My, God!

That sick, green face. Lizard eyes, flashing yellow hatred peered down at her. The creature's mouth yawned open and revealed incisors that glowed white. A shudder ripped through her body as those teeth snapped shut inches from her head. She struggled for breath, but the panic closed in tighter around her throat.

Gasping, Skye twisted her face away. But its breath. The pungent, cloying smell wafted to her. Peppermints and cigarettes.

A noise broke into Skye's thoughts. Then she realized the high, keening was coming from her.

"Okay, Skye. I don't like this. You need to calm down. Take several slow, deep breaths. Relax. You are no longer in the hall, but in a safe place."

Skye took a couple of jagged breaths. She tried to latch onto Kathy's soothing voice. But those eyes and teeth— Her heart thudded against her chest. A chill slithered over the sweat against her brow and back.

"Skye. Concentrate on the light. Inhale. Feel the light flow into your lungs and spread through the rest of your body. With each breath, your body grows more languid, heavy, and relaxed.

"The minutes are reversing to a safer place. They're rewinding back until it's the day before. Think of a clock's hands moving backward, circling again, again. Midnight. Six. Now eight in the morning. You're going back even further. One, then two days. A week. Whatever you saw will not be there. You'll be completely safe. Now tell me where you are."

"I'm in a hallway."

"...the same one?"

As she walked down the dark, grainy corridor, her nose twitched against the sting of antiseptic in the air. She crept forward, the tile cold against her bare feet. "No. This one's different. It's gray." Dread feathered the back of her neck. "But I've been here before. It's too familiar."

"Do you see anything?"

Skye looked around. She wasn't supposed to be in this part of the building. She knew it but she continued down the long corridor, mindful of the waiting silence. "There're double doors at the end of the hall."

A cry slipped from one of the rooms. She froze. The sound grew in strength. Unable to halt the urge to uncover its cause, she edged nearer to the room.

From the other side of the closed door, a moment of thick silence followed. Then a scream cut into the air. The sound went on and on, echoing inside her head. Then abruptly, it stopped.

She stumbled back.

Another scream broke through the room and into the hall, more strident than the last.

The pain and terror from inside the room lashed at her. Her stomach twisted. A whimper rose up her throat along with the taste of bile. She struggled to swallow. Barely managed.

"What's going on?" Urgency hardened Karen's voice.

With a shaking hand, Skye clutched at her throat and stared at the door in horror. "It's that other person."

"The one from before in our last session?"

"Yes, but now they're screaming. The pain. My God, they're in such pain!"

"Go to the door and open it. This time push yourself to see what's happening inside."

Skye shook her head vehemently. Her toes curled against the chill floor, while the hospital gown around her body scraped against her skin as she took a trembling step backward.

"Open the door," Kathy ordered.

Another step away from the door. Fear crawled like a mutated centipede along the flesh of Skye's back. She already knew the person behind the screams, but by God, she didn't want to be a witness to the sick happenings going on inside. "I can't. I won't. I'm too afraid."

"Then if you won't go into that room, look around you. What do you see? Anything different?"

"Just the file folder in a plastic bin beside the door. I can see the name on it from here."

"And the name?"

"The same as every other time." Frustration and despair thickened Skye's voice.

"Tell me anyway."

"David Bishop."

~~*~~

Friday afternoon and two days later, Skye pulled her pickup to a stop and eyed the wrought iron gates, banning the lower classes like herself from entering the neighborhood. She disliked being forced into meeting Bishop at his home, and she particularly disliked bossy men.

Jay had tried to control her, mold her into a woman he expected a police officer's wife should be. But no more. She'd gotten used to being her own boss and in charge of her life, not having some man tell her how to run it. Granted, her life was a mess at the moment, but it was *her* mess.

It was far too soon to reveal anything about herself to Bishop. She needed to learn more about his personal background, his weaknesses, his strengths before she trusted him. His father seemed harmless enough, but an error in judgment on her part could jeopardize more than her own life. She had to think of her son. He was far more vulnerable.

She just hoped Bishop held some answers. She eased down

her window. A draft of hot air rushed into the cab. She blinked as the fierce heat burned against her face, her exposed skin and burrowed through her clothing, making her wish for the winter months and bearable temperatures. After checking the menu at the gate, she punched in Bishop's number into the security's keypad and waited.

"Hello?"

Despite the intercom's static, she recognized Bishop's deep, scratchy baritone.

"It's Skye."

"Just drive on through, turn at the first left and it's the house at the end of the Cul-de-sac."

The black, arched gates eased open on silent hinges, and Skye drove into a subdivision filled with perfectly manicured bushes, trees, and lawns. The buzz of a weed-wacker and the scent of freshly mowed grass drifted through the air as she drove past a lawn maintenance truck and two workers sweating under the sun.

When she reached the cul-de-sac, she stared at Bishop's sprawling two-story mansion. Okay. Mansion might be stretching it, but the place probably would be the biggest house she'd ever step inside of.

It was a little intimidating. She'd never lived in a perfect house or socialized with the perfect people inside them. Heck, the two-bedroom condo she'd owned with Jay would have fit inside this opulent home five times over.

At least Skye knew Bishop wasn't so perfect, but somehow she didn't find the knowledge soothing as she guided her pickup around the gray stone, horseshoe driveway and parked in front a pair of massive, wooden double doors.

She stepped out of the truck and walked around to the entrance where two very wet noses attacked her from both sides. The noses were attached to two friendly and furry golden retrievers.

Okay. She'd exaggerated on the attacked part. More like investigated. Smiling, she scratched around the ears of both dogs, which sent their bottoms wiggling and their tails wagging that much more.

"I hope they're not bothering you."

Tensing, she looked up and found a man with gray-brown hair and a tall, lanky frame standing by the front door with a half-smile on his face. Seeing Gordon and not Bishop, she relaxed. A reprieve...for the moment.

"Not at all. I love dogs. I just never had the opportunity to have one." She met Gordon's eyes, the same deep brown color as his son's, but unlike Bishop, Gordon's eyes held a softness, almost a sadness in their depths. "Nothing beats a pair of adoring brown eyes and unconditional love when a person walks in the front door after a hard day."

"The smaller of the two is Maggie, and Dozer's our male and the one I'd watch out for. He may look furry and harmless, but that one's no gentleman." An ironic smile lifted one side of his mouth. "His name's short for Bulldozer, because he'll bulldoze his way through anything. Even knocked me on my butt a couple of times."

"I'll remember that." Skye grinned back, then followed Gordon and both dogs into the house's blessed cool interior and across the empty, marble foyer. "You're son's expecting me, isn't he?"

"Oh, yeah. He's in the green room. It's out through that door." He nodded to his left. "And on your right. Then you go down— I'll just show you. It'll be easier."

Skye stiffened, under the impression there'd be three of them the entire length of her visit. "Aren't you going to join us?"

"Maybe in a bit. I just came over to set up David's new computer system—the boy has no head for electronics—but I'll drop by in a bit with some iced tea." Gordon paused in the hallway. "You should have brought your son. I love kids."

"He's over at a friend's house right now. I don't want him missing out on making new friends." She wasn't about to tell the man that this would be the last place she'd bring Tyler. She didn't trust Bishop, so why would she trust him in the same house with her son?

"That's a shame." Gordon led them along an arched hallway and turned down another. "I don't get much opportunity to be around children, what with David never getting around to making that a priority."

Skye didn't have anything to say to that, but she could imagine Bishop's lack of appreciation for having his laundry vocalized in front of strangers. "I can't picture life without mine."

Gordon paused at an open doorway. "Same, except there have been times where I wanted to strangle the little turd."

A smile quivered on her lips. Somehow she couldn't see the man strangling his much larger and younger son. Actually, she couldn't see too many people getting the best of Bishop, but she liked the idea. She liked the idea even more if she were the person to do it, because maybe then she'd be able to get him to tell her the truth about his so-called magic.

"What's that, Dad?" Bishop called from what Skye guessed to be the green room

"Nothing." Gordon winked at Skye. "Just talking about the dogs."

They stepped into a room, and Skye now realized why Gordon had called it the green room. Philodendron, Ficus, Dracaena—too many plants for her to identify—flooded the room in a jungle of greens. Wicker furniture with pale yellow cushions added to the illusion of being in a mystical world.

She stared, disconcerted at the tranquil, earthy atmosphere. From what little she'd gauged of Bishop, nothing about him was soothing.

Three walls of glass revealed the outside world, where a myriad of colored flowers framed a Pebble Tec pool, whirlpool and rock fountain. From the swimming area, a pristine lawn rolled across the rest of the yard. Mesmerized, she inhaled crisp, cool air into her lungs, feeling as if she were outside on a beautiful spring day when in truth it was the middle of the summer with sweltering temperatures.

"My son may not have a head for electronics," Gordon murmured from beside her, "but he does know his plants."

Then he slipped from the room with both dogs, leaving her alone with his son. She met Bishop's questioning gaze. "It's beautiful."

"Thanks."

Casually dressed in faded jeans and a white T-shirt, and even with his severely cropped hair, he looked somehow more approachable than the other times she'd faced him. Appearances didn't necessarily mean the truth.

"So." He strode over and stopped a bare two feet away, pushing into her personal space. "Are you going to tell me the truth as to why you've been following me?"

His entire presence flooded her senses, the breadth of his shoulders, the clean, musky scent of him. He towered over her, while his close proximity leeched her self-confidence. Somehow she managed to stop herself from stepping away to widen the distance between them.

"Followed? I seem to remember you were the one following me." She arched a brow, pleased at the confidence in her voice. "Is your ego that big?"

"Skye, please. No games." He rubbed a hand along the short stubble of his hair. "Are we talking blackmail?"

Beneath the frustration and anger in his voice, she heard what she suspected might be fear.

"Why would you think blackmail?" Skye asked, searching for that same fear in his eyes. "Unless you have something to hide?"

CHAPTER 7

SKYE MIGHT HAVE pushed Bishop too far.

A pulse throbbed along the hard line of his jaw while his gaze narrowed. Even angry, Bishop's angular features and tanned complexion added to an attractive face, but such a façade could hide a multitude of character flaws like her ex-husband. Rattled at the intensity of his gaze, she took in an unsteady breath.

"How much?" he asked.

She shook her head, realizing she might be going about this all wrong. "Money has nothing to do with it."

"Then what?"

"I need to think this through."

Desperate to widen the space between them, she walked over to the glass wall and watched the water bubble over the rock fountain and into the pool. The scene's tranquility didn't soothe but amplified the turmoil and uncertainty jumbling inside her head. Even after having a couple of days to think about it, she still hadn't been able to figure out what the heck she was going to tell him.

She cleared her throat and decided on honesty. "Your show," she said, still staring at the fountain. "It's not magic. Not really. At least not what the public believes."

Silence. Now she had his complete attention. Tension, thick

and unmistakable, hummed in the air around them. She'd managed to shock him. Maybe even frighten him.

"Come off it," he finally protested. "That's insane."

"Insane?" She turned on her heel and met his look of disdain, but she wasn't fooled by the expression. "It's called telekinesis to be exact."

"Really?"

At his sarcasm, Skye tensed. "Would you like me to prove it?"

"Hey, kids. How's it going? Feel like some iced tea?"

Both turned as Gordon, smiling and holding a tray with a pitcher of iced tea and glasses, stepped into the room. Maggie and Dozer, tongues lolling and tails wagging, stood on either side of him.

Another pause of silence, loud and awkward, followed Gordon's question. Then Bishop took the tray from his father, raised an eyebrow and said, "Skye here's telling me that I have telekinesis of all things."

The older man's smile dipped. "Oh, crap. I'll come back another time."

Gordon and the dogs disappeared into the bowels of the house.

"I think we scared him away," Skye murmured.

Bishop stared back with obvious displeasure before he placed the tray on a glass coffee table. "And I wonder why?"

"So are you going to deny you have telekinesis?"

"Telekinesis is fiction. It's obvious you've been watching too many horror movies."

Hands balling into fists at her sides, thoroughly frustrated, Skye transferred her frustration to the garden shears lying on the tile floor next to some clay, potted flowers. Taking a deep, calming breath, she centered her mind, focused on the shears and willed them from the floor. The shears lifted into the air and arrowed toward the window, then hovered for a moment as a better idea came to Skye.

She sent Bishop a nasty, little smile. "Need a haircut?"

The shears jack-knifed from the window and hurtled toward Bishop. A cushion from one of the chairs rushed into the air.

A soft whoosh. Two feet from Bishop, the pillow blocked a savage attack to his face. The shears stabbed the pillow. Metal tips pierced through to the other side. The cushion still impaled by the shears fell to the floor.

"Are you trying to kill me!"

Bishop closed the distance between them and grabbed her elbow. He hauled her against his chest until his face was inches from her own. His breath fanned her cheek, feathering the downy hairs along her temple.

Skye glared at him. "Of course not. I had total control over those shears. If I'd wanted to kill you, believe me, I'd have done it days ago. And I wouldn't have used a pair of garden shears. I was trying to prove a point. And I did. That move with the pillow was no magic. You did it all by yourself."

For several tense seconds, he held her there. She didn't struggle, but stared back, chin hitched in the air, knowing the expression in her eyes dared him to try something. The heavy beat of his heart pounded against her breast, while the scent of coffee and sandalwood aftershave washed across her senses. Their lips were mere inches apart. For a wild second, she thought he was going to kiss her.

Suddenly, Skye became aware of him as a man—all hard muscle, sinew and testosterone—and to her dismay desire tightened her breasts and curled in the pit of her stomach.

He shoved her away. "What is it you want? Money? To be in my act? Well, it's not going to happen." He sliced a hand through the air and backed away. "You're a fool if you blab this to anyone. No one's going to believe you."

"You don't understand." And he might never, not with the atmosphere and people surrounding him. Bishop thought in terms of material gain, of using a person to get ahead. Years ago, Skye's mind might have worked that way, but her needs had grown far simpler. Survival. Love. Truth. "I don't want anyone else to know, and I don't want anything from you but answers."

"Answers to what?"

"To why we have the same powers. And why we share a past."

"Past? That makes no sense. I've never met you before."

That wasn't something she wanted to hear. "You must remember. Somewhere you must have a memory of me. Doesn't the name Skye Hunter sound familiar to you?"

He stared back, his face devoid of expression. "I'm sorry, no."

"But..."

"Why are you so insistent that you know me?"

She rubbed the back of her neck, suddenly exhausted. All this time she'd hoped, prayed Bishop held the answers to the strange, inconsistent images from her past. "I was under hypnosis when repressed memories started surfacing. Your name came up during more than one session."

"That's impossible. I would remember you."

"What about being in a hospital? Did you have an operation when you were a child?"

He shook his head, his thick brow knitting into a frown. "Never. What does a hospital have to do with anything?"

"I think you were in a hospital room. I heard you screaming."

"Did you see me?"

"No."

An indefinable expression flickered in his eyes. Possible disbelief? Or fear? Skye swore it was fear, but the emotion disappeared too quickly, and he was far too adept at hiding his thoughts.

He walked over to the coffee table and poured a glass of iced tea. "This person screaming has to be someone else."

"I'm not mistaken." Frustration thickened her voice and warmed her skin, while the burn of tears bit against the back of her eyes. When he offered her the glass, she declined with a jerk of her head. "And I'm not making this up."

"I'm sure you're not. What else came out when you were hypnotized?"

The inflexible light in his eyes and stubborn thrust of his jaw did nothing to sooth Skye's growing agitation. She didn't dare mention the lizard-like creature. He'd consider her crazy if he didn't already. "Nothing."

"That was it? Someone with the same name as me was inside a hospital room?"

He'd done it again—given her the opportunity to tell him everything. Images filled her head of hate-filled yellow eyes and snapping incisors, while a cold reptilian claw against her naked shoulder snaked into her memory.

And his reaction if she blurted it all out? He was barely tolerating her company right now. Add stories of lizards in hospitals, and he'd be calling the police and throwing her out within seconds.

Skye might feel like she was losing this battle, but she sure as hell wasn't going to show Bishop. The pressure against her eyes eased as she straightened her shoulders and inched her chin upward. Forget the tears. They'd only make her look weak. "Yes, that's it."

Lips thinning, he rubbed a palm against the length of his glass. Then he shook his head. "You've got the wrong man. There's hundreds if not thousands of men named David Bishop. It's obvious you've mistaken me for someone else."

"No, I haven't. You're the only one with the same, inexplicable powers."

"I don't know what to tell you there." He set his glass back down on the table with a snap. From his rigid posture, he didn't like what she was telling him. Simply because he didn't like discussing his powers? Or because of another, darker reason?

The sound of a shoe scraping against tile carried into the room.

"Dad."

Gordon stepped from the hall and into the room. Skye tensed, unable to read beyond the man's bland expression and guess as to how much he'd overheard.

"Can we have some privacy?" Bishop asked. "Is that too much to ask?"

"Sure," Gordon muttered and disappeared again, but both dogs entered the room to sit by Bishop.

When the sound of Gordon's footsteps disappeared, Bishop sighed. "You'll have to excuse my dad. He's always been overprotective. It doesn't seem to matter how old I've gotten or how long I've been on my own."

Exactly how overprotective? Enough to eavesdrop? Skye

wondered exactly how far the man would go to guard his son. Maybe Gordon wasn't the innocent-looking, mild-mannered, old man he appeared. Skye needed to file that thought away in case their paths crossed again.

Absently, Bishop patted Maggie and Dozer's golden heads while some of the tension left his face. "Where were we?"

"We weren't anywhere." She swallowed, determined to keep the disappointment from her voice as she watched Bishop stroke both dogs. Could a man with two trusting and gentle dogs who obviously adored him be so dangerous? She didn't think so, but she'd been wrong before when it came to judging people. She didn't have to look further than her ex-husband. "I think it would be best if I left. We're not getting anywhere."

She turned to go, but at the doorway, David caught her elbow. Arching a brow, she flicked a glance at his large hand. He started to say something, but instead shook his head and let her go.

"I'll walk you to the door."

She muttered, "Fine."

Leaving seemed the best option, but she'd have insisted on staying if she'd thought she could get more answers. Heck, she hadn't learned a thing today, and she was more confused than ever.

Without a word, Bishop opened the door and she stepped over the threshold and into the stifling summer heat. Sensing his gaze on her, she didn't glance over a shoulder to check but walked to her truck and slipped inside. When she turned the ignition, the engine stuttered, caught and shuddered as if about to die.

Please, no. She twisted damp hands around the steering wheel. She couldn't have this heap break down here of all places. This beautiful, immaculate neighborhood amplified her short-comings as a mother and provider and screamed at how low her life had sunk.

After she pressed on the gas and shifted into drive, the truck stuttered forward, then after a loud cough rumbled into life. With a prayer of thanks under her breath, she turned onto the street.

Once out of the neighborhood, though, Skye didn't relax. She was no closer to finding the truth than yesterday. And for the first time, she didn't have a plan.

Bishop said he didn't remember her or anything to do with her, but he was lying. She couldn't prove her suspicions. He'd covered the lies well behind a cool, remote façade. For the briefest moment, though, she swore she'd seen fear in his eyes.

Exactly what was he afraid of? And why?

~~*~~

"So are you going to follow her?"

In the living room, his dad stepped up beside him as David watched Skye get in her car and drive off. David didn't look over but continued to stare outside as he reached into his pocket and pulled out a tube of antacid tablets.

"Not this time."

"Good." His dad nodded toward the window. "She's trouble."

"Tell me something I don't know."

"She'll chew you up and spit you out."

"Again. That's something I already know." David pulled two tablets from the tube and stuffed them into his mouth. He ground both between his teeth and swallowed.

"Hmmm, she reminds me a lot of your mother. That woman had me tied up in so many knots that I didn't know whether I was coming or going."

"But you loved her."

"And you know where that got me. Oh, well. No doubt, she's happy with her current husband." His dad folded his arms, rocked back on his heels and grunted. "Well, we all know you're not going to take my advice—never have when it's important. So when are you going to see her next?"

"I..." David couldn't keep away from Skye if he wanted. The woman and mystery around her both fascinated and repelled him. Of course, there was this undeniable attraction. He hadn't wanted a woman with this much intensity in years. Why not act on it? Hell, by using sex, he might get the real truth out of her. He'd been told he was good at getting a woman to come long and hard. He sighed. "Soon. Real soon. But next time there won't be a pair of garden shears nearby."

"I'm not going to even ask what that's about."

Gordon walked from the room. David shoved the remaining tube of antacids back in his pocket and stared out the front window for several minutes, unable to shake off Skye's meeting. He still didn't believe her. She wanted something. She'd been holding back, not telling him everything. He'd seen the hunted look in her eyes for the briefest of moments.

He'd also done some holding back. She'd asked if he remembered her, and he'd skated around the truth. Even today, her name continued to fill him with dread. He didn't know why other than it related to his past. But he'd be damned if he was going to delve into a history that could ruin his future.

Skye didn't know it yet, but David had every intention of uncovering her secrets. He'd worked too hard to get where he was to have her do or say something to pull his life down around him.

He knew exactly what to use against her.

Sex.

God knows, she was attracted to him. He'd seen the heat in her eyes. Damn. He was going to enjoy every minute of getting those secrets from her lips.

CHAPTER 8

"I THOUGHT I MIGHT find you here," a deep, scratchy baritone voice whispered against the back of Skye's neck and sent a shiver racing across her skin.

Bishop.

He stepped up to the crowded roulette table beside her. Tall, rugged looking and oh-so-dangerous to her self-control. Heck, one look from him and she was feeling as if she'd lost a couple of IQ points.

Three days after meeting him at his home, Skye sat at one of several roulette tables at The Pharaoh. Tonight, she needed cash—desperately. Other than selling her body or robbing a convenience store, the only other means to get it fast was at a casino. So far, she'd managed to get enough money to last for a good month.

"You know, I could turn you in," he said by her ear this time, which sent another little shiver along her flesh. "Mary Ann."

Tension cut across her back and shoulders, and she almost forgot to breathe.

Impossible. She'd been so careful. How could he possibly know?

"Shocked I learned your alias?"

"I rarely get shocked," Skye managed in a smooth, controlled voice. Her stomach twisted and threatened to empty its contents. "How did you find out?"

"I thought it was time to pull in a favor I have with someone in security."

She continued to stare at the players setting their bets for the next game and forced herself to remember her identifications appeared perfectly legal. No one could prove she was anyone but Mary Ann Summers. "And what do you plan on doing?"

"Not a damn thing."

At the unexpected surrender in his voice, tension oozed from her muscles and her breathing returned to something almost normal. "And why's that?"

Shifting in the leather chair, she turned to him then and wished she hadn't. Those incredible deep brown eyes of his bored into her and made her wonder if he could read her thoughts.

"If I turned you in, I wouldn't get a chance to really uncover what the hell is going on." He lifted a brow and nodded toward the roulette wheel. "Running a little low on cash?"

"That's between me and my wallet." This time Skye sent him a cool smile.

She wasn't about to admit she needed the money to get her truck back from the garage. To her horror, the transmission had gone out and left her scrambling for additional funds. Driving around in a taxi in this city added up fast, not to mention the added expenses of a hotel room and food—just plain everyday necessities.

Thinking of her financial crisis sent her heart thumping, but she ruthlessly forced herself to calm down. She needed to look at the big picture. Money was the least of her problems.

"Is this your day job?" Bishop asked.

"It is now." She never thought to get herself a normal job, knowing that it wasn't an option—too many risks with people becoming a fixture in her life. Coworkers and friends asked questions and expected answers from the people in their lives.

Some might consider her no better than a thief, and Skye was fine with that. Frankly, she'd do far worse than steal when it came to ensuring her son's well-being.

"Mind me asking what you did before playing roulette?"

"I mind, but if you promise not to ask any more questions, I'll tell you."

He arched a brow and smiled. "How about I keep my curiosity to myself as long as we're at this roulette wheel?"

She laughed, shook her head, and found herself relaxing under his amused gaze. The man had far too much charm. Enough magnetism to get her into trouble if she didn't watch herself. "You never give an inch, do you? Well, if you must know, I was an accounting clerk."

"Really? I never would have guessed. You look too exotic for the office."

She wrinkled her nose. "I think I'll take that as a compliment. Otherwise, I'll suspect you were thinking more in the lines of a hooker."

Bishop laughed. "God, no. You've got far too much style to be mistaken for a hooker. A high-class call girl—now that might be something I could see." The humor dropped from his voice, and something dark and smoky curled around his words. "You've got the damn legs for it. I wouldn't hesitate to pay."

Sudden raw, sexual awareness heated her skin and quickened her breathing. From the intensity in David's expression and tension animating from his large body, she suspected he felt the same. Her heart stumbled over a beat. A warm flush crept up her neck and into her face as the scent of sandalwood and male drifted toward her. With a brown suede, stiletto heeled shoe dangling from the toes of one foot, she shifted and crossed a bare leg over another. The short hem of her form-hugging dress rode up her thighs, and she tugged the chocolate material down. Never had she felt so conscious of being a woman.

Before she said something stupid, she turned back to the table and watched the dealer sweep this plays chips, including her own, off the layout.

David sank down in the leather, swivel chair beside her, placed his money on the felt outside of the playing area and nodded to the dealer. "I'll have five stacks, please."

"What are you doing?"

"Buying in of course." He leaned over and placed a stack on a corner bet, his arm brushing against her own.

Warily, Skye stared at the sharp, masculine lines of his profile. He wore a pristine, white long-sleeved shirt, untucked at the waist, a pair of jeans and brown casual shoes—probably all designer labels.

"I thought I'd give this table a shot." He tapped a finger on top of his chips, sat back in his chair and winked. "But if you find me too intimidating, there's always the craps table. After all, you've got a much better chance at winning against the house with craps than roulette."

The man acted far too confident and with probable cause. Because of his glamorous career, lethal looks, and large bank account, he probably acquired cars, women, and any number of gadgets with little effort. Well, it was about time someone dismantled that gargantuan confidence and turned it into something more manageable, and she was the perfect person to do it.

"I've already played several games of craps. This table'll do me just fine. I've been far too lucky tonight to even think of moving."

Today, she'd come away from playing craps with enough to cover the truck and most of the monthly expenses, but she'd decided to add a nice financial cushion for any unexpected expenses.

She'd developed a certain skill to appearing "lucky," but there was always an ever-present chance of flagging the casino if she outplayed the odds repeatedly. Security and all available cameras zeroing in on her were the last things she wanted.

"Sounds like you expect your luck to continue."

She gave him a sideways glance. "Of course."

"Overconfidence can play against you."

"Really?" Skye couldn't believe the man had the gall to say that when he dripped with the stuff?

"Reeeally."

At the challenge in his eyes, her jaw tensed. "I wouldn't try anything if I were you. I'll win against you every single time," she bluffed.

He arched a brow. "So competitive. Are you like that in every-thing?" Curiosity and something distinctly wicked flared in his dark, far too knowing eyes. "What about in bed? Do you always have to be the one in control?"

For a moment, the bold question robbed her of speech. It didn't help when sudden images of their naked bodies and entwined limbs flashed in her mind. She straightened her shoulders and flipped a thick lock of hair over her shoulder.

"And what's wrong with that?" She sent him a half-smile, deliberately lightening her voice with amusement, not about to reveal how much his interest and words flustered her. The man's ego didn't need any help. "That way I know I get what I want."

"There's nothing wrong with letting someone take the initia-tive, but every now and then I like to be the one on top."

"I'm not interested in your sex life." She lifted her hand over her mouth and faked a yawn. "Any more detail, and I'll be bored to tears."

Dark and sinful, his laughter washed across the distance between them. He placed an elbow against the arm of his chair, leaned toward her and whispered, "You can always try me out for a test run. I might even teach you a few moves if you're naughty enough."

"I think I'll pass."

Even when she swiveled in her chair to face the table, she sensed his eyes on her. Skye forced herself not to squirm in her chair or pull up the bodice of her sleeveless dress. She liked the idea of learning a couple new maneuvers far more than she wanted to acknowledge.

"Maybe another time."

Skye opened her mouth to argue and deflate a bit of that ego of his, but she closed it. She wasn't going to play his little word games, not when she was getting too caught up in the sexual banter between them. She couldn't afford such distractions.

Instead, she tried to refocus on the table and the betting. She watched the roulette wheel spin, the ball ricochet off one pocket and then the next. As the wheel slowed, the blurred numbers grew with clarity.

"There's something about a roulette wheel I find mesmerizing," Bishop murmured. "Strange as it sounds, even as a child when I first saw one on television it intrigued me."

Skye looked over and found Bishop staring at the wheel with a fascinated expression that must have been similar to her own. "I know. I'll play poker, craps, and even slots, but I inadvertently always end up at the roulette table. I'm drawn to everything about it, and I don't know why."

"I guess we do have one thing in common."

For several seconds they stared at each other. The buzz of conversation, the hum and clatter of slot machines faded. She felt a sudden, inexplicable bond with Bishop, almost as if they'd shared an experience deeper, more profound than this moment...

Crazy.

She thrust the thought aside and focused on the table in front of her. She hadn't come to Vegas for a personal relationship.

With no winners this spin, the dealer swept up the losing chips, and Skye placed two stacks on the outside six lines. The dealer spun the wheel and let the ball drop. She pushed images and sounds to the background and stared at the ball. As the wheel slowed yet further, she mentally pushed the ball into the ten pocket. The ball landed, quivered and stayed. Then suddenly, it jumped from the pocket, bounced and landed in the number two pocket. By the time she recovered from her surprise, Skye didn't have time to move it back to ten without it looking odd.

Slowly she uncrossed her leg, turned to Bishop and warned, "Don't."

"Don't what?"

"I'm not buying that innocent look."

Finally. Progress. She'd managed to get Bishop to reveal his telekinesis without stabbing him with a pair of shears. Now she needed to see how far he'd take it, and she had an idea a dare might be the perfect bait.

She shifted in her chair and looked around. Across the table, a young girl with pink-streaked hair and matching lipstick and nails sat with a face flushed with excitement. She didn't look a day over twenty-one, and Skye suspected this was her first time betting at a roulette table in Vegas.

When the girl placed a couple of chips on number nine with a tentative hand, a wicked idea formed in her mind. Skye slipped from her chair and stepped back to allow another player to take her place.

"Cashing out already?"

"I think my luck just ran out, but do you know what? I think that girl with the pink highlights might be far luckier than I've been tonight."

Bishop glanced at the girl and back at Skye. Understanding flared in his brown eyes, and he smiled a little half-smile that looked far too cocky. He slipped from his own chair, retrieved his chips and stood beside her to watch the table. "I don't know about that. The little, bald-headed guy next to her looks far luckier with his chips on six. Retired, probably with a fixed income. I bet he probably needs the cash more than her."

"You think so? I beg to differ." Skye met the challenge in his eyes and straightened her shoulders and grinned back.

Pleasure bubbled up into her chest. Months, maybe even years, since she experienced such emotion. All because of Bishop.

Mentally, she shook herself from the thought. No analyzing. Just take the moment.

One. Two deep, cleansing breaths. Then she peered between the shoulders of the gamblers seated in front of them and mentally zeroed in on the ball after the dealer's drop. The wheel slowed. The ball clattered across the pockets, hesitated, then plopped into the nine pocket. And it—or should she say Bishop—did exactly what she expected. The ball jumped immediately from the pocket and into six. She forced it out of six and around the wheel until it landed back into nine. Once in the pocket, she used her mind to keep it there.

"You're working far too hard at keeping that in the hole. It doesn't want to be forced," David whispered. His lips brushed her ear lobe as he spoke, while his breath warm and moist whispered against her neck.

Much to her dismay, Skye lost her concentration, and she knew that's exactly what Bishop wanted. The ball jumped again and landed on six. By the time she rammed her elbow into his side, heard his soft whoosh of breath, too much time had passed for her to get the number back into the nine pocket.

"Number six, black," the dealer called out.

"Well, by God!" The elderly, bald-headed man slapped his hand on the table with a thump. "Will you get over that?"

Leaning closer to Bishop, she whispered, "That was just luck."

"I'd call it skill."

As she shifted and lifted her head to glance up at him, his lips brushed against her temple. He was far too close. So near, she smelled cinnamon on his breath.

She'd never revealed her telekinesis deliberately with another human being or felt this comfortable or this connected. To be able to share her secret with someone else who understood, lifted her spirits and tugged at her heart.

She met his gaze, and until now, hadn't realized his brown eyes held deep rust colored flecks around the irises. She also hadn't realized just how nicely they fit together height-wise. In heels, she didn't have far to inch up and touch her lips to his or press up against his hips.

Hunger washed across her flesh and seeped into her body while getting air into lungs seemed far harder than moments before.

"We have a winner!"

Both of them blinked and drew apart, but sexual awareness still throbbed in the air between them. Bishop's face seemed a bit flushed, his breath a bit quicker, and his eyes a bit more dilated than moments before. It seemed she wasn't the only one caught up in this crazy attraction.

On the next spin, Skye concentrated harder. The girl had chosen twenty-one. Not the smartest move when it came to odds and the roulette, but that didn't matter, because fate—or more like Skye—was helping her.

When the ball quivered on twenty-one and threatened to slip out because of Bishop's power, Skye frantically searched for a

way to distract him. She jabbed him in the ribs with an elbow...
again. Not the most original idea, but it worked. The ball stayed
in the pocket, and the girl squealed with delight.

"Hey!" Frowning, he looked insulted if not for the tell-tale
gleam in his eyes. "Cheater."

She smirked. "I like to win."

"And stay on top."

Skye decided to ignore that comment. "I think that makes us
even."

"Oh, I think we should try one more time for a tie-breaker.
My retired guy probably has to struggle to pay his prescription
and medical care."

"You're on." She'd never done something as crazy as this, but
she couldn't resist seeing the excitement and wonder on both the
man and girl's faces.

The next number was fifteen for the girl and a corner bet by
the elderly man. Skye focused, determined not to get distracted
by Bishop's next strategic move on her person. When he draped
an arm around her shoulder, she was fully prepared and tried
to shrug him off. Then he used a thumb to caress the sensitive
skin below her ear, and after a moment, he moved from there to
play with her silver earring. The gentle touch sent a shiver racing
down her spine.

From the corner of her vision, she saw his wide smile. So he
was enjoying himself, was he? She couldn't help but do the same
and found herself grinning like an idiot.

The wheel slowed. With her mind, Skye pushed the ball into
number fifteen. Then suddenly the ball popped out. Skye tried
to sweep it around the wheel again to fifteen, but some invisible
force fought back. The white ball skirted across the pockets and
dropped into two and held, no matter how hard Skye tried to use
her mind to pull it out.

"Yes!" A woman with sleek, black hair and a scarlet top, clapped
wildly and glanced around the table with wide-eyed amazement.

Skye stiffened. The woman wasn't supposed to win. A bet on
number two had nothing to do with either the girl or the man.
"Did you?"

Confusion flashed across Bishop's face as he slid his arm from around her shoulders, exposing her skin to the casino's cool air. "No. I haven't a clue what happened."

Skye shivered and crossed an arm around her stomach while unease crept along the back of her neck. "You don't have some inside joke going on here I'm not aware of?"

"No. I was battling the ball from your mental hold when something seemed to grab it."

Searching his face, Skye saw genuine puzzlement in his dark eyes and believed him. "That's odd."

He frowned as he glanced around the table. "Unless someone with the same ability is playing with the two of us."

Skye followed his narrowed gaze. The pink haired girl had two friends on either side of her. The elderly man sat alone. A man, possibly a husband, stood to the right of the raven-haired woman. Several people, all looking like innocent tourists, watched or walked by the table. The back of a man disappeared into a crowded aisle.

There was no way to identify the person behind the stunt.

Fear pressed against Skye's chest with such force that it momentarily cut off the breath from her lungs. Skye backed away from the table. She wasn't being paranoid. Not this time. Someone else had moved the ball on the roulette wheel.

That someone was a threat and knew all about her. She sensed it deep in the pit of her stomach. That person had stood within hearing, even touching distance.

Panic lashed at her mind. Her hands fisted.

Too much emotion. Too much pressure. She glanced over at a glass of what looked like a Bloody Mary on the edge of the table. Her control disintegrated. The glass exploded, spraying liquid and ice on the table, across Bishop's chest and a man to the right of him.

"What the hell!" someone cried out.

Several others gasped.

A hot wave of mortification swept into Skye's face as Bishop's once pristine white shirt turned into an ugly tie-dyed red. She prized her composure, worked hard and long to keep her feelings under the radar. For months she hadn't broken anything—until now.

But someone had followed her here. If they knew her location, that would mean...

Ty. My God. She'd thought he'd be fine with Jamie, but he wasn't safe. Neither one of them were.

CHAPTER 9

"SO WHAT'S THE situation?" Ferguson asked from the other end of Peter's cell phone.

Seated behind the wheel of his parked rental, Peter squinted against the fading sun and pulled the car's visor lower. If it wasn't for the vent blowing cold air, he'd be sweating like a stuffed sausage on a grill. "I found her at the Pharaoh."

It had taken Peter a week longer than he'd expected. The woman had been far harder to find than most.

"Anything else?"

"She went over to a David Bishop's house."

Silence. Peter stilled, sensing the shock on the other side of the line. Strange. Why did the name Bishop bother this prick so much?

From across the parking lot, Peter stared at the Pharaoh, a garish, pyramid-type building. The casino squatted in front of him, while the Vegas sun reflected off its windows and gold paint. Ugly just like the rest of the city. How the hell anyone lived here was beyond him.

Peter cleared his throat. "After she left, a few minutes later a man came out of the same residence."

"Go on."

"I think the guy was Bishop's father. I'm guessing. He had

gray hair, the same type of facial features but a skinnier build. I was too far away for a positive ID."

"Damn it!"

"What's the problem?"

"Gordon's the problem."

Peter frowned and glided a hand across the steering wheel. "Who's this Gordon?"

"None of your damn business! I'd tell you if it was. I would have thought you'd have figured that one out by now!"

Peter's nostrils flared, and he fisted a hand around the wheel. *Bastard.* He was almost tempted to keep his mouth shut on his other news. "There's something you should know."

"Yeah, what?"

"Do you know of anyone else interested in Skye and her son?"

"No." Anger seeped from his voice. "Why?"

Peter paused and let Ferguson wait for a moment. The prick wasn't as powerful as he liked to think. "Someone else is following them."

"Well, find out who the hell they are. That's what I pay you for!"

The line disconnected.

"Asshole," Peter muttered and tossed his cell on the passenger seat.

He started the car and pulled out of his parking space. When he turned the steering wheel and guided the car out onto the street, pain cut across his left shoulder and down his arm. He scowled. Two years now, and neither bone nor muscle had healed correctly from where the bullet had torn through both. The pain always reminded him of his past life.

A life ruined because of Skye Hunter.

Oh, but soon, real soon, he'd more than ruin Skye's life.

~~*~~

Someone rapped sharply on the hotel door.

Skye tensed, digging her fingers into the t-shirt she held in her hands. She twisted the material, while fear bit into her back and shoulder muscles.

My God they'd found her. After all the months, all the running, it came to this moment.

She looked over at Tyler flung across the width of the bed with his head propped up on a hand and his gaze attached to a television program. The show's volume, moments ago sounding normal, blared into the confined room.

They'd been in their hotel room less than fifteen minutes.

After she fled the Pharaoh and rushed over to Jamie's apartment, she'd found Tyler safe, unaware and unharmed. But she hadn't relaxed, not with a jumble of scenarios on what to do next running inside her head, and she sure as hell wasn't relaxed now with someone pounding on her door.

"Ms. Summers?" a male voice called from the hall outside.

Standing by her own bed, Skye dropped the shirt into her open duffle bag and kicked off her high-heeled shoes. She hadn't even had the chance to change out of her dress and into some jeans. "Tyler, get in the bathroom."

He blinked and glanced at her. "What's wrong?"

"I don't know yet. Just get in the bathroom to be safe." Bare feet silent on the carpeted floor, she edged away from the bed.

"Mom. We're fine."

"Tyler. Now."

He must have recognized the seriousness of the situation from her low, clipped voice, because he scrambled off the bed and disappeared into the bathroom. After the door closed and the lock clicked into place, Skye turned off the television. The room's sudden silence itched across her spine.

Breath catching roughly against her throat, she moved to the door. "Who is it?"

"Security."

She peered through the door's viewfinder. A clean-shaven man in a business suit stood in the hall. Nothing about him looked familiar. "What do you want?"

"Can you step out into the hall please?"

Damn it. This wasn't looking good. "I'd rather not."

"Ms. Summers, I don't think you realize how grave this situation is. I don't want to involve the police, but I will if I have to."

Security or liar. Either way, he looked like he didn't intend to move from the door.

She flexed her fingers, then rubbed her damp palms against her silk-clad hips. Possibly just one man. If he tried anything, she could take him. Still, the knowledge didn't slow her heart rate as she gripped the deadbolt and snapped it open.

She took in one slow, soothing breath and exhaled in a quick rush. Next, she clutched the doorknob and twisted. Legs braced, heart thumping, she swung open the door. All her energy focused on the man in front of her. One suspicious move and she'd slam him against the wall with her telekinesis.

When he didn't aim a fist to her face or point a gun at her chest, she glanced up and down the hall for any others.

Empty.

For now.

Stuffed into a suit one size too small, the man—no, more like pro-wrestler look-a-like—stared at her with cold eyes. "You're going to have to leave the premises."

Shifting, she gripped the door jamb with rigid hand and remained in the threshold, while the open door butted up against her back. "I don't understand."

"We've had security cameras watching your activity on the casino floor."

Dread, bitter and foul tasting, coated her mouth. "Why?"

"We believe you're using a cell phone or some type of device to trigger the roulette wheel and dice."

"That's crazy!"

Then Skye remembered Jay. He must have asked the hotel's security questions about her. Still, Jay knew how to get information without making waves. It didn't make sense—

Bishop.

The reason for getting singled out had to be because of Bishop. Who else but him? He knew someone in security. He'd asked questions, uncovered her alias and alerted security a second time. The hotel must have been watching her for days. Management would be crazy not to when two different men started asking questions about some woman gambling and residing in their hotel.

Pressure tightened across her chest. "Did David Bishop have anything to with this?"

"I'm not at liberty to discuss this with you." But with the mention of Bishop's name, she saw the man's eyes flicker.

"He did, didn't he?"

"Management wants you to vacate the building and surrounding property within the hour."

"And what if I don't?"

His overly large forehead creased into a frown. "We haven't pursued why you're using an assumed name, but if you decide to cause any problems, we might just have to do that."

"So you're threatening me?"

"Now look here, Ms. Summers. We don't have to explain anything to you. The hotel wants you out of here, and if you decide to fight us on—"

"Mom?"

Glancing over a shoulder, she found her son several feet behind her. He stood in his stocking feet, his hands balled into fists at his side, uneasiness, and fear glittering in his eyes. He looked far too vulnerable. He didn't deserve the deck he'd been dealt.

"Hey, sweetie."

"What's wrong?"

Skye smiled with difficulty. "Nothing serious. At least nothing that can't be fixed." She turned back to the security guard as her son snaked an arm around her middle. At Tyler's protective gesture, she straightened and squeezed his hand pressed against her side. "We'll be out in an hour."

After she closed the door, Tyler let go of her waist and sat down on the edge of the bed. "Something's wrong. You can tell me now he's gone."

She met Tyler's solemn gaze, and the pressure against her chest tightened into a dull ache. Would there ever be a day when she didn't disappoint Tyler? "We just have to find another place to live."

He nodded. No anger. No surprise. He picked up his portable game player from the bed and pulled his duffle bag from the closet. He'd been through this drill before.

Sighing with resignation, she grabbed more clothes from one of the dresser drawers to stuff in her own bag. She'd planned on leaving the Pharaoh after the incident with the roulette wheel, but she hadn't expected to be thrown off the premises. She could thank Bishop for that.

Maybe she'd do just that.

~~*~~

Less than an hour later, Skye stood in the middle of the entryway to Bishop's home and hit the doorbell with a thumb. She hit the button again. Then thinking that might not be enough to get him out of bed, she pressed down again with a trembling hand.

The porch light glared from above, spotlighting her figure for anyone to see. Thank God, a security gate separated them and Bishop's house from the general public. She'd also checked numerous times on the way here for a tail and hadn't found any, but then that might not mean much. Bishop had managed to follow her pretty well without her knowledge, and he'd been a novice.

The shakes had soon started after she'd dumped their luggage into the back of the pickup and pulled out of the parking lot of the Pharaoh. Security could have easily been someone far more dangerous, like the person playing mind games at the roulette table earlier that day.

The door swung open. Braced on long, muscled legs with a smattering of hair, Bishop stood in the doorway. A pair of ragged shorts rode low on his hips. Nothing else covered his chiseled abs and chest. His half-naked body and close proximity snapped off the air momentarily going into her lungs. Her mind floundered for words.

He blinked against the light, then frowned. "How did you... You must have remembered the security code." He rubbed his fingers across his forehead. "Why are you here?"

"I need a place to stay."

His face turned impassive. "So what does that have to do with me?"

"Since you're the reason why I was kicked out of the Pharaoh, I think it's more than fair that you give me a room for my son and me."

He leaned a shoulder against the door jamb and arched a brow. "Oh, no. There's no way in hell you're staying here."

"Tough."

Thank God the word came out sounding ruthless instead of desperate. She didn't dare show Bishop any weakness, though right now her frayed emotions were close to shredding into a pile of rags.

Staying at another casino wasn't an option. Whoever had watched her at the roulette wheel would expect her to show up somewhere on the strip. And even if she did enter another casino, she'd be kicked out. Word would be already out about her illegally working the tables.

David stepped out of the house and closed the door. "What are you going to do? Camp out in my front yard? I don't think so."

"I have no intention of doing anything on your 'front yard'. Two of your rooms will do nicely. My God, you've got enough space in there for several families. An adult and one child aren't going to make much of a difference." Bishop owed her something by prying into her life and messing with it to the point where he'd inadvertently gotten her kicked out.

She glanced over her shoulder where the driveway lights illuminated her pickup. Even though shadows clung to the cab's interior, she made out the top of Tyler's head in the passenger seat. Her son meant everything to her. He needed a safe place right now. The security alone here would be worth the price of staying in a house with an angry owner.

Skye turned back around to find Bishop shaking his head. "Sorry. You've managed to take care of yourself and your son all these years. You can keep on doing it without my help."

The idea of driving back out into the night to some unknown destination sent a wave of panic through her body. It wasn't going to happen. Not tonight. "I don't think you understand. If it wasn't for you, we'd still be at the Pharaoh." A lie, but he didn't need to know that she'd been ready to flee anyway. "Do you have any idea how my son must have felt when hotel security demanded we leave?"

"I had nothing to do with you being evicted."

"How can you say that?" Finding her voice rising in accusation, she lowered it. Panicking wasn't going to get her anywhere. "You said yourself that you knew someone in security at the hotel. If you'd kept your questions to yourself and not stuck your nose into my business, we'd be fine."

"I think you're the one who doesn't understand." He stepped toward her until his dark, brown gaze locked with hers and the heat radiating from his body clung to her own. "I just wanted to find out who the hell you were." Sincerity flashed in his eyes and the hard lines of his face softened. "I had no intention of getting you kicked out of the hotel. That's all on you. If you hadn't lied about your name and used more than luck at the gaming troubles, you wouldn't be in the trouble you are in now. I just happened to accidentally hurry things along."

"Happened? Oh, I don't think so." Skye wasn't about to back down now. She stepped toward him until her breath brushed against his jaw and neck. "I understand fully. You're the one that doesn't get it."

"And what's that?"

"Simple really. If you don't let us stay here, then something's going to go wrong with your magic show."

He tensed. "What the hell is that supposed to mean?"

Skye lifted her lips into a fake smile. "I'll mess with your performance. When your retriever floats in the air to the right, I'll make sure he floats to the left. If something disappears, I'll make it reappear. It's called telekinesis, remember?" Sarcasm dripped from her last few words. "Can you imagine what type of chaos I can create?"

All lies, but Bishop didn't know that. She was counting on it. She lifted her chin and stared back, proud she didn't flinch or step away from the animosity radiating from his male bulk. But her composure was so close to disintegrating. For the last several months she'd had to deal with all the running and looking behind her shoulder and worrying about Tyler. Add the materialization of a new threat—a person with the same telekinetic powers playing a sick game of roulette—and they all threatened to smash her fake bravado.

"Shit! You're crazy. Do you know that?" David squeezed his hands into fists at his sides as if to stop himself from wrapping them around her throat, while a muscle pulsed by the corner of his jaw. "Why the hell me? What makes you think you can trust me?"

"I can't." She shrugged a shoulder. She wanted to. God knows she wanted that. "But I trust you more than anyone else. It's obvious you don't know what's going on. For one, you're a bad actor, and for another, if you'd wanted me dead or incapacitated, I wouldn't be talking to you now."

~~*~~

David glared at her, searching for signs of weakness or uncertainty, but her raised chin, stormy eyes and grim expression didn't give anything away. The woman was drama with a capital D and probably pig-headed enough to follow through on the threat. A threat he couldn't afford to dismiss.

He'd wanted her close, but not this damn close. She'd be under the same roof, down the hall, near naked. With her underfoot, she might be liable to dig into his past and anything else she found an interest in when it came to his life.

By being in the same house, he didn't think he had the self-control to keep off her even if he wanted to. To hell with his self-control. If she wanted to force herself into his house by blackmail, then he'd retaliate. Seduction sounded like the perfect way to strike back. Devious, yes. But he'd never admitted to being some moral citizen above reproach. He'd have her under him squirming with passion and spilling all her secrets.

He grunted. "You win. For now." When the truck door groaned open, he glanced over her shoulder and found her son stepping onto the driveway. Damn, but for one crazy minute, he'd forgotten about the boy. Seduction might be a whole hell of a lot harder than he'd first thought. "Go get your son and your stuff."

He opened the door and allowed Dozer and Maggie to slip outside. Everyone needed to get used to each other if they were going to reside under the same roof. When the boy came around the truck and started walking up the drive, grudgingly David stepped down the stairs with both dogs to greet him. He had to remember the kid was innocent. Skye deserved his anger, but the boy didn't.

A high whine emitted from Dozer.

"Heel."

Tail wiping the cement, Dozer sat, but quivered in obvious anticipation, while Maggie sank down on her haunches beside the other retriever. David didn't want to scare the kid with two large dogs battling for attention.

When the boy, who lurched forward from the weight of his duffle bag, stumbled to the stairs, David smiled and reached for the bag. "It looks like you could use some help."

The boy clutched the bag and veered away from David's hand. Distrust and something old and weary glittered in his eyes, while the porch's light magnified the boy's pallor. David's smile congealed. What fun. He'd just invited one of the Munster kids from that old sitcom into his house.

Skye caught up to her son with her own, huge, duffle bag. Unlike the boy, she hefted the thing as if it didn't weigh much more than a couple of grapefruit. He decided to store that bit of information in his brain for any future altercation that might crop up.

Skye paused to scratch behind Maggie's ear. "Hey, girl." She grinned up at David. "Which is this one again?"

At her unexpected and genuine smile, David, to his horror, found himself scrambling for a coherent reply. "Maggie. They're both harmless." He said the last for the boy, who reached over and slid a tentative hand across Dozer's crown.

"He's so soft," the boy murmured in awe. "Does he do any tricks?"

"A few."

Just then Dozer decided to drop and roll, his act of playing dead ruined by the rapid swish of his tail.

"I like him." When he reached down to scratch the dog's belly, the bag knocked against the boy's ankle and plopped onto the ground.

"Come on, Ty. You'll have time to play with him inside." She turned to David and arched a brow. "Where to?"

Grunting, David pivoted and climbed the shallow stairs and walked into the house.

In the entryway, David heard, "Holy cow, Mom, look at that," behind his back. He knew Tyler referred to the stained-glass roof of the entrance above them, but he didn't pause as he led them down the hall and in the opposite direction from his bedroom. He didn't dare have Skye anywhere near him with the boy under the same roof. Hell, when it came to her, he had little self-control and was liable be on her like a rutting dog, angry or not.

He stopped at the doorway to one of the guest bedrooms. "There's an adjoining bathroom to the right. From the bathroom, there's another bedroom, which Tyler can use. Kitchen's down the hall from where we came from and also on the right."

As she followed her son into the bedroom, the air around him whispered with her distinct fragrance of lavender and another elusive scent. Trying to distinguish the smell, he caught himself closing his eyes and quickly snapped them open.

"I'll see you tomorrow," he murmured, before escaping to the other section of the house. Other than his father, David never had anyone over for any length of time, never mind a mother and her son.

Shit.

He stalked through the house and into his bedroom. He didn't try to go back to bed, knowing the futility of getting any sleep. Instead, he changed into a swimsuit and let himself outside. But even when he did an hour of laps, he didn't feel tired. After rubbing himself down with a plush towel and tossing it on a lounge chair, he re-entered the house but didn't bother with a light. Moonlight guided him through the rooms and into the kitchen and glistened off the chrome appliances. A shot of brandy might do something.

IDENTITY

Brandy bottle in hand, David closed the cabinet door and turned to find a dark silhouette of someone else in the kitchen with him.

CHAPTER 10

HEART THUNDERING, DAVID fumbled with the bottle in his hands and somehow managing to catch it around the neck before banging it on the counter. "Shit! What are you doing here?"

"I just came in for a glass of water." Sudden light flooded the room, and Skye stepped away from the kitchen switch. "I didn't mean to scare you."

"You didn't." David blinked to adjust his gaze.

Her eyebrow arched upward as she stepped further into the kitchen and ran a finger along the edge of the island made of cherry cabinets and black granite countertops.

"Okay. Maybe a bit. I'm not used to having anyone else in the house at night."

Skye had pulled her hair from its pony tail and let the thick, chestnut strands flow past her shoulders in waves. A vision of those same strands across his pillow flashed in his mind. Desire tightened his groin. She hadn't even been in the house for a night and he already wanted to climb on her.

Yeah, he planned on seducing her, but not this soon. He'd wanted to give her a good day to adjust to his house with her son. He also didn't want to look that desperate.

"That's a bit hard to believe."

"Why?" As he ran his gaze over her body with interest, he crossed the kitchen's cool, marble tile. To hell with the brandy. With Skye, he needed his wits.

She'd changed into a navy tank top and blue and white plaid boxers. Even with her feet in a pair of thick, white socks bunched at the ankles and her face void of makeup, she looked sexy as hell. It was beyond him how, when she wore something so masculine.

She searched his face with cool, hazel eyes. "I would think women and you are pretty inseparable. I'm sure the groupie thing is pretty hard to pass up."

He shook his head, not really wanting to admit her assumption upset him. From one of the cabinets, he took out a glass and filled it with ice and water from the chrome refrigerator. "I'm not a player. Ah... I see your surprise. Believe it or not, the constant attention gets old. Far faster than you'd think."

Glass in hand, he stopped two feet in front of her, leaned a hip against the counter and offered her the water.

Shadows clung below her eyes and the translucent quality of her skin hinted at exhaustion. She took the glass. The way she deliberately avoided his fingers bothered David, and because it bothered him, it annoyed him that much more.

He sighed. Maybe he had been a little rough on her. "About the hotel situation... I'm sorry. Like I said, I never had any intention of getting you kicked out. I'm not that much of ass, but what the hell am I supposed to do with all your threats?"

She searched his face, her gaze guarded above the glass as she took a swallow. "Yes, well, I might have come across a bit pushy."

This time he was the one who raised an eyebrow.

"All right. A lot."

He noticed she hadn't retracted her threat. The woman was damn prickly. Something or someone had made her that way. The question was—who or what? And did he really want to find out?

She cleared her throat. "Thanks for taking us in."

That was something at least. "You didn't give me much of a choice."

"That's true." She lifted the corner of her mouth into an ironic smile. "We might have ended up in the garage instead."

Poised, confident, she stood with her chin raised and thoroughly in control—even in a pair of pajamas.

Jeeze. What would it take to crack that damn composure? Dynamite?

David's gaze narrowed. Maybe something far simpler.

Shit. He'd wanted to kiss her from the moment he'd caught sight of her on the casino's floor.

He was tired of being the one always out of control—something that had never happened with any other woman until Skye blasted into his life. But not tonight. Tonight, she'd be the one losing control.

Giving her a day to get situated was a stupid idea anyway. He needed her off balance—now. And at this point, he didn't care if he looked desperate.

Skye's lips parted as he moved closer. The air conditioner on his damp skin didn't cool his suddenly heated skin.

She edged backward.

He inched forward.

"Okay, Bishop." The ice-cubes rattled in her glass as she set it on the counter with a snap. "That's close enough."

"Why? Am I getting to you?"

"Of course not."

He stroked a knuckle along the tender skin below her ear. "Then why is your pulse fluttering like a terrified mouse?"

"That must be your imagination." Her throat flexed as she swallowed, but she didn't step away. Her nipples pressed against the thin cotton of her shirt, tempting him to cup and caress both breasts until they tightened even more beneath his touch.

"Really?"

She raised her hand as if to pull his away, but he caught her wrist and brought her palm to his mouth. He licked the fleshy part below her index finger, inhaling her distinct lavender and feminine scent. At her indrawn breath, doubts about her lack of sexual interest in him scattered. David smiled against her hand with satisfaction.

Soon. If not tonight, there'd be another time when he'd have her spilling her hidden agenda from between those delectable lips.

He lifted his thumb from her inner wrist and brushed his mouth over her rapid pulse. He tasted salt and a possibility of something more. From above her hand, he watched for a reaction as he murmured against the warmth of her skin, "What is it about you that keeps me off balance and ties me in knots? You don't know how much I want to pull off your clothes and take you here on the floor."

Skye's chest rose and fell in quick succession as the color of delicate rose bloomed into her cheeks and melded with the dusting of her freckles. The desire that flared into her eyes hit him in the gut.

David wanted her, wanted her more than he could remember wanting a woman.

His grip on her wrist tightened. He wrapped his free arm around her waist and applied pressure to the small of her back until her body grazed his. The cool cotton of her shirt and shorts brushed against his bare stomach and legs.

He released her wrist and caught her chin between a finger and thumb, urging her to look up and meet the hunger he knew burned in his eyes. "I think you like being this close."

He didn't wait for an answer. Hell, he knew, she'd come up with an argument if he gave her more than a second. He lowered his head, and the touch of her lips dragged a rattling sigh from his own. The taste of her, warm, female and alluring urged him to take more than a fleeting kiss. He held off. Savoring the moment. The anticipation.

Her sigh mingled with his. The touch of her hand against his bicep, tentative at first, grew bolder as her fingers glided up to his shoulder.

"You have the most incredible skin. I've wanted to touch it from the minute I first saw you." When he trailed his fingers along a two-inch scar by her temple that disappeared into her hair, he frowned. "What happened here? Did you do that Skydiving? Or something not so hair-raising? Maybe mountain climbing or horseback riding?

"Nothing so dramatic," she replied with a throaty, awkward sounding chuckle. "I actually don't remember. I probably fell out of a tree or off a bike."

She dropped her hand from his shoulder and made to pull away but David didn't release his grip from around her waist. He was far from done with her.

"You should be more careful." He slid his fingers from her temple to the curve of her cheek, and then swept a thumb along the line of her jaw. When he cupped her neck with one hand, her pulse thrummed against his palm.

David shifted, feeling himself grow hard with need. Her breasts brushed against his chest. He found the cotton strangely erotic against his naked skin.

"I need more." His voice came out rough and raw with emotion as he searched her face. She wanted him too. He saw the awareness in her eyes, sensed the hunger in the air around her. Anticipation radiated from her body. "This isn't enough."

"It is for me."

"I think you want more."

"I think you've got an inflated ego," she whispered against his lips, but she didn't draw away as he kissed the corner of her mouth and tugged on her lower lip with both teeth until her mouth widened.

"In a minute, I'm hoping you won't be able to think."

He captured her lips. This time though, he needed more than a simple caress, a simple taste. He longed to have her blind to anything but him, his touch, his hunger.

He swept his lips across her mouth again and again, testing their texture, their warmth. Her mouth opened wider against the pressure of his, and her tongue mated with his, inquisitive, daring, and bold.

David cupped her slender shoulders with shaking hands and pressed closer. Her breasts flattened against his chest and her hips rubbed against his erection. His grip on her flesh tightened as desire surged through his veins, clouding everything but the need to slake his hunger on the woman in his arms.

With Skye's hands roaming roughly over his back, David

turned and lifted her onto the kitchen island. She opened her legs and cradled his hips between her thighs. The feel of her heat against his cock ripped a groan from his mouth as he caught the back of her skull in one hand and kissed her. Thin fabric blocked him from plunging into her right that second and taking her until they both came.

A snuffle and soft woof sounded from somewhere in the kitchen. One of the dogs brushed against his calf. David nudged the animal aside with a leg. There was no way in hell he'd let a dog get in the way of what he wanted.

Skye. The woman twisted his inside, made him forget everything but the need to take her, to mark her as his.

Another bark broke over their labored breathing. This one sounded louder and more impatient.

David broke off their kiss and glared down at Dozer sitting on his haunches and sweeping the floor with his tail. Those big brown eyes didn't fool him. The dog always liked to be the center of attention, and now was no different.

Skye's fingers dug into his arms and she pushed him away. "Okay, Bishop. This is crazy."

Reluctantly, he eased back from her body. He took in a shuddering breath, stunned at the depth of his reaction.

David noted her flushed cheeks, swollen lips and the unmasked need glittering in her eyes before she lowered her lids. "Crazy? Maybe... But one more minute and crazy would be the last thing on our minds."

Skye opened her mouth, closed it, then opened it again. "This can't happen again."

She didn't look so in control now. Somehow David didn't find anything satisfying about cracking her composure like he'd thought. Yeah, he'd gotten to her, but it didn't compare to how much she'd pushed him over the edge. Forget control. He'd lost anything resembling it the moment she'd kissed him back. While his plan to get secrets from those lips... Hell, they'd hit the dust along with that control.

With his gaze locked on hers, David wrapped both hands on her knees and caressed the delicate skin of her inner thighs with his thumbs. Skye grabbed his hands with trembling ones of her own but didn't pry them off. Encouraged, David inched his fingers slowly up her thighs, savoring the texture, the warmth and the tremor beneath his touch.

Longing swept across her face, and she bit down on the corner of her lip. Their breathing carried across the room while the sexual tension between them thickened and escalated. Her reaction, unmasked, unmistakable, and so damn responsive stoked the hunger burning through his body.

Then her face tightened, wiping out her brief look of hunger. She shoved at his chest.

He dropped his hands and stepped backward, fighting the disappointment and frustration from entering his voice. "Why? You want it. I want it."

Skye slipped off the counter and moved across the kitchen. Only when she stood on the opposite side of the island did she face him. Gone was the passion, the longing in her eyes. She stared back with impenetrable, hazel eyes. "I can't have any distractions. I'm here to find out what happened to a missing part of my past. You're a key." She warded off his response with a raised hand and shook her head. "No. Don't even try to convince me otherwise. It won't work. I know what I'm talking about."

"Enough to stake your life on it?"

"I already have," her words, barely audible still carried across the distance between them. She winced and rubbed the bridge of her nose. "Forget I said that. I'm tired and talking about things that don't make sense."

"Forget? Why?" He stepped around the dog and grabbed his bottle of brandy. To hell with his wits. They'd disserted him the second he pulled Skye into his arms. He grabbed a glass from a cabinet and lifted both in her direction.

"I don't drink."

David lifted a brow but didn't say anything. Somehow that didn't surprise him. Hell. Alcohol might jeopardize her prized self-control.

He brought glass and bottle over to the kitchen island, poured himself a good inch and downed it in one swallow. The liquor, though smooth, burned down his throat and hit him in the gut. He blinked and fought back the cough itching the back of his throat.

"Why would you stake your life?" Carefully, he set his glass down on the counter. "That's a pretty loaded statement. Seems to me that's exactly what you meant. Why is your life in danger? Because of someone after you? You're obviously hiding from someone." Those lips, still reddened from his kisses, thinned into a stubborn line. Her lack of a response burned his gut even more than the brandy. "Damn it! You're staying at my house. You've blackmailed me, made me question my life. I think I have a hell of a good reason to want to know why."

"I need a drink."

He didn't comment but got another glass out from the cabinet and poured her a shot. The glass scraped against the granite counter as he slid the drink her way. She grabbed it and downed the brandy in one smooth swallow. No wincing, no flicker of emotion in those large, hazel eyes. If not for that brief moment in his arms, David would think the woman was ice personified.

Wiping her mouth with the back of her hand, she raised her chin, her body rigid and oddly regal in her tank top and boxer shorts. "They want my son."

"Who?"

"If I knew that, do you think I'd be standing here?" She shook her head, weariness dipping her shoulders. "Sorry. I didn't mean to bite your head off. The whole subject's hard to take."

"What happened?" He kept his voice neutral, but the muscles of his back and shoulders bunched with shock and unease.

"Two years ago Tyler was kidnapped. We'd been in a department store. I'd turned my back for a second and..." She rubbed the bridge of her nose again, then seemed to mentally shake herself. "God, fate, a miracle, what have you, protected him. The man who grabbed him was killed in a car crash several miles from the scene. Buckled in the back seat of the car, Tyler came away from the accident unscathed. I have no answers as to why Tyler was snatched. The perpetrator did have a record, but nothing like kidnapping."

"And?" He shook his head and forced himself to remain on this side of the island, mindful of the sudden animosity in Skye's voice. If he offered any type of comfort, she'd just lash out. "How is that related to now?"

"I thought everything was over when the kidnapper was killed, but they tried again when Tyler was walking home from school. At first, I believed we were dealing with a pedophile. That completely changed with this second attempt. It made me realize more than one person was involved and that they were organized."

"What about the police?"

"The police?" She grunted, disgust flashing in her eyes and curling the corner of her lip. "They think I'm paranoid—thanks to my ex. During the divorce, Jay fought me every step, even made it out that I was making everything up about people being after Tyler. In order to get custody I had to be seen by a psychiatrist."

He shook his hand and circled his glass with his hand and felt like shit. His life seemed so damn superficial and uncomplicated. No wonder the boy had appeared far older than his years.

"I'm sorry, Skye. I really am. It sounds like you've been in hell, but I still don't understand why you're dragging me into your mess."

She laughed. Her words hoarsened with rancor. "Believe me, I wouldn't have, but I'm desperate. I know it all ties to my past—these memories I started uncovering during my sessions with the psychiatric."

"And I'm in those memories."

"Yes." She walked around the island to his side, her face growing earnest. "I know what I'm recalling is connected with our powers. I'm sure of it. I also think you were adopted like me. Am I wrong?"

"No. I was adopted, but thousands are kids are adopted each year. That's hardly a connection."

"When you add telekinesis," she insisted, "I think it's a huge connection."

David stopped himself from softening. Yeah, she'd been hit

hard by life, but she'd deliberately set out to involve him. He didn't want to be embroiled in someone else's chaotic life. He liked how his life was. It might be superficial and uncomplicated, but it was his. Irritation thickened his voice. "But you have no proof of our association? And now you've got these people focused on me."

"No. It's all about Tyler and his powers."

"If you believe it's all about Tyler, then why chase me down? Why turn my life into your mess? Especially when everyone thinks these people don't exist."

"Don't look at me that way. I'm not paranoid! I know you've got something hidden in your past. Something locked inside your brain." She stared at him with fierce eyes and grabbed his upper arm as if to punctuate her point. "Have you talked to your father as to who your parents were? Maybe we're from the same foster home?"

"Foster home? I don't think so."

Straightening, she pulled her hand from his arm. "Why not ask your father?" She stepped backward and tossed her hair over one shoulder with a finger. The intensity of her expression didn't ease. "I know he's hiding something. Did he ever tell you where you got your powers from? Can you tell me that? Or what about adoption papers? I bet you anything he won't have them."

With her last comment hanging in the air, she pivoted and disappeared from the kitchen.

CHAPTER 11

HUNKERED DOWN IN the middle of the green room, David ripped out the plant from its nursery pot with too much force. Damp dirt splattered into his face and across the floor. He hit his glass of iced tea resting on the wrought-iron coffee table with the back of his hand. The contents went flying, while the plastic glass clattered onto the floor and cracked.

"Damn it!"

Clumps of soil now mingled with the tea on his shirt and shorts. He wiped his face with a forearm, inhaled dirt and tea, and sneezed.

His mood darkened to black. He'd woken up in a foul mood. Last night's encounter with Skye still rankled. His morning ritual of tending to his indoor garden, which usually soothed, exasperated his already disjointed thoughts.

Did he ever tell you where you got your powers from? Skye's words shredded his already frayed composure.

He hated the question.

The two times he'd asked, his father had grown antagonistic and vague. David had dropped the subject that last time when he'd turned nineteen. He'd convinced himself the reasons didn't matter.

David's power had given him a career, admiration, and envy

from his fellow colleagues, a magnificent home and every material comfort imaginable. But now Skye threatened it all. If she exposed his telekinesis, his show would disintegrate into a lie, his fans would see him as a fraud. No one would regard him in the same light again.

He frowned. Determination cut across his jaw, while he wiped at his palms to get rid of the dirt. Somehow he managed to rub the soil deeper into his skin. Unlike his skin, his life wasn't going to be stained with controversy and disgrace. It would continue as usual. Uncomplicated and superficial.

Yes. Damn it. He'd lived with the lie all his life and would continue to do so until he died. Nothing or no one was going to change anything. Particularly Skye. After all, she was only one woman. He was giving her far more power than she deserved.

Grunting in disgust, David jerked to a stand. He strode across the room and went in search of a towel.

When David stepped from the garden room, the murmur of the television drifted from the media room further down the hall. Earlier that morning, his father had shown up to watch the game an hour after Skye and her son had disappeared out the front door.

Skye's words came back to burrow into his brain. *What about adoption papers? I bet you anything he won't have them.*

David wondered if he really knew his father. He opened the linen cabinet several feet before the entrance to the media room and grabbed the top towel. Maybe the only knowledge David had garnered over the years was edited and fabricated to suit his father. Years of his father teaching ethics and morals might have been hypocritical lies.

David snapped the linen door closed. He strangled the towel between his hands.

"Holy crap! What's wrong with your eyes, man? He was safe." His father's disgruntled voice carried into the hall.

David's grip on the towel loosened. His dad wasn't some dark, sinister character. What the hell was he thinking? Skye was playing with his mind, and doing a damn good job at it.

Shaking his head, he walked over to the room's doorway and

stopped in its threshold. Sunlight streamed through one of the windows and highlighted his father, predictable as always, sitting in his favorite, leather upholstered recliner. By the chair, both Dozer and Maggie lay sleeping on the tile. Neither stirred from the sounds of his father and the television.

"Dad?" David leaned a shoulder and hip against the door frame and crossed a leg at the ankle. His father continued to glare at the screen. Ever since David had bought the seventy-five-inch television, he'd been unable to keep his dad away. "Dad!"

His father jerked around and slapped a hand against his chest. "Would you stop sneaking up on me? You did it as a kid and you're still doing it."

David twisted his mouth to keep a smile from forming on his lips. "I'll be louder next time." He uncrossed his ankles and pushed off the door frame. "Why don't you just move in here? There's plenty of room."

His father frowned. "I like my place just fine. I can do what I want when I want."

"You can do that at my place. And anyway, you're here most of the time. So it wouldn't be much of a change. You'd just spend less time driving back and forth." David walked further into the room. "I know you get lonely."

"I don't get lonely." His father clutched the leather arms, the whites of his knuckles contrasting with the age spots dusting his hands. "I like my company. I like my condo. I like everything about it."

"If you like it so much, then why are you always here? You don't sound too happy either."

Gordon muttered something under his breath. "I'm happy." He gave David a smile that looked more like a pained grimace. "You just don't know what happy looks like."

"Fine. I guess I don't." Doubts of his father's past and sinister secrets scattered. Complicated wasn't a word that would ever describe his father. What the hell had he been thinking? David shook his head and laughed.

"What's so funny?"

"Skye has this crazy idea that we're somehow connected. Maybe from a foster home."

His father's scowl deepened. "What type of nonsense is she talking about?"

"She has these memories of a hospital and of me being there with her." David tossed the towel on an end table. "She heard me screaming."

Leather creaked as his father sifted within the chair's depths. He dug his fingers deeper into the arms. "The woman's nuts."

"Is she? I wonder. You see..." David rubbed the back of his neck and hesitated. Once he spoke the words aloud to someone other than himself, they couldn't be retracted. "It's her name. Skye Hunter. The first time I heard it aloud, it was like being hit with a damn truck. I got this sick sensation. I—" He dropped his hand to the side. "There's no other explanation than having met her sometime in my past."

"She's feeding you a line of crap." His father's lips curled up at one corner in obvious disdain.

"I've kept telling myself that too. But why? It doesn't make sense." David strode across the room to look out the window. Bougainvillea petals had dripped onto the ground by the grass border. Vibrant pinks now beige puddles with singed edges. He placed his right hand on the glass and stared at the brief flare of condensation that outlined his splayed fingers.

His hand looked ordinary, like the rest of him, but inside nothing about him was normal. Even after living with it for as long as he could remember, the power at times humbled and amazed him

"The time before you took me in, everything's real hazy," David murmured. "It might be from any number of reasons. An unhappy, early childhood. The passage of time. Still, I get this feeling I should be able to remember more."

From behind, his father grunted. "If you ask me, you need to keep away from her. She's making you obsessed with your past."

"Obsessed?" David lifted his hand from the glass pane and turned on his heel to see the scowl hadn't left his father's face.

"If I am, I think I have cause. She has the same powers. She levitates. Moves things. Do you have any idea the odds of having two people with telekinesis and the same background?"

His father's face emptied of expression.

David ignored the look and cleared the frustration from his throat. "I need answers. I want to know how long I've had my telekinesis. Was I born with it? I can't seem to remember."

"Crap, David. I can't remember the time of day on most occasions, never mind my own childhood. That's normal the older you get."

"You must know if I inherited these powers from my parents?"

His father massaged his temple and brow with a thumb and forefinger. "I thought we went through this years ago. I know nothing of your biological parents. You were sent to a string of foster homes, but the majority of the time you spent it at the foster center. Simple as that."

"And the foster center? What was it called?"

"This is ridiculous! You know that?" His father struggled from the lounge chair, punctuating how age and his battle with cancer had whittled the vitality from his body. He stepped around both dogs.

David stopped himself from softening. "I'd like to know."

"We're talking years here, David. I don't know the name. All I remember was that it was on the outside of Boston."

"What of my adoption papers? I don't have them. You never gave them to me. You must have them somewhere."

His father opened his mouth and snapped it shut. "Of course."

"I'd like to see them."

"Well... They're..." His father crossed his arms against his stomach, avoiding David's gaze to glance at the television screen. "They must be in my safe-deposit box."

David's heart rate stumbled then raced to a wild tempo. The sound of the baseball fans roared in the background and grew as jarring as the disappointment that banded around his chest.

His father was lying. David knew him too well to think

otherwise. He wanted to pretend, to ignore the signs coming from his father, but they glared back at him.

"That's great," David replied, pretending nothing had changed. He'd always believed he could trust his father above anyone else, but his father's words had revealed the opposite. "The banks are open. We can get them now."

"For God's sake, David. The last thing I want to do is go to the bank. I was enjoying a ball game until you waltzed in here with all your questions."

More lies hidden by a blanket of avoidance. "Sorry, Dad, but I really want to see those papers."

"What is with you today? It's that woman. That Skye, isn't it?" He took in a ragged breath, while a dull flush crept up his neck and into his face. Anger pulsed and radiated across the distance between them. "It's the past, David. It doesn't matter. This woman is playing games with your head. She's pure drama. Just like your mother. They thrive on it."

David stiffened. "Teresa was never my mother. And unlike Teresa, Skye loves her son."

"I don't care!"

David turned and picked up the towel from the table as an excuse to avoid meeting the fury in his father's eyes. Flecks of dirt fell from the towel like his doubts about Skye's stories.

Simple questions didn't garner complicated reactions, which reinforced David's belief—there were no adoption papers.

"What are you hiding?" David asked, forcing his gaze back to his father and any telling reaction.

The muscles of his father's throat flexed in a swallow. "There's no talking any sense to you right now." He grabbed his iced tea glass from the end table by the chair he'd vacated. "I've got errands to do. I'll see you later."

David stepped back to let his father pass. How typical. His dad always ran from conflict. This time, though, David wasn't going to be brushed aside—

The doorbell pealed through the house.

His dad paused in the middle of the room. "Who's at the door? It can't be yard maintenance."

"It's probably Skye. She knows the code to get into the neighborhood." David rocked back on his heels. "She's staying here with her son for a while."

His father's lips dipped at the corners. "So that's how it is."

David's own mouth tightened. "That's how it is."

Not waiting for another snide comment, David turned and strode to the front door. The click of claws against tile echoed behind him. The dogs sped past and reached the front door first.

When he opened the door, both dogs converged on Skye and Tyler.

"Dozer. Maggie. Down."

"They're not bothering me." Tyler dropped to his knees in the foyer and wrapped pale arms around Dozer's neck. "He's so soft."

Skye smiled down at her son and skimmed her fingers over the dark sheen of Tyler's hair. She'd pulled her own hair back into a sleek ponytail. The style accentuated the long column of her neck, while sunlight filtering through the window by the door highlighted the porcelain texture of her skin.

She was beyond beautiful. The black tank top and white shorts accented the slope of her hips and curve of her breast. A slender woman, but with enough flesh over muscle and bone to grasp in the heat of passion. The dusting of freckles across her nose and cheeks gave her an otherworldly aura. Last night she'd also tasted and smelled beyond perfect.

"I've always wanted a dog," Tyler murmured against the Dozer's coat. "But we were never able to have one."

Skye's smile faded and a shadow—guilt David suspected—crossed her delicate features.

She loved her son. To have had something like that with Teresa would have softened David's edges, even made him think of a relationship with the opposite sex as a worthy goal. But David had dumped all hopes of marriage and falling in love by the time he'd hit thirteen with no sign of Teresa, no card and no phone call to acknowledge his birthday.

He wasn't about to open himself up to that abuse again, and Skye was no exception. He'd never trusted Teresa, and pretty much everyone else in his life, except for his dad. Until today, his father had been the one person he'd trusted.

And now? Now, he didn't know if he'd ever truly trust his dad again.

Skye glanced over Tyler's head and met his gaze. Her eyes sharpened. "What's wrong?"

"You were right," David said in a cool, emotionless voice. "There are no adoption papers. I don't think there ever were."

Her soft inhalation echoed in the foyer. "And the foster home? The place you came from? Do you have a name?"

"No. But it's somewhere outside of Boston."

Her lips curved into a radiant smile. "Finally something! I'd hoped, prayed for a lead. For too long I've wondered if I've been as paranoid as everyone else believes me to be. But now, I know I was right by going with my gut."

"Yes, well." He tried to shake off the numbness etched inside his head. "Now you have a place to start."

"And starting right this minute is perfect." She squeezed her son's shoulder as the boy rose to his feet. "Do you have a computer?"

"It's in the den."

"I'm sure we can find the home on the internet. A quick search is bound to pull up something relevant."

"You're not going to be able to do that now," his father said from behind him.

CHAPTER 12

SKYE TURNED TO find Gordon standing in the foyer.

Her hand slipped from her son's shoulder. "Why?"

Gordon shrugged. "There's no way to get on the internet with David's computer. He's got a virus. I never finished cleaning the hard drive."

"You never told me that," David murmured with a distinct edge to his voice.

Gordon's mouth tightened. "You never asked."

"We can go to the local library instead." A downed computer wasn't going to stop her from digging into this foster home. "I'm sure they have internet access. We should be able to find something."

An indefinable emotion flickered in Gordon's eyes. "Well, if you ask me I think you're chasing after a bunch of nonsense."

"Well, Dad, I'm not asking you." David rubbed a palm over his severely cropped hair. "I think Skye's got a good idea."

Grunting, Gordon stepped between Skye and David. "I'd like to come."

"Why?" David asked, a crease pulling at his brow.

Gordon glanced at both of them. "It'll be interesting to see what you find out."

The muscles in Skye's shoulder, taut before, bunched

painfully as she met Gordon's bland expression. She wasn't fooled. Animosity oozed from the man's pores.

The whisper of a headache across her brow intensified. Why the sudden change? It didn't make sense. Unless... Gordon wanted to sabotage getting any information on the foster home?

David moved toward the front door. "Come on, Tyler. You'll be the first ever to sit in the back of my SUV. I've got a DVD player all hooked up too."

Interest flared in Tyler's eyes. "Does your SUV go as fast as your Lexus?"

With a gentle, almost indulgent smile, David looked down at Tyler as he opened the door. "I'm afraid not, but I promise, I'll take you for a spin in the Lexus."

"Cool."

"I'll meet everyone outside." Skye brushed damp tendrils of hair from her temple. If she was going to be staring at documents and computer screens she needed a mild painkiller. "I just need some water. This heat's a killer."

Skye hurried down the hall. In the kitchen, she swallowed two ibuprofen and chased them down with half a glass of water. When she returned to the foyer, she found Gordon blocking the front door.

She paused. Disapproval deepened the lines of his face and pulled his gray brows into a frown.

Fantastic. She was in no mood to deal with a confrontation.

"Is there a problem?" Skye asked.

Gordon's lip curled. "You're the problem."

Ouch. You couldn't get more direct than that. She grabbed the strap of her purse with stiff fingers. She never once predicted Gordon's outright hostility, which was a mistake. After all, the son had been downright rude to her on occasion. She shouldn't expect anything less from the father. "Excuse me?"

"I'll make it short." Gordon straightened. "I don't know what you're saying to David, but I want you to stop. All of a sudden he's interested in his adoptive parents and why he's different."

"Are you talking about his telekinesis?"

He snorted. "If that's what you want to call it."

"Maybe you should lighten up when it comes to your son. It's natural to want to know your history—what makes you who you are."

Gordon took an intimating step toward her and glared down at her. "How about you just leave well enough alone? None of it's your business."

"You're wrong." Her grip tightened on the strap of her purse. She refused to be intimidated. "The part that relates to me is my business."

"This is different." His voice turned harsh. "You need to keep David from digging into his past. It's dead."

"I can't do that. He's a grown man. He'll do what he wants, no matter what I tell him."

Gordon grunted. "You have no idea what the hell you're getting yourself into."

"Is that a threat?" Skye thrust her chin out, not caring how antagonistic she looked. She suspected his anger and frustration masked a number of dark secrets she could only guess at.

But were those secrets enough to kill for? For a moment, Skye wondered what the man was capable of. Then she thought of the attempted kidnappings. Maybe she'd made a grave error. Gordon might be involved far deeper than she'd ever imagined.

Skye stepped back from the man. Uneasiness prickled the back of her neck, but she quickly shook off the feeling. It didn't matter. Skye intended to peel away the secrets from the past, no matter how intimidating Gordon became.

"Take it however you want it," Gordon finally said. Then he turned on his heel, opened the door and didn't wait to see if she followed.

~~*~~

"Like I said," Gordon muttered from behind David and Skye in the computer room of the library, "you're chasing shadows and little else."

Seated in front of computer monitor beside David, Skye compressed her lips to smother a retort. For the last two hours, David's father had been hovering around them like a crazed bat.

She glanced to the right where Tyler sat at another table playing one of the computer games the library offered. Unlike Gordon, her son had found something to amuse himself.

She rubbed the back of her neck and blinked against the fluorescent lights that glared from above and revealed every crevice across the Formica table, every chip on the room's walls and every black scuff mark on the faded linoleum floor. The bright lights hadn't helped the strain of staring at a jumble of words.

On her left, David twisted around and peered at his dad. "Dad, we've been through this before. I'm not—"

"Yeah, I know. You're not asking for my opinion." Gordon's breath drifted over her shoulder.

Peppermint. The scent whispered beneath her nose. Skye's brow knitted. Anxiety tightened around her chest. What was it about that scent? Something familiar, but elusive. Her frown deepened. No matter how hard she grasped at the memory, it hung tantalizingly outside her reach.

Clothing rustled as Gordon shifted from behind. He said in a voice low enough not to disturb the other people in the room, "You might as well pack it in. If you haven't found anything by now, you're not going to."

"Okay, that's enough." Frowning, David shifted and glared up at his dad. "How about you find something to do other than breathe down our necks?"

"Aren't we in a foul mood?" Gordon rocked back on his heels. "Fine. I'll leave. Anything's got to be better than staring at a bunch of newspaper articles. Maybe Tyler will want to join me and have a look around."

"No! He's fine." Skye lowered her voice, conscious of several turning heads as she swiveled in her chair to face Gordon. "I don't want to ruin a good thing. He's occupied just fine right now."

"The kid's got to be as bored as I am."

She met Gordon's simple, direct expression and wondered... Did the man have some dark, ulterior motive to leave the room with her son? No visible signs of insanity gleamed in his eyes.

No hint of a crazed madman lurked beyond their depths. An ordinary, aged man with sloped shoulders stared back at her.

Skye didn't care how normal the man looked. She still didn't trust him. "I don't care."

Jaw tightening, Gordon muttered, "Fine."

She watched him disappear from the room, glanced over at Tyler, still occupied with the computer, and sank back in her chair. But she didn't relax as David added another string of words to the search engine and pressed the enter button. Seconds later, a new list appeared. Another click from David revealed a newspaper article about a recent explosion at a pharmaceutical company.

Skye leaned forward and frowned, her mind not really on the article on the screen. "What do you know of your father?"

"What type of question is that?" he asked in a guarded voice. He twisted in his chair until his thigh brushed against her knee.

She stopped herself from shifting away, knowing such a move would reveal how much his nearness bothered her. "Ever since Tyler was kidnapped, I've always been super cautious, and I'm just wondering if your dad and Tyler... If Tyler would be safe with—" Sighing, she shook her head. "It doesn't matter."

David arched a brow. "You're wondering if Tyler would be safe with my dad."

"No..."

Understanding swept across his face. "You think my father has something to do with the kidnappings?"

"I didn't say that."

"But you're thinking it." He laughed and covered her knee with a large palm. "You're way off. Ethics and my dad go hand in hand. If you had to trust anyone, he'd be the one I'd pick." An inexplicable expression flickered across his features as he pulled his hand away. "Well....you can count on him. So don't worry on that end. My dad was a cop. A good cop. And proud of it too. He was forced to retire early, though, because of a bout of cancer that he eventually won."

Abruptly he turned back to the screen, but the warmth of his palm lingered on her skin. Just as quickly, Skye faced the computer, suddenly overwhelmed with admiration and another, indefinable emotion building inside her chest.

She liked David. Beneath the smooth-talking flirt was a man with loyalty, a man who valued his family, a man she could become very fond of.

Nope. She wasn't going there. 'Like' was fine. 'Like' was as deep as she was going to get when it came to this relationship.

His leg brushed against her thigh, and his shoulder, far too wide and muscular, pressed against her own as he leaned closer to scan the article. As he worked the mouse with an agile hand, the tendons of his forearm rippled with each click and sweep of the mouse.

Skye inhaled an unsteady breath as the warmth of his body blanketed her in a layer of growing awareness. Being this close reminded her of the other evening and the way he'd kissed her.

Tender. Knowing. Experienced.

Okay. She needed to pull her thoughts from David and her unwanted attraction toward him.

She shifted to the right and closer to the screen, which added a few more inches of blessed space between them. Ruthlessly she forced her attention back to the computer. Sexual fantasies would only get her into deep trouble.

Skye scanned the article of the explosion, frowning on why such an irrelevant piece would be pulled up by using 'foster home' as a keyword search.

While David guided the mouse, the screen scrolled downward. On the right corner, several words superimposed into her brain.

"No. Wait!"

Skye caught his wrist. The rough texture of his hair, the muscles beneath her fingers punctuated his masculinity and sent a new wave of awareness skittering across her senses. Unnerved at her reaction, she released her grip.

At the glare from a woman with thick-framed glasses and white tuffs of hair, Skye cleared her throat and said in a lower voice. "Look." She tapped on the screen and avoided David's questioning gaze. "Another explosion happened at this pharmaceutical company fifteen years ago. The place—Miltronics—is on the outskirts of Boston. Even more interesting is that the blast affected a nearby foster home."

David clicked the hyperlink that led into a more in-depth article. "Mmmm. It looks like chemicals from Miltronics leeched into the well water surrounding the facility. Even with the contaminated area being quickly contained, almost two dozen deaths happened a little after. All inexplicable. About half were elderly and the other half were children. And get this—the children who died—they were all from a nearby foster home."

Spine snapping into a rigid line, Skye searched the article hungrily. "And the foster home? Is there a name?"

"October House."

He whispered the words, thick with unease. A sudden chill peppered her exposed skin as the air-conditioner kicked on and air surged through the room.

David murmured, "That name..."

"...sounds familiar."

Their gazes locked across the short distance between them. Tension thickened to a palatable degree. The room and the people faded from Skye's peripheral vision, while sounds lowered to an indecipherable buzz.

"October House," she said the words aloud, savoring them, testing the syllables on her tongue. The name tasted bitter, foul.

She glanced at the screen and the image of the home. The place was surrounded by a wrought iron fence and a yard filled with dead, overgrown grass. Skye wondered if the fence's spiked tips were a way to keep people in or out? The place looked uninviting, from the steep, faded gray roof to the three stories of red and battered brick. Windows, many with boards painted dirty rust, stared at her with knowing, mysterious eyes.

Simple, old, and not so innocent. But vaguely familiar.

She closed her eyes and superimposed the picture's image inside her head. Taking in a steadying breath, she focused on the house, grasping for a hint of what the interior rooms looked like, for a memory of other children or teachers in the halls.

A shadowed bedroom with twin beds lifted from the gray

mist. Skye closed her eyes tighter, desperate for a clue, a picture of a past.

The murmur of voices. Children—

Reptilian eyes snapped into focus. A creature with a grotesque, green head thrust its face inches from her own. Hatred spewed from the depths of its diamond-like pupils. Slowly, almost as if the thing drew pleasure from terrorizing her, the creature opened its mouth. Incisors, sharp enough to rip open flesh with one savage bite and twist, glowed white. Drool slithered from the cavernous mouth.

My God!

Opening her eyes, Skye cried out and jerked back in her seat. Fear launched her heart into a wild crescendo as she grabbed the arms of her chair. She was half conscious of people glancing her way, but she didn't care. The threat of the image still bombarded her.

"What's wrong?"

She shook her head and rubbed her brow. Still, her heart continued to thump wildly inside her chest.

"Skye, talk to me," David urged, his voice thick with concern as he caught both her hands and cradled them inside his much larger ones.

Did she dare trust him enough with this? The sincerity in his face didn't look staged. But would he believe her? She'd never told anyone.

She disliked the way her hands trembled inside his, and how it revealed her tenuous control and vulnerability. The fear was too real and raw to mask. She cleared her throat, hesitated a moment, then said, "Whenever I try to remember any great detail of my childhood this thing appears inside my head. It's this sick, creature with yellow, reptilian eyes. Every time it happens, I swear I'm about to have a panic attack."

"Are you talking about a lizard?"

"Yes." She stared at her hands still encased in his and watched how his thumb swept gently across her knuckles. She waited for some scoffing remark, a derisive laugh.

"But it doesn't look quite like a lizard, does it?"

Her quick intake of breath rasped against her lungs. "No..."

"More like an alien than anything else."

"How do you know that? How *could* you know that?"

David's grip on her hands tightened, and he shifted in his chair until his knees touched hers. "Because I have the same images."

Her eyes widened. She clutched at his hands. "My God. What does that mean?"

He pressed her palms down on her knees and rubbed their backs before holding them in place. "I don't know," he murmured, "but I can tell you it's not good."

Skye sat unmoving, unable to comprehend a rational tie between aliens and the two of them. It was all too bizarre to take in.

"You've been telling me the truth all this time." David's deep, husky whisper draped over her senses.

Having someone else believe her was a salve to her battered soul, it soothed, it nurtured, it made her believe once again in herself. The idea of not being eternally alone turned the rigid muscles in her arms and legs into trembling appendages.

She blinked back tears. "Yes, I have."

For the first time, Skye saw belief in his brown eyes.

"I'm sorry."

His simple apology chipped at her composure far more than any derisive comment could have.

She took in a steadying breath, finding herself growing weak from the understanding and compassion in his eyes. Now was not the time to get all emotional.

"You know," David mused, "the odds of the two of us encountering an alien is astronomical."

"Just as astronomical as having telekinesis."

David withdrew his hands and rested them on his thighs. He shook his head, while skepticism creased his brow. "But what the hell does it all mean? The idea of alien abductions is outright crazy."

"Maybe, but I won't know until I uncover the secrets of the house and the explosion at Miltronics." Skye glanced back at the screen and knew October House held far more depth than the two-dimensional image staring back at her.

"What are you planning?"

"To go back to Boston, of course. Will you come with me?" The question hung in the air, and Skye couldn't do a thing to take it back. Stupid. So stupid. She should never have asked.

The gentleness in his face evaporated and a cool veneer settled over his features. "I'm not interested in digging up my past."

"Even for the truth?" She couldn't believe he'd willingly let go of a history filled with lies.

"Even if I wanted to, after all these years, it'll be impossible to find anything. Too many children, too many false paths to investigate."

A noise from outside stopped Skye from arguing. The sound carried over the hum of the computers and rustle of papers.

A shout broke into the library air.

Skye glanced over at Tyler's chair.

He'd disappeared.

CHAPTER 13

DAVID FLINCHED AS another cry echoed into the room. Dread scurried across his flesh. He shot to his feet and met Skye's alarmed gaze. "What the hell?"

She launched herself from her chair, knocking the metal and plastic to the floor with a clang. Her shoes squealed against the tile.

He banged a shin against the leg of her chair in his hurry to get across the room. Skye was faster and reached the exit as Tyler whipped around the doorway. The boy slammed into her.

"Mom. Mom!"

She stumbled back and caught Tyler's arms to steady the both of them as several people rushed from the room. The boy's flushed face and wild eyes stoked David's alarm. David strode up beside Skye and placed a reassuring hand against the small of her back.

"What is it?" David asked.

"It's Mr. Bishop."

David's breath hissed into his lungs and his fingers latched onto the fabric of Skye's shirt and twisted. "What's wrong?"

"He's on the second floor fighting with this man." Tyler gulped in a lungful of air. A shudder raced through his frame as he clutched Skye's elbow. "They started arguing. And this man—this man grabs Mr. Bishop—"

David brushed passed both of them, stepped through the threshold and into the main section of the building. He rushed across the large expanse of floor and around several people forming a small crowd. They were all peering along the balcony of the second floor. He glanced up and to the left.

Oh, shit.

Pain tore savagely into his chest.

His dad's upper torso rested precariously over the railing, while a large man draped over him like some dark, violent angel. The man shoved his father further over the metal bar. His dad snatched at air, then grappled with the man's shoulders.

The silent struggle lasted seconds.

With one quick twist of movement, the man flung his father over the metal railing. David didn't have any time to act or react with any strategy. Panic splintered his ability to focus all his energy on his telekinesis. He pulled what power he could and wrapped it around his father in an attempt to levitate him.

It wasn't enough.

His dad slammed against the cement floor. The sickening thump echoed against the large room.

"He's got a gun!" A woman yelled on the outskirts of the crowd.

Chaos erupted. People pushed, shoved in the opposite direction of David. He didn't see a gun. He didn't care. He needed to get to his dad.

Two steps. Eight. Another five and he dropped to his knees at his father's side in horror.

"Dad!"

His father lay on the floor as if broken. His leg twisted at the knee in the opposite direction than it should. David's gaze skirted away and searched desperately for movement to reveal a sign of life.

Nothing.

Blinking back a wave of faintness, he moved his mouth, but numbness cemented the words against his throat.

Earlier, David had been such a bastard. He couldn't take back the callous words he'd thrown at his father.

Now it might be too late for apologies. Any excuse seemed lame and hollow. Shame squeezed around his chest.

"They've called an ambulance."

David nodded sharply, knowing Skye's gentle voice and words were meant to soothe. He wanted to go after the attacker, but he couldn't leave his dad lying broken on the floor alone and without family. David also didn't dare move him for fear of a spinal injury with the odd angle to his dad's leg.

"Come on, Dad. Hang in there."

Still nothing. Fear bubbled up his throat and threatened to choke the breath from his lungs.

Wait. No. Right there. This time David noticed the slight rise and fall of his chest.

Jesus. Thank God.

David covered his father's spotted and worn hand with his own. Warmth, not the chill of death, stole against his palm.

But for how long?

As he watched the paramedics wheel in a gurney, David was forced to back away so the two-man team could do their job.

He couldn't remember a time where he'd felt this damn helpless.

~~*~~

Peter wrapped his hand around the steering wheel, pleased at the steadiness of his grip as he followed the ambulance from the library. With his other hand, he wiped the sweat from his brow, which still itched from the shoulder-length wig he'd yanked off minutes earlier.

The second he'd slipped from the library and any witnesses, he'd stuffed the wig in his backpack. Both now rested in the trunk of the car and would disappear inside an overflowing dumpster on the other side of the city.

But right now, he wasn't interested in either as he kept a respectable distance behind the other vehicle. He was more concerned at reaching the hospital without being detected by the paramedics, police or any curious pedestrians.

He glanced in his rearview mirror and noticed a white, nondescript car turn the same corner in his wake.

The phone attached to his hip vibrated against his belt. Peter ignored it. The distinct ring told him Ferguson waited on the other line. He could wait a little longer, especially with what Peter had to tell him. The prick wouldn't feel overly fond of him after this latest development.

Peter had fucked up. Not what he wanted to admit to himself, never mind Ferguson.

What the hell had happened? The situation had blown up into a mess. The way the skinny bastard had blocked Peter with his wrist and elbow had thrown him. Then he'd punched Peter's left shoulder—the one which had never fully recovered from a bullet wound—and momentarily disabled him. The man's background wasn't civilian, not with the way he'd expertly maneuvered Peter's attack. He'd bet his ass on it.

The plan had been a quick kill for two purposes. One to keep the old man from talking. Two to show Skye she didn't have any place safe to go. No matter where she went—in the most public arena or hidden in some dank, remote hole, he'd find her, and she would know it.

Hopefully, he'd be out of the hospital within the hour. If Bishop's father wasn't yet dead from the fall, he'd soon be dead from complications. Peter had never walked away without completing an assignment, and he didn't plan on starting today.

He was growing to hate this job. For the first time, he'd screwed up. And he knew why. He'd made this personal.

"Skye."

The four-letter name tasted rancid on his lips. Because of her, he'd lost everything.

Well, they said revenge was sweet. Soon, real soon, he'd find out if there was any truth to the saying.

While everyone still reeled from the old man's death, Peter would strike again. They wouldn't see him coming, not so soon after this last attack.

Which was exactly how he wanted it.

And this time, he wouldn't fuck up.

He glanced in his review mirror and noticed that same car a good distance behind. The car's appearance—white, generic, and easily forgettable, flagged Peter more than anything else could.

The ambulance pulled into the Good Samaritan Hospital, but Peter drove past the emergency and parking entrance. He wasn't about to involve a third party in his plans. The hospital would have to wait a few more minutes while he shook off his tail. If not for the urgency of finishing off the old man, he'd permanently eliminate the person stupid enough to think Peter hadn't noticed.

His gaze narrowed as he turned down the next street. Moments later, the car did the same.

Just who the hell was tailing him?

~~*~~

"Do you know of anyone who would want your father dead?"

David stood by the double doors leading into the hospital's emergency room with Skye and a police officer. Behind him, Tyler sat slumped in the corner of the waiting room, watching the television bolted to the top corner of the wall.

For hours David had sat, paced, stared at the blank wall and watched people come and go in tears, pain and fear while waiting for word. So far, he hadn't received any himself. Not even a quick reassurance or consultation from the medical staff. Ah, but they'd made damn sure his father had insurance.

"No. I can't think of anyone." David cleared his throat, but the action didn't remove the shakiness from his voice. The scene of his father being tossed over the balcony kept on replaying again and again inside his head, inflaming his sense of helplessness. "Other than a few retired friends, he pretty well kept to himself."

"You're sure?" The cop, Gomez according to the name badge on his khaki uniform, adjusted his belt with a fleshy hand. Keys jingled and a set of handcuffs flashed against the hospital's artificial light.

"Yeah."

"Well, several witnesses didn't hear or see any altercation between your father and the assailant before the attack. They did say that the man was focused solely on your father and getting him over the balcony. From my understanding, your father gave him a pretty good fight."

"Like I said, he didn't have any enemies that I knew of." David couldn't read past the officer's hard expression as Skye shifted beside him.

But why would someone push his dad over a balcony? An act of random violence? It didn't fit. Even random violence had some token of motivation. Also, a lunatic wouldn't have slipped from the scene with such finesse, and the cop was probably thinking the same thing.

David then thought of his father's job as a cop. His dad could have easily ticked someone off while he'd been on the force. But his dad had retired years ago. Attacking his father now after all this time also didn't make any sense.

Gomez glanced down at the notebook in his other hand, then turned his jaded gaze on Skye. "Now Miss Summers... It is Mary Ann Summers, correct?"

"That's right." Skye's hand curled around David's elbow until her nails cut into his flesh.

"How is it that you're related to the victim?"

"Through David."

When her nails dug even deeper, David didn't flinch. He might not know many details of Skye's life from before they met, but he'd learned enough to decipher the unease radiating from her voice and body. Realization crept into his thoughts like termites, slow and insidious, and he eased her hand from his arm.

Really, what did he know of the woman other than what she wanted to tell him?

"What is it?" Gomez lifted a black brow.

David shook his head, still feeling the phantom bite of Skye's nails on his skin. "Nothing."

Conscious of keeping his face void of expression, he shifted away from Skye. Bitterness coated the back of his throat as understanding abraded his thoughts.

After two kidnapping attempts on her son, Skye had run from Boston to Vegas. She then had started poking into David's history, thinking his past was connected to the violence. Somehow she'd inadvertently involved his father and revealed a hidden connection.

Memories of a white car following him or Skye on two separate occasions flashed across his mind's eye. Not a coincidence as David had thought. The kidnappers must have been watching far more closely than anyone had imagined and had decided to shut up his father for good. That or give them all a warning to stop digging.

Hell, it made sense. More sense than anything else David had come up with.

"Were you able to identify your father's attacker?"

"No."

Gomez glanced over at Skye.

She shook her head and tucked her fingers into the back pockets of her shorts. A pained expression swept across her face. "Everything happened so fast."

David dragged in a ragged lungful of air. "What about other witnesses? Did anyone see anything?"

David didn't get it. Why go to such lengths in a public place and risk discovery? Not only that but if they knew anything about his father, they'd realize he wouldn't betray a confidence. Unless... They were too afraid of the chance, no matter how slight, of his dad revealing something to Skye.

Gomez rubbed a palm along the length of his baton and shook his head. He nodded toward Tyler still sitting in the waiting room. "Other than the boy there, no one's come forward yet. The guy had on a baseball cap and straggly, shoulder-length hair that hid much of his face. Neither helped in getting a positive ID. Sorry." The words were nothing more than platitudes. "I gave you my number. If anything comes up, give us a call. I can't promise you anything."

When the cop left, Skye's fingers glided over David's forearm, a tentative attempt to console him as she whispered, "I'm sorry. I tried helping, but there were too many people running all over the place and in the way. I couldn't get a good view of your father or his attacker to use my telekinesis. I never thought..."

The harsh hospital lights amplified the ashen hue to her skin. He met her eyes faded from fatigue and sorrow, but neither emotion eased his growing resentment.

How could she look so innocent and contrite? He curled his hands into fists in an attempt to keep them at his sides. He wanted to either shake her or shove her away.

"Thought what? That your kidnapper would go after my father? But why wouldn't he? You kept on digging and digging into my past. You led this—this crazed attacker right to my dad."

Skye stepped back, a screen of indifference washing across her features. "Excuse me?"

"David Bishop?"

At the voice, David turned. A man—doctor if David could go by the green scrubs on his tall, athletic frame—strode toward them with a clipboard in one hand. The door from the emergency room he'd just left swished closed with a hollow sigh.

"That's me." David searched the man's solemn face. "My father. Is he going to be okay?"

The doctor's lips firmed briefly. He glanced at the clipboard in one hand and adjusted his rimless glasses with another before his face softened.

Shit. A tight, unforgiving band squeezed around David's chest. "What is it? He's not—"

"No."

David's heart crashed against his ribs. For a minute, he'd thought the worst. He nodded toward the emergency room. "So can I talk to him?"

"You can't right now. He has a compound fracture, two cracked ribs, a broken leg, and a concussion." The doctor met and held David's gaze. "He's currently in a medically induced coma."

CHAPTER 14

AFTER THE DOCTOR left, tension radiated from David and etched hard lines into his face. Even knowing he'd brush off any attempt at comfort, Skye found herself ignoring all common sense and saying, "He'll be fine. You'll see."

"And you're an expert on these things?"

Skye lifted her chin, opened her mouth, but then saw his haunted eyes. Maturity didn't coincide with retaliation, especially against a person in such deep pain. "No I'm not, but your father seems very stubborn and not one to give in easily."

"Really?" He pulled out a roll of antacid tablets. "And how would you know that? Are you a mind reader now?"

Now he was getting nasty. Skye dug her teeth into her bottom lip. The man was hurt. She needed to remind herself of that, but if he made one more comment—

"Mom." Tyler rose from the chair in the corner of the waiting room. "Can I get a drink from the machine?"

She frowned and looked around until she saw two vending machines against the wall less than thirty feet away. Two hospital employees, probably nurses wheeled an empty bed down the harshly lit hallway. Skye wondered if they'd just come from the morgue. She shivered. No. She didn't dare let her thoughts go down that tangent.

"Sure." She dug in her purse, pulled out a five and handed the bill to him. "How about water or juice? I'll go with you."

"Mr. Bishop."

At the sound of a female voice, Skye turned.

"We're having problems with your father's insurance carrier," a woman said, her name tag proclaiming her Jane from administration. "I'm sure you'll be able to answer a few questions that billing has."

The corners of David's lips dipped. "Sure. I'll be back in a bit," he said the last to Skye before he stuffed two antacid tablets in his mouth, pocketed the roll, and followed the woman out of the waiting room.

The air conditioner kicked on, sending a wave of frigid air racing against Skye's exposed skin. She rubbed at her arms and turned back to Tyler. He was gone. Stiffening, she pivoted and glanced down the hall. What was Tyler doing by the vending machines with a man?

The man bent down and said something to her son, angling his back in such a way that it obscured his features. His brown, shaggy hair seemed at odds with his pristine, white doctor's uniform. His lab coat didn't relieve her growing unease. She'd always had this crazy, inexplicable fear of them, along with stethoscopes and needles.

Skye's gaze narrowed. Tension cut into her shoulder muscles. An innocent looking encounter, but Skye had lost much of her innocence years before. Having an unfamiliar man so close to Tyler chilled her, even with the lack of fear in Tyler's face.

The man placed a large hand on Tyler's shoulder. His fingers curled over slender bone and muscle. With one quick move, he could latch onto Tyler's throat and snap her son's neck before Skye could react.

Panic pressed into her chest and ripped the breath from her lungs. The lights above flickered, turned off, then flared back on. "Tyler. Come here!"

Her son turned toward her while the man pivoted and drifted down the hall in the opposition direction.

"Hey," Skye called, alarm sharpening her voice. "You!"

The man didn't glance back.

The heels of her shoes slapped against the floor as she hurried down the hall after him. She passed the fire-extinguisher on the wall. The glass panel cracked with a loud protest. She took two more steps toward his retreating back but paused by Tyler's side. She met his son's scowl and stopped.

Skye didn't dare confront the man and give him a chance to retaliate, not with Tyler so close at hand. Yeah, she might use her telekinesis but with her heightened emotions, she was more liable to break a window than stop an attacker.

David's father was already lying in a hospital bed because of her. Did she want even more chaos? Skye swallowed down the guilt and remorse, but it bubbled up and threatened to choke the breath from her lungs.

"What did he want?"

Tyler's frown deepened. "Nothing."

"Nothing?" Skye couldn't keep the skepticism from her voice. "Then what did he say? I saw him talking to you."

"He just wanted to know if I had change for a five."

"That's it?"

"Yeah." Tyler stared at the vending machine. A plastic water bottle dropped into the dispenser without him touching a button.

"Don't do that." Quickly she glanced around the hall. No one seemed interested in the two of them.

"But I paid." His voice thickened with frustration.

"It doesn't matter if you paid." She folded her arms across her chest. "If you use your powers too often, it becomes a habit. Something you'll have hard a time breaking. Then one day you'll do it by reflex right when someone's watching."

"But it's not the same as the computer."

A shiver raced across her flesh. Memories of the last time Tyler played on their home computer, delved into Complink's computer system with his mind and the media blitz that followed still haunted her, would probably still always haunt her.

"True." How to explain? He'd paid. Been completely ethical. The last thing she wanted was for Tyler to think of himself as flawed. "But we're special and not quite like everyone else. People feel uncomfortable around different."

That didn't come across any better. Exhaling loudly, she stepped back, turned and almost slammed into a warm body. She stumbled as David steadied her with a hand to her elbow.

His gaze darted over her face. "What's wrong?"

"I thought..." She glanced down the hall. The fluorescent light from above flickered. The man had disappeared. "Nothing."

They followed David into the waiting room, but when dinner time came and went, they left him to go in hunt for some food for Tyler. When they came back after eating, David hadn't moved from one of the olive green chairs lining the wall. The waiting was obviously eating away at him. New shadows of weariness clung beneath David's eyes and cut deeper lines on either side of his mouth. Even with a good six feet separating them, Skye felt the anxiety rolling off his body in large waves.

Whatever anger she'd stored from his previous comments, had dissolved long ago. If she'd experienced the same situation with Gordon as with Tyler, Skye knew she would have lashed out.

"You need to eat and get some rest," she insisted, sinking into a seat opposite from David. "Don't you have a show tonight?"

"I can't." He swept a palm over his cropped hair and shook his head. "And I already called the casino to cancel."

"You won't be much help to your father if you're exhausted."

Tyler dropped into the chair beside her and took a deep swallow from his water bottle, then wiped his forearm against his mouth. The pallor in his face matched David's and emphasized the precariousness of their future.

She'd uncovered a new clue with the name of a foster home, October House. But with that new clue, a deadly attack against David's father had followed. What would the next clue bring? An attack that left someone dead this time?

Maybe she should give up, move from Vegas and start somewhere new. Skye rubbed the back of her neck. Who was she fooling? She'd last months before her past caught up to her. A new city wasn't going to solve her wrecked life.

"Mom. When can we leave?" Tyler's shoulders slumped with weariness. "I'm tired."

"Why don't the two of you go back to my place and get some sleep? I'll stay here."

Skye shook her head, then tucked a wisp of her hair into her ponytail. "Come with us. Try to at least get a couple of hours of sleep."

His lips thinned as he latched onto the faded arms rests. He glanced at the double doors leading into the emergency area.

"Didn't the doctor say that there wouldn't be any change for the next twenty-four hours?"

He turned away from the doors and nodded.

~~*~~

Peter stopped and faced an eight-foot adobe wall. The sun had long since set. The branches of the mesquite tree beside him camouflaged his silhouette from the grasping fingers of street lights, while a moonless night also aided tonight's quest. He tossed a plastic bag of boneless meat over the fence. The package landed on the other side with a soft thump. He'd thought of getting hamburgers from a fast food joint but had changed his mind. All that sauce and those additives were bound to be terrible for the dogs' digestive system.

He grabbed a thick tree limb, placed the heel of his shoe against the trunk and pulled himself up, ignoring the scrape and prick of branches. After getting a good balance, he caught the top of the adjacent wall with a hand and leg, then straddled the fence. A quick glance on the other side revealed gravel and landscaped desert shrub. The neighboring street and yards were empty.

He landed less than a yard from the bag of meat. After grabbing the package from the ground, he walked casually down the street.

Headlights flashed briefly on Peter before the car turned toward the community's main entrance. The driver exited the electronic gate, unaware or uncaring of the lone pedestrian.

Amazing how people who considered themselves intelligent

thought a fence and security gate would keep out the criminal element. If a person wanted in a house bad enough, nothing was about to stop them.

Peter smiled. He wanted in a certain house really bad.

~~*~~

Gripping the counter with one hand, David stood in the middle of the kitchen with an empty shot glass in the other. Head bowed, he stared at the floor. A good fifteen minutes earlier, Skye had tucked her son into bed and disappeared into the guest bedroom next to Tyler's.

Silence cloaked the house. The quiet punctuated his father's absence. Even though he never moved into David's house, he'd been a permanent fixture.

Jesus. The man was the only person he had on this earth.

He grabbed the scotch, poured another shot and downed it in one swallow. It stung the back of his throat and all the way to his stomach.

The third shot went down smoother and masked the pain binding his chest. He fought back the temptation for one more, and instead, put the bottle back in the cabinet. Getting drunk wouldn't get his father out of the hospital.

He'd been instrumental in the attack on his father. By allowing Skye and her son into his life, he'd inadvertently brought them also into his father's. He needed to get her out of this house and his life.

Both dogs started barking outside. The noise pierced the stillness of the night—the third time they'd gone into a full fledge barking frenzy in two hours.

David strode to the kitchen door and opened it. Any more of this and the neighbors were liable to call the police. "Damn it, Dozer. Maggie. Get in here, now."

He flicked on the porch light and stepped outside. The dogs quieted and trotted from around the side of the house. The gurgle of the waterfall and the soothing music of wind chimes carried across the night. Deeper shadows clung to the palms, fence and shrubs.

Nothing moved.

Until tonight, the dogs didn't bark at empty air.

Despite two false alarms, David moved cautiously across the backyard and peered along the side of the house. Two large shadows loomed toward him. He relaxed. Nothing other than the city's trash receptacles against the wall. He glanced at both dogs wandering over the yard and sniffing the ground.

Nothing odd in that.

After the dogs padded into the house, David shut and locked the door, then slid the doggy panel closed to keep them inside for the rest of the night.

For a few minutes, they'd distracted him from his father. But now the magnitude of his dad's health sent a wave of panic rolling through David.

Standing by the kitchen, he glanced toward his room. The hallway stared back, black, hollow and unwelcoming. Battling sheets and an empty room held little appeal. The scotch hadn't done a damn thing to calm his mind or dull the ache in his chest. He stepped into the hall and looked in the opposite direction and toward the media room. For a moment he thought he heard the television. Then he realized the sound was a phantom noise, triggered by hope and nothing else.

Gnawing panic scoured his chest. If his father died...

He swept a shaking hand across his scalp, the stubble of his military cut barely giving in to the touch. From the hall, he saw the clock on the microwave glow a few minutes past three. He had yet to get any sleep. The next shift at the hospital was at seven. That would be about the time they'd stop the dipervin drip on his father, which would allow him to wake from his chemical coma. Then the staff would be able to gauge the extent of the damage to his father's brain.

Hours still.

He turned to snap off the kitchen light and found Skye only a few feet away. "Jesus, Skye! That's twice now you've scared the hell out of me. You should have clued me in you were right behind me."

"I was afraid to interrupt. You looked like you were deep in thought."

He backed up a step and rested a hand against the wall, grappling to control the rapid beat of his heart. What would have happened if the person had been his father's attacker?

Hell. He'd have been dead.

The kitchen light reflected empathy in Skye's doe-like eyes. David bristled, pressing his palm harder against the smooth surface of the wall. He didn't want pity, particularly Skye's.

She'd involved his father in her thirst for the truth. He couldn't prove it, but his father didn't have enemies, none until she'd shown up. Yeah, his dad was a cop, but he was a retired cop and had been for years. If someone had been holding a grudge against his dad they would have acted on it years ago. Yeah, there was a chance someone from his father's past had surfaced, but David discounted it, because there was just too much of a coincidence with Skye showing up and his father being attacked.

David couldn't afford to have Skye in his house any longer, a distraction, a possible aggravation, and a dangerous element. If his dad survived, he'd be staying in David's house and in desperate need of family. He didn't dare let Skye anywhere near his father again, not with a violent cloud following her and her son.

"I want you and Tyler gone in the morning."

She flinched.

He'd cut through her cool layer of composure, but the victory gave him little satisfaction. He didn't care about games. Not anymore. His life and that of his father's was far too serious to play a competition of wills.

"Why am I not surprised?" A smile danced across her sensuous mouth, but bitterness added an edge to her voice.

She still wore the pair of shorts and shirt from earlier that day and hadn't yet changed into those dangerously disturbing boxers and tank top of hers. He found her too much of a distraction though. Her femininity, the sensual allure of her scent beckoned, incited the male need to imprint himself on her.

David mentally shook himself, not daring to delve into the hunger eating at his insides. "I don't want you near my father. We both know I'm not being unreasonable in the request. I have to focus on my father's safety and no one else's."

She rubbed the back of her neck and sighed. Her shoulders slumped. Any person other than Skye and David would have thought it was from defeat.

"I'm sorry for your father. I'll claim some responsibility, but not all of it." She inched her chin upward, which he swore held a shadow of a tremor. "Life isn't that simple. And you know what? Blaming me isn't going to clear up this situation. I think it's pretty safe to say that this guy was after your dad and no one else. Yeah, I might have led him to your dad, but something in his past is the real reason for the attack."

David curled his fingers into a fist against the wall. He ground his teeth together to cut off the biting retort that just wanted to spring loose. Damn it. He wanted to argue. Prove her wrong. But he couldn't. He suspected she might be right. He inhaled frustration and helplessness and pushed off the wall.

"Yeah, there might have been something in my father's past, but it was dead and buried for years until you decided to jab it with a damn shovel."

Nodding sharply, she stepped backward and clenched her hands into fists. "Fine. We'll leave in the morning."

As she turned to go, the finality of her words hit David.

"No. Wait." Alarm sharpened his words. David wanted her gone, but he violently balked at the idea of never seeing her again. This was a woman that fascinated him with her tenaciousness, her uncompromising ability to face adversity. The realization that he cared for her slammed into his gut.

He dragged in air, but it did nothing to rid him of the panic at the idea of never seeing her again. One night. Just one night with her. With a tremor in his hand, he caught her elbow and pulled her around to face him.

The muscles of her arm stiffened beneath his grasp, but he didn't let go.

"Wait for what?"

He drank in the hurt and bewilderment in her face before she quickly screened both expressions. "I can't let you leave. Not yet."

CHAPTER 15

SHE JERKED BACK from David as if slapped. "Let? Excuse me? No one *lets* me do anything. I let myself—"

"Damn it, Skye. Just shut up and don't argue for once." To hell with it. If she slapped him, so be it. David could live with that, but he couldn't live with him blowing off the last chance to be with her.

With one step, David devoured the distance between them. He clutched her upper arms and hauled her up against him. The swell of her breasts flattened against his chest. Their heat burned through the material of his shirt and stoked his growing hunger.

Their gazes clashed for an instant. Then he took her mouth in a kiss. Tonight he would not be denied. He'd wanted Skye for far too long.

He caught a finger beneath her hair tie and slipped it free. Chestnut hair tumbled to her shoulders, their silken strands twining between his fingers. The scent of her hair drifted in the air, and he closed his eyes, drinking in the musky scent of woman and flowers.

For a brief moment Skye yielded, her lips softening and molding against his, but then she grew rigid within his arms. With both hands, she grasped his shoulders and dug her nails into his skin. He reigned in his desire and shut his eyes tighter. The last thing he wanted to do was scare the hell out of her.

David forced himself to slow down, to give instead of take, and skimmed his mouth over her own, a gentle whisper that sampled the texture of her lips, the flavor of her mouth. A strange mix of toothpaste and sin. Her breath altered, turned rapid and uneven, while a shudder rippled through her body.

The pressure on his shoulders eased, and her mouth softened and turned inquisitive as she leaned into his embrace, surrender in the soft sigh of her breath.

Thought dissolved into pure sensation as pleasure and excitement burned his flesh and quickened his pulse. His hands trembled as he cupped her face with both hands and glided his thumbs along the line of her jaw and moved to the downy softness below her ears. Skye's pulse fluttered wildly beneath his touch, revealing her desire as her hands slipped from his shoulders and danced across his back.

The knowledge that she wanted him stoked the desire burning through his body. He shifted restlessly. The kiss tantalized but did nothing to cool his growing ardor.

"I want you," he whispered against her lips, skimming her mouth with each word. He kissed her jaw, the indentation between her ear and neck, the silken curve above her collarbone as he slipped a hand beneath her shirt to caress the taut muscles of her lower back.

She shivered and clutched his shoulders. "I can't..." Her protest couldn't mask the need in the husky tremor of her voice. "There's Ty. He's—"

"Asleep."

"But—"

He silenced her protest, taking her mouth once again in a slow, thorough kiss, tasting her desire and her doubts. "One night," he urged as he wrapped his fingers in her hair. Hell, she had no clue what he'd do to be with her. "Give me one night."

Skye's entire body quivered against him. David tensed, dreading the thought of her rejection. All his life he'd had women succumbing without any great effort, but none of that mattered, none of *them* mattered compared to the woman now in his arms. To him, Skye had become an obsession.

Her fierce determination, her loyalty to her son were qualities he couldn't help but admire. But what drew him to her more than anything was the vulnerability in her doe-like eyes that even her prickly edges and rigid control couldn't completely mask. Damn, but she did things to his insides, twisting them in places he didn't think could be twisted.

Skye twined both arms around his neck and grazed her teeth lightly against the curve of his neck before inching up and pressing her mouth over his to whisper, "One night."

David took in a shuddering breath of relief, bent down, caught Skye around the knees and waist and hefted her up into his arms. He glanced down the darkened hall where both Tyler and Skye's bedrooms were, then he turned on his heel and walked in the opposite direction where shadows thickened. He pivoted down another hall and didn't falter. He wasn't about to slow and give Skye an opportunity to change her mind. In the morning he'd worry about recriminations, but now... Now, he'd focus on pleasure, desire and Skye.

He stepped into his room. Moonlight slanted through the open blinds and cut across the king-size bed. He nudged the door shut with his heel. Loosening his grip, he eased Skye to her feet, and relished the feel of her soft curves as she slid down the length of his body.

David looked down into her upturned face. Shadows clung beneath her eyes and below the curve of her cheeks but the light from the window exposed the hunger in her gaze. His chest tightened. He dipped two fingers between her skin and shorts and tugged the waistband until her stomach flushed with his hips. The warmth of her body against his groin pulled a growl from his mouth.

There was only longing... Longing to lose himself in her softness, in her heat and her hunger.

He locked the door.

~~*~~

Skye shivered in the circle of David's arms as he lowered his head and took her lips in a long, devouring kiss.

Devoured. That was the only word Skye could think to describe it. David consumed her thoughts. He shattered her common sense and defenses until only desire and yearning— pure sensation—inundated her body and mind.

Yes, tonight she might have tossed all logic into the trash, but she didn't care. All she cared about right now was the feel of his hands slipping beneath her shirt to cup her naked breasts, the way his mouth melded over her own and how his flesh quivered beneath her fingers as she trailed them up across the indentation along his spine.

David nudged her backward across the carpet inch by inch until the backs of her legs hit the edge of his bed. All the while his hands roamed her body, gliding over the slope of her shoulder, cupping the weight of her breast and running restlessly up and down the curve of her hips.

He opened the top drawer in the nightstand and pulled out a square package. Oh, God. She'd been completely lost in the moment that she'd forgotten about protection.

After tossing it on the bed, he towered over her, his breath harsh and ragged as he pulled his shirt over his head and flung it on the ground. Sighs mingled with the rustle of clothes as they groped, pulled and tugged clothing off each other. Then there was naked skin against naked skin and pure pleasure.

She fell back onto the mattress and David dropped down beside her. Shadows and moonlight drew out the harsh contours of his face, the rugged sweep of his jaw. With an index finger, he caressed the arch of her eyebrow, the curve of her cheekbone.

"You're beautiful, you know that?" He leaned over her, his head and the wide breadth of his shoulders coating her in deeper shadow. "Do you know how much I want you?"

Such awe in his voice. The depth of the emotion melted her limbs into the mattress. She lifted her own hand and traced a finger along his bottom lip. She smiled. "How about you show me?"

He dragged in air with a sharp hiss. The moment his lips

touched hers and his body settled over her own, her smile dissolved. His scent skimmed across her senses. Their breath collided, their tongues mated. He tasted what a man should taste like, hot, bold and forceful.

She arched upward, her curves yielding to the harder, more angler lines of his body. The ridge of his erection burned against her skin, and she shifted and parted her thighs as anticipation, almost painful in intensity, curled low in her stomach.

But he eased lower, his lips trailing kisses along the hollow of her throat and past her collarbone. The hair on his legs rubbed against her skin as he flicked his tongue across the tip of one breast. The wet touch of his mouth closed over her nipple. She gasped, closing her eyes, sinking into a whirlpool of desire. Just when she thought it couldn't get much better, David slipped his other hand between her legs and caressed her wet folds with teasing, relentless strokes.

Ecstasy hovered, tantalizing close. Skye's breath hitched against her chest, while sweat broke out across her flesh. The pulse and stroke of his thumb and finger drew her deeper and deeper into a well of sensation. She clutched at his wrist, wanting more but wanting him inside her too. Then it didn't matter as her body convulsed, pleasure splintering every muscle and pore in her body with a kaleidoscope of sensation.

As she lay panting, her body shivering with the aftermath of her climax, David cradled her in his arms, kissed her temple, the corner of her mouth and said, "This time I want to watch you come with me in you."

She blinked up into David's face. Even though the night obscured his expression, sexual tension radiated from his shadowed form. She swept a hand across the mattress and clutched the condom package with trembling fingers.

She ripped open the wrapping between her teeth, her hands trembling with a new urgency. His indrawn breath rasped against the night as she rolled the condom over his cock. His heat burned into her hand, his hardness and size intimidated and enthralled.

"Oh, Jesus, Skye..." His touch grew clumsy, hurried, almost

rough as he swept his hands over her hips, kneaded her buttocks and positioned her...

Skye cried out as he plunged into her. She arched up and wrapped her legs around his hips, meeting each thrust with equal fervor. Her hands scaled the rippling muscles of his back, moved lower to grip the powerful thrust of his hips.

"That's it." His breath whispered against her temple as he cradled her throat with a hand and scraped his teeth against her earlobe. "Come for me."

His words wrenched her into a whirlwind of ecstasy. She scratched her fingernails across his sweat-slicked shoulders. Every muscle grew rigid as she dove into a vortex of sensation again. She buried her face in the pillow to her side, muffling the cry that ripped from her lungs.

Then he came into her, his big body convulsing above her, his arms banding around her waist and shoulders, and a low moan rumbling from deep in his throat.

David slumped against her, his weight pressing her into the mattress. Then he swung them both on their sides with his arms never slipping from her body.

His heart thundered against her breast as Skye tried to regain some semblance of sanity. She was afraid to draw away and crush the moment, afraid the wonder and satisfaction would disintegrate once she slipped from David's arms.

"I'll be right back," he murmured against her hair.

When he withdrew from her body, she flinched at the sudden cool air that rushed across her skin. Feeling awkward and unsure, she slipped under the covers. She detested both emotions; they only magnified frailties she'd tried so hard to smother.

The mattress dipped, and David disappeared into the adjoining bathroom. A moment later, the muffled sound of dogs barking filtered into the room. She sat up and started to slip from the bed, but David stepped back into the bedroom.

"They'll stop in a minute." He paused on the edge of the bed and rested one knee on the mattress. "It's nothing. They've been doing that all night."

"Are you sure?"

The barking stopped as abruptly as it started.

"See? Absolutely nothing."

She curled her fingers around the edge of the bed sheets. "I should go."

David sank down on the bed and urged her back down amidst the rumpled bedding and pillows. With one quick move, he pulled her up on top of him. "Not yet."

She clutched his shoulders, unable to dampen the excitement lacing her blood as his hard-muscled body and legs brushed against her. His arousal burned against her belly and sent her pulse leaping wildly. One touch, and she wanted him all over again.

Skye curled her arms around David's neck and let herself be consumed by the sexual hunger quickly blinding her to all but the moment. She was rapidly finding out she couldn't say no. Not to David.

~~*~~

Flat on her back, Skye opened her eyes and stared at the ceiling fan. The blades cut through the air slowly, silently. Sunlight streamed through the blinds and across the thick-beamed, mahogany bed. She shifted, sending a protest through most of her muscles and twisting the white, cotton sheets around her legs. The air conditioner kicked on and sent a chill across her naked body. Shivering, she pulled the covers up to her neck. With her gaze locked on the ceiling, she slid a hand across the mattress and found the place beside her empty and cool to the touch, confirming what she already knew.

David had left long before. Yet, his scent clung on her skin and the bedding, while the imprint of his body lingered on her flesh. Shifting, she noted the dark, wood dresser, and deep, chocolate lounge chair in the corner of the room, which spoke of masculinity and money, and a man who liked casual elegance. A book of poetry rested on the nightstand. The man was an enigma, hoarding his thoughts and his past, leery of intimacy, yet at the same time, Skye sensed he desperately craved it.

She closed her eyes. Memories and images of the last night filtered through her mind, causing her to stir restlessly.

Now that she'd reclaimed her sexuality with a man she found not only intelligent but wickedly handsome and completely distracting, she craved sex that much more. Not good at all to her way of thinking. The distraction would only impede her from focusing and uncovering the secrets from her past. Subconsciously she must have known that, having avoided her attraction to David until last night. She sighed with resignation. This hunger for David didn't involve just a physical fascination with the man, no matter how much she wanted to tell herself otherwise.

Sorrow shadowed her thoughts and banded around her throat. She blinked the sudden moisture from her eyes. This morning she would leave with Tyler. She couldn't avoid or delay the inevitable. Really, there was no point in remaining even if David wanted her to stay.

David would continue to spurn her questions and the mystery behind his adoption. She couldn't change him, and with his father grasping precariously to life in the hospital, David wouldn't start unearthing answers now.

She tugged his pillow into her arms and stuffed her nose into the mass. His scent intensified and for a moment she let herself indulge in the idea of hope, of pretending she was normal, of thinking she could have the luxury of falling in love.

She didn't dare start caring for the man. Not now. Not when she was going to be walking out his front door for good. That would be completely asinine.

She glanced at the clock on the nightstand. Nine o'clock. Thrusting the pillow away, she jerked into a sitting position. By now Tyler would be up and having breakfast. Her son might have already gone to her room to check on her.

How the hell was she going to explain this to Tyler? She'd done things before she'd considered foolhardy, but this one ranked up there with the best of them.

She stared at the closed door and the empty bed beside her. Somehow she'd have to slip from David's room and make sure Tyler didn't catch her on her way to her room.

After shoving her arms and legs into her clothes, she eased

open the door. Seeing no one, she slipped into the hall, then moved down the hall on silent feet. The cool tile seeped into her skin.

At the thick silence enveloping the house, Skye frowned. She would think Tyler or David would be making some type of noise. Not even the murmur of the television echoed through the rooms.

When she reached the hall to their rooms, she paused. Tyler's door stood closed. Odd. She'd never known him to sleep this late. Normally he'd be up for a good two hour by now. Unease prickled across her nape as her gaze locked on the door and she inched across the last few feet. With trembling fingers, she grasped the cool, metal doorknob. She turned the knob. The latch clicked open. The door swung open on silent hinges.

She stared across the room. The bed, covers flung aside, was empty. The impression of Tyler's body curved into the mattress and wrinkled sheet. One pillow lay discarded in the middle of the floor while the other rested against the floorboard.

The sliding glass window yawned open. The screen had been ripped out. A hot, desert breeze flicked at the cotton drapes.

She backed away from the room, her heart crashing against her ribs.

Someone had taken Tyler.

CHAPTER 16

ALOUD SPLASH FROM outside brought Skye running into the backyard. She blinked from the glare of the sun's rays against the pool's sparkling water. Seeing someone swimming, she quickened her pace, and delight bubbled into her chest. The emotion quickly fizzled and turned rancid.

David speared through the water, his broad shoulders and dark head unmistakable. Not Tyler's like she'd hoped. She blinked back tears.

The fountain's gurgle joined the spray of David's hands and feet hitting the water's surface. From the mesquite tree overhead, a mockingbird sang a litany of musical notes. The scene portrayed an image of normalcy and tranquility, but nothing was. Nothing ever would be.

Had it ever been?

She stepped further into the backyard, only half-conscious of both dogs snuffling for attention. She absently stroked the head of one. Tyler had always wanted a dog.

And now...

She folded her arms across her middle and pressed them against her stomach, but nothing curbed the painful twisting of her insides.

David vaulted from the pool. Water streamed down his chest

and stomach and pasted his navy trunks against his hips and upper thighs. He wiped his hands over his face and frowned. "What's wrong?"

Skye blinked, struggling to focus. She opened her mouth. Words didn't come.

David's frown deepened. He grabbed a towel from the lounge chair, rubbed the water from his arms and chest with quick, rough hands, and strode across the pool decking. Unease darkening his eyes, he stopped in front of her and cupped her elbow, his hand damp against her arm. "Skye, say something. I can't do a damn thing unless you talk to me."

"They took Tyler. There can't be any other reason. Tyler'd never leave on his own violation."

"They?"

"The pigs who tried kidnapping him before. The ones who followed us from Boston. The ones—" Her voice rose and frayed with growing hysteria. "Oh, God. I don't have a clue who they are."

"That's impossible. The neighborhood's got the best security system in the city. Plus, there're the dogs... Shit." Color leached from his face. He flung the towel back on the lounge chair and rushed past her.

Skye hurried after him and stumbled to a halt when she reached the doorway to Tyler's bedroom.

As David stepped into the room, she peered inside, wild hope rippling through her body on the chance she'd hallucinated the last few minutes. But no. The bed in the corner of the room remained barren with the sheets ripped away and tossed onto the floor. She grabbed a discarded pillow from the carpet and inhaled Tyler's distinct scent of soap and shampoo, innocence and wonder.

David leaned out the window and checked right, then left. The ceiling fan shifted hot air from one place to the other. The heat closed in around her. He pulled back inside and turned to face her. At the bleak look in his face, her vision clouded. She clutched her throat. The muscles in her legs quivered and drained of strength.

The fan sped up, whirling faster and faster as the panic rose inside her. The blades cut a path through the air again and again until they blended together in a circle of motion as the motor cried in protest, the volume rising—

"Skye, stop it! You're going to kill someone if you don't get control of your telekinesis." David stared at the fan with narrowed eyes. Abruptly, the motor stopped humming and the blades slowed.

She blinked.

"Here. Sit down." David caught her around the waist before she landed on the floor and urged her down in a plush, navy chair by the side of the bed. "Put your head between your legs."

Gentle fingers pulled her hair from her face as she bent over and rested both hands on her knees. She took in large, heaving gulps of air. The sudden oxygen tore into her brain. A brief, black rush of nothingness closed in around her, but somehow she managed to shove it aside and let the moment pass.

Skye raised her head and found David on his knees in front of her. His large hand gripped the arm of the chair, and she smothered the urge to touch him. She should never have stepped within two feet of him. The guilt wouldn't go away. How could it? "While I was having sex, someone grabbed him. What does that make me?" A note of hysteria crept into her voice. "Can you tell me that!"

"Skye, the man was a professional. How else can you explain it?" A muscle pulsed along the ridge of his jaw while he stared back with raw, pain-filled eyes. "He got through security. He knew about the dogs. He played me. By getting both animals so worked up over the course of the evening, he knew I'd ignore them eventually. So don't start blaming yourself. I'm guilty more than anyone. Tyler was under my roof and my protection."

"Words don't get my son back," she shot back, digging her nails into the arms of the chair. She stared at the carpet where she superimposed Tyler's image on it. If she could just make him materialize in the flesh... "I don't understand. His telekinesis. Why didn't he use it to fight back?"

David slipped a lock of hair from her cheek and curled it around her ear. "I'm sure he had a reason."

When realization dawned, Skye dragged in a rattling breath of shame. She folded her hand into a fist. "Because I told him not to." Bitterness thickened her voice. "Isn't that just perfect? Time and again I'd nag at him not to use his power. I made it so damn easy for them to take Ty."

"Don't say that, Skye. You did what you thought was best. You were trying to protect him."

"But don't you see? I didn't protect him." The pain in Skye's chest accumulated until it became an unbearable crushing pressure. David's silence told her more than any hollow attempt at consolation. Who could argue against the truth?

David stood and stepped away from the chair. Skye frowned, noticing a sudden stillness in his expression. "Look at the mirror," he ordered.

The odd note in David's hushed tone snapped her head around. She glanced above the oak dresser. Letters were scrolled in bold, black marker across the top.

You can't run from your past. You were a bitch then, and you're a bitch now.

Skye's stomached twisted and rolled. She gagged and barely managed to keep the contents inside her body.

"Do you know who wrote this?" David asked, his voice thick with anger and outrage.

"No."

"Whatever they have against you, it has something to do with your past. It's almost like they're sticking it in your face, the way they came in while you were in the house."

Skye gripped the arms of her chair. Tension cracked up her spine. A new wave of nausea rolled inside her stomach.

"Are you sure it's the people who tried to kidnap your son?"

"I don't know. There's so much anger in the words. The only person who I've truly pissed off was my ex, Jay." Despair swelled into her voice. "But I thought that was all in the past. Unless he's somehow involved in the kidnappings... After all, he's shown up and threatened blackmail, but to kidnap your own son? It just doesn't make any sense."

"Maybe you're making it more complicated than it is." David

stepped toward the dresser and with a finger, he traced the line of black marker underlining the word bitch.

"You might be right. He did show up earlier at the casino wanting money."

"Blackmail." He said the word as if it tasted foul on his lips. "I'll call the police."

"They're not going to do anything."

David turned and stared at her, his eyebrows clashing. "Why?"

"Because Jay was a cop." She ignored the shock that flashed across his face. "I don't care what you say. They stick together. He might have been kicked off the force, but he's still one of them." She pushed her hair away from her face, and turned away, unable to look at him directly in the eye. She found it impossible to shake off the feeling of shame that settled across her shoulders at how she'd fought just as dirty as Jay during the divorce. "Boston police don't particularly like me either. With what I uncovered through Jay's illegal activities, I forced them into a departmental investigation. The media loved it and the police hated it."

She attempted a smile. "Who wants a scandal? They surely didn't, and they particularly didn't want to blame themselves for their ineptness, so they decided to blame someone else, and I was the perfect target. A single, white female lacking power and a voice."

"I'm sure if we talk to someone, they'll listen."

Skye tightened her grip on the arms of the chair as she blinked the moisture from her eyes. "There's more." Even knowing his expression would mirror her own feelings of disgust, she forced herself to return David's gaze. "Under my divorce decree, I'm not supposed to leave the state unless it's approved by the court. By leaving Massachusetts, I've broken the law and stand to lose custody of Tyler. No one in their right mind is going to take my side of anything."

David strode across the room and sank on the arm of the chair. With unmistakable tenderness and a face void of disgust, he cupped her cheek and rubbed a tear from under her eye with a thumb. "We'll find him."

A quiet and welcome resolve enveloped her. Anything was better than the guilt and despair that corroded hope, because she needed hope. Without hope...

Before her thoughts turned darker, Skye sprang to her feet and away from David. She paced the room, needing to refocus and reclaim the strength and resolve she'd always prided herself on. Both characteristics she'd relied on since the day Tyler had escaped death and a kidnapping attempt. Her son desperately needed a mother who would fight for him, not a weak-willed woman wallowing inside an acid glass of despair.

"I know I'll find him." She lifted her chin. "Because I know where he is."

Still seated on the arm of her chair, David looked up at her. "And that's?"

"Boston of course, where Jay slithered back to. Right there on the mirror it says I can't run from my past, and my past is all in Boston."

Skye's chin dipped as her icy resolve wavered. She glanced at his hands gripping the chair's arms. Capable, far stronger than her own. By leaving Las Vegas, she would be leaving David. She quailed at the idea of never seeing him again. The feelings she'd tried so hard to keep at bay when it came to David threatened to tumble free. Less than a month and he'd burrowed his way into her life. "Come with me. I don't want to do this alone."

David's eyes darkened. Silence draped the room and indecision flickered across his face.

"I need your help, David."

"My father."

Her jaw tightened, and she struggled to keep her face neutral. The last thing she wanted was for him to see how his words bruised those vulnerable places she tried so hard to keep hidden. She might understand his need to take care of his own, but that didn't dampen the pain.

Head raised, shoulders rigid, she stared at him across the few feet that separated them. Feet? Hardly. They were miles. Too many miles to cross without her son.

He rubbed at his face and shook his head. "I can't."

"Or won't?"

His face tightened.

She knew she'd pushed too far. "I'm sorry. That was unfair. I'm asking too much with your father in the hospital."

"My father's the only family I have."

"The same with Tyler." She nodded abruptly and backed away.

One night of sex. She'd been like all his other women, no different. A woman from his past and little more than a pleasant, distant memory. Right this minute, she truly hated the idea of how easily she'd succumbed to the heat in his eyes and touch. "So this is it."

He rose from the chair and made to step toward her.

She forestalled him with a hand in the air. "Don't. I can't handle your touch." She sent him a wobbly smile, feeling hurt, used and alone, but she wasn't about to reveal any weakness to him. "Maybe I'll see you around."

Skye didn't wait around for his reply but pivoted and hurried from the bedroom.

~~*~~

David watched Skye disappear down the hall. He didn't follow but continued to stand in the middle of the bedroom. Pain banded around his chest. Shit. He rubbed the heel of a hand against his temple as a headache pounded into his skull.

He should be relieved. Wasn't that what he'd wanted? To be left alone? After all, he'd always found Skye a complication, a barbed cactus hooked into his side and a constant pain, no matter how deeply he found himself attracted to her.

He'd ignored her soft words, her plea for help. What else could he do? His father lay in the hospital, his life in balance. David couldn't leave the only person who ever had cared for him. His mother hadn't stuck around. His dad didn't deserve someone else skipping out.

But he'd let a woman, vulnerable and terrified for her son, walk away to face a violent threat alone.

He swallowed down his guilt, but it rose back up like bile. If he were any type of man, he'd follow her or stop her from going. But not him. Because that would mean he'd have to delve into his past and the subsequent lies he knew he'd find. He couldn't do it.

CHAPTER 17

BANGING FROM THE trunk reverberated through the interior of the car. Peter grunted. From behind the wheel, he adjusted the rearview mirror. The sun's rays bounced off the top of the trunk, which remained closed. No thanks to the kid inside.

Damn. The chloroform had worn off. He couldn't continue driving on the interstate with the kid rattling the back. Eventually, someone passing might see or hear.

"Hey!" he yelled over the hum of tires on asphalt. "You need to calm down, slugger."

From the sudden silence in the back, the kid had heard him. Good. In an hour, Peter would pull off and check. If the kid hadn't taken a leak, he'd give him some water, but only enough to keep the boy from dehydrating, because he sure as hell didn't want the stench of piss inside the car.

The orders had been to keep the boy alive. Peter didn't much care either way.

What he did care about was Skye's reaction. He would have loved to see her face the moment she realized her son was kidnapped. He hoped the terror was eating away at her insides right about now.

Payback was a bitch.

The pounding in the trunk turned frantic.

What the hell was the kid doing? Using his legs like a damn battering ram?

Shit. Several hours out of Las Vegas and he had to play babysitter. Peter turned off at the next exit. Fifteen minutes later, with no sign of life for miles, he pulled down a dirt road that looked more like a cow path. The car bounced over packed dirt and dead shrub, drowning out the noise coming from the trunk until he stopped the car. After grabbing a flashlight from inside the glove compartment, he popped the trunk. As he stepped outside, desert heat coated him in its grip while a layer of dust did the same to the car's exterior.

Hinges sighed as he lifted the lid with a cautious hand. He flicked on the light and shone its beam cautiously into the interior. On his back, Tyler lay bound, gagged, blindfolded and curled up in a fetal position. Seeing the boy hadn't dislodged the pillowcase around his head, Peter relaxed.

He'd been warned the kid was dangerous without a blindfold. For now, Peter decided to believe Ferguson. It might have been the odd note in the other man's voice that had convinced him. Peter didn't want to take any chances. He'd seen some crazy shit over the years.

"We've got a long ride ahead of us. No more moving around like some damn worm on a line. Got that?"

He grabbed the front of the boy's shirt and yanked the kid upward. The boy stiffened as if about to go into convulsions. Peter slipped the flashlight under his armpit, then slammed his fist into the boy's face. Body once rigid, slumped. The boy's head dropped backward, exposing the vulnerable column of his throat. His neck gleamed ivory against Peter's flashlight. One quick twist and the boy would be no more.

Sighing, Peter dropped the kid back in the trunk and slammed the top closed. It wasn't yet time.

Peter got behind the wheel, drove back along the dirt road and once again entered the stream of highway traffic. He shifted into a comfortable position against the vinyl seat and checked the review mirror once again. No movement, no sound. Still, he had one hell of a long drive. He fiddled with the radio until a station cleared. Monotone voices filled the car's interior, while silence continued from the trunk.

~~*~~

David sat silently, waiting, watching. Next to him, his father lay beneath a white, disinfected sheet, the rise and fall of his chest in tune with the rhythmic beep of the machine to the right of the hospital bed.

People rarely came out of comas intact. Panic and pain banded around David's chest. If the old man couldn't function to his full capacity, he knew his father would shatter. Being reliant on David would poison his self-esteem until he became a brittle shell of his former self.

His dad might care about being partially paralyzed, but David didn't. He just wanted his dad back. Alive. They'd been through so damn much.

Afraid to have faith or believe in miracles, David stared at the man who'd raised him, who'd sacrificed a rising career in the police department and relationships with the opposite sex. All because of a young son latched to his leg and a need to place his child above all else.

Gray, translucent skin covered a web of veins across his father's temples and cheeks. A bruise, tinted red and purple, marked one cheek, while a bandage covered his temple and outer eyebrow.

His father's eyelids flickered.

David snapped forward in his chair. There again. Barely a breath of movement from his lashes. But there. Not his imagination.

"Dad," David whispered.

His father's eyes flickered open.

David's heart rate drummed against his chest as he cupped his father's aged hand. Pleasure welled up his throat and made it impossible to speak.

His father turned his head against the pillow. When his gaze caught on David, he blinked. Then a frantic flash of desperation flared in the liquid depths of his eyes. He moved his lips around the tube. A hollow, unnatural groan emitted through the plastic.

More sounds issued from the tube as he dug talon-like fingers into David's flesh. His father grimaced as pain lashed across his features.

Oh, shit. David grappled with getting air into his lungs. The pain, the vulnerability in his father's face. David needed it to stop, he needed—

"Nurse." With his free hand, David hit the call button by his father's bed. "Nurse!"

The door swished open. A woman in her late thirties, dressed in green hospital garb and with a faded tattoo on her forearm walked briskly into the room and around the other side of the bed.

"That tube's got to hurt. Can't you take it out?" he asked as his father clawed at his mouth with his other hand. "He wants to say something."

"I'm afraid not." She sighed in resignation as she gently but firmly grasped his father's wrist and placed it down by his side. She shook her head, sympathy softening the angular lines of her face. "They're always like this when they come to. Always wanting to chat like a bunch of magpies. I tell you— Now stop that," she admonished, grabbing his hand again before he reached for the mouthpiece. "If you need to talk, I've got an ABC board with letters of the complete alphabet. All you have to do is point to form the words you want to communicate."

His father slapped at her hand.

"Mr. Bishop," she raised her voice, getting his father's attention. "You're jeopardizing your recovery. You need to calm down. You've been in a chemically induced coma because of the swelling inside your skull." The nurse continued to tell him the situation in a soothing but authoritative voice as she checked his vital signs. With each word, the wildness in his father's eyes faded.

David sank back down in his chair, his father's rigid fingers of his other hand still latched onto his. "Do you have that board?"

She came back a moment later with a flat board. "It's not the most innovative, but it works."

The moment David shifted closer to the bed and held up the board, his father started jabbing his finger at the black letters. An unnatural flush darkened his brow and cheeks.

"Dad. Slow down a bit."

His father's brow creased. A tremor rattled his arm as he poked a finger again and again.

A.D.O.P.T.

David frowned. "I know I was adopted."

His father made a noise against the tube, which sounded strangely like disgust. David shoved down his impatience. "I don't understand what that has to do with your attacker. Did you see who pushed you over the balcony?"

Y.E.S.

"Did you recognize him?"

His father jabbed at the board again.

N.O.

David grunted in frustration and noticed the nurse had disappeared from the room. Probably because she knew how irritating the damn board was in communicating.

His father exhaled through the tube, amplifying his fragility and the artificial quality of his breath. David rubbed the back of his neck. Helplessness seeped like acid through skin and muscle and deep into his bones.

More jabbing.

S.K.Y.E.

David's chest tightened. "She's gone."

Parched skin tightened across his father's knuckles as he clutched the board's edge and stared at David with brows drawn into a fierce, gray line.

"Skye thinks her ex-husband kidnapped her son. She followed them to Boston."

His father shook his head violently and shifted on the bed. The rustle of skin against cotton sheets meshed with air flowing through the plastic tube. A grimace of pain cut across his father's face.

G.O.

"Go where?" Was his dad disgusted with him for bringing Skye into their lives? David could understand how—

G.O.

"Dad, I don't understand."

D.A.N.G.E.R.

"I know you're in danger."

His father rapped on the board with his knuckles.

S.K.Y.E. G.O.

"You want me to go after her?"

A frantic nod from his father. Then another round of jabbing on the board.

M.I.L.T.R.O.N.I.C.S.

"Miltronics," David whispered. Foreboding scurried across his spine. He remembered the name from the article in the library. The foster home. The explosion. It sounded like his father was warning him that Skye was in danger and it all had to do with Miltronics.

A burst of energy exploded from his father. His hand slammed against the board, ripping it from David's grasp to clatter on the ground. An invisible force wrenched his dad from the mattress. His limbs turned rigid beneath the thin cotton sheet. He convulsed, his eyes blank and sightless.

David jerked to his feet. A frigid wave of shock kept him momentarily frozen in place.

The nurse rushed into the room and slapped at the code blue button above his bed. "Mr. Bishop. You need to leave."

"I can't leave him like this."

"*Now.*"

David backed away from the bed. Panic hit him in the chest. The heart machine flickered along with the overhead lights.

Snap.

He glanced across his father's body to the window. A ragged crack had sliced a path across the glass. Fisting his hands at his side, David struggled to smother the maelstrom of emotions bombarding his head. He needed to haul back on his telekinesis before he killed his father or someone else.

Pop.

Shit. He had to get out.

A new fracture bloomed on the window and etched a dozen jagged stems outward across the glass.

Now.

Linoleum squealed as he pivoted on his heel. Stomach rolling, he hurried from the room and paced a path across the waiting area. He didn't sit in the same, worn chair like the previous time with Skye.

No. This time, David stood alone when he desperately needed Skye's strength and sympathy. He walked over to the window and glanced outside to the concrete parking lot from the fifth floor. Even though the sun had since risen, gray clouds filled the sky, and shadows clung to the cars, light poles and buildings beyond.

Go.

The one word echoed inside David's head. His father had warned of danger, had mentioned Miltronics and the need to go after Skye. David rubbed the back of his neck, but the action did nothing to ease the tension knotted around his muscles.

Even when his dad was near death, unlike David, he'd focused on someone other than himself, concerned with a woman and a boy he hardly knew.

David dropped his hand to his side. What type of man had he become? Not one his father would be proud of. For too long he'd buried his head and never looked beyond what people could give him. Skye was no different. All he'd cared about was how she might screw up his life, and because of that, he'd let a woman cross the country after a kidnapper alone. He hadn't once tried to talk Skye out of it.

"Mr. Bishop."

David jerked around and discovered the same nurse had slipped into the room behind him. His gaze skirted away from the sympathy in her face and focused on her tattoo, a faded design of flowers and swords. Seeing her empathy would only weaken his already tentative control.

"We had to put your father under again. This time we were forced to switch from Diprivan to Ativan, which complicates the situation."

Tension ground into the muscles of his back. "Is he going to be all right? Did he just have a heart attack?"

"His heart's fine. His reaction can be typical in some cases, but at this point, I can't tell you with any confidence what the outcome will be. I do know it's very likely he'll be under for a minimum of two weeks."

"And what are the chances of him *not* waking up?"

The woman sighed. "Of course, there's always that likelihood." She glanced down the hall, which led to another section of the hospital. "We have clergy if you need to talk to someone."

The nurse's words felt like a knife to the gut and underscored his father's fragile link to life. "No, I'll be fine."

A lie, but he wasn't about to expose his despair and regrets to a woman who'd heard it all before from others.

"Can I sit with him?"

"Of course."

David retraced his steps and stopped at the side of his father's bed. It was like the last hour had never happened. His father lay as motionless as before, much of his frail body hidden by sheets and a hospital gown. Oxygen hissed in out of the tube, the heart monitor beeped, and the silence between hung in the air, thick and cloying.

Edging closer to the bed, David stared down at a man who'd fought like hell when he'd been struck with colon cancer. The battle had taken a lot out of him. So much so that David wondered if his dad had the will to fight this new battle.

How the hell could David look at himself again? He'd been a selfish bastard for as long as he could remember. Unlike Skye. He'd never met a woman so fearless. Even when things looked so damn hopeless, she hadn't given up hope. Not Skye. The only option she chose was to fight back.

By doing nothing, he was condoning what they'd done to his dad and to Skye's son. Turning a cheek, not because he thought it was the right thing to do, but because he didn't want to get involved and upset his carefully constructed life.

Go.

His father's urgent plea reverberated inside David's head again.

Maybe it was time he acted like a man. A man who gave a damn.

CHAPTER 18

SKYE FLIPPED OFF the last of the lights and dropped down in a recliner in the corner of Jay's living room to wait. Less than an hour ago when she'd knocked on Jay's door and received no response, she'd used her telekinesis to slip past the locks and get inside. After scouring the two-bedroom apartment for Tyler or any sign of his presence, she'd found nothing. Not one hint her son had stepped through the front door.

Jay had been hard to find, but she hadn't expected an easy search. For two days she'd hunted around Boston and the surrounding areas for Jay, his friends and anyone who'd crossed paths with him at some time in his life. Much of his old police colleagues proved useless, except for Mack Bennett, the only cooperative person she'd encountered. Even though he'd never stepped over the line while she was married, he hadn't hidden his attraction, and she'd used it today shamelessly, flirting and charming her way to getting Jay's address from him.

Night had fallen, and light from the parking lot lampposts speared through the window's blinds to score paths across the opposite wall. She gripped the armrests and dug her fingers into the worn, gray velvet.

The rapid, drum of her pulse thrummed inside her head while her gut burned with anxiety. What if Jay didn't take Ty?

What if all along someone else had their eye on her son? A serial killer bent on his own sick agenda? Her breath backed into her throat. She couldn't think that way. If Jay didn't have Tyler, he'd know who did. He had to.

Savagely, she bit down on her lower lip to keep the tears at bay. Letting her heart and her emotions crowd into her conscious wasn't going to get her son back. She needed a cool head and the brains to outwit Jay.

The scrape of a shoe on cement sounded from outside the front door. Skye rolled her shoulders and straightened in the chair. Calm. Cool. Jay needed to know she was in complete control.

She would find Tyler, and God help Jay if he got in her way.

The key grated in the lock. Her breath whispered between clenched teeth. The deadbolt turned, a slight slide of metal against metal. Tension slashed into the muscles of her shoulders and back. The door opened. Skye didn't move. Jay stepped into the foyer, closed the door with a shoulder and turned toward the living area, a six-pack of long-necks in one hand.

He hadn't seen her yet.

She stared at the lamp on the end table beside her and focused. Light flooded the room.

Jay blinked, then stiffened. "What the hell."

As he took a step backward, their gazes caught and held, his narrowed, suspicious, hers unblinking, without expression. At least that's what she hoped he saw.

"Hello, Jay."

"What are you doing here?"

"I've come for Tyler."

"Tyler?"

She dug her nails deeper into the chair until her fingers hit the wood concealed beneath. Her composure cracked. Damn him. She was tired of his games.

Jay set the beer on a scratched table against the wall and glanced down the hall to where both bedrooms were.

"Don't bother. It's not there."

His expression grew bland. "What are you talking about?"

"The gun in the nightstand by your bed. Not the most original place to put a weapon, but then you were never the imaginative type." Lips twisting into a resemblance of a smile, she picked up the revolver in her lap and dangled the trigger guard with an index finger.

His face tightened. "Aren't you the smart one?"

She frowned, sensing a deeper meaning beneath his snide tone as she crossed her legs and eased the gun back to her lap. "How much were you hoping to get?"

"What are you talking about?"

"Blackmail. Your plan to use Tyler to get money from me." Saying the words aloud turned her stomach. How low could a person go? She couldn't even fathom how Jay could use an innocent child, never mind his own son, for personal gain. "After all, you showed up in Las Vegas looking for cash."

Jay laughed. Shaking his head, he latched onto the neck of a beer and pulled it from its case. "You're way off. Tyler's the last person I'd want."

"I seem to remember a different story." Memories flooded her, painful and raw and not dulled by time. "You fought me every step of the way. You were determined to get sole-custody."

He twisted the top, tossed the cap up, and caught it in mid-air. "That's the past. Things worked out better for me going solo. I like my life the way it is now."

She glanced around the room, at the dirt smudges bracketing the doorways and handles, the worn, beige carpet. She wrinkled her nose at the sway-backed, gray sofa opposite her. Patches of velvet were scraped off from overuse. "Really? Seems to me you've lowered your standards."

After he tipped the bottle and downed several swallows, he wiped his mouth with the back of his hand. "You haven't changed a bit. Still a bitch."

His words... She'd heard or seen them before. Oh, God. Shock slammed into her chest. An image of the mirror in David's home flashed in her mind's eye. *You can't run from your past. You were a bitch then, and you're a bitch now.*

He'd lied like every other time he'd opened his mouth. Jay had been the one who'd taken Tyler, not some faceless kidnapper. He'd had Tyler all this time, while she'd be going insane with fear.

Clutching the gun's handle with a rigid hand, she jerked to a stand. "You sick bastard."

She glared at Jay from across the room. Anger rolled through her body with such force that it choked the breath from her lungs. The emotion built until she drove it from her body and directed its power at Jay. She yanked him off the ground with the force of her rage and shoved him through the air. The bottle flew from his hand, spewing foam and liquid into the air before it dropped and rolled across the carpet. His head and back hit the wall with a loud thud.

Shoved up against the wall, feet dangling centimeters above the floor, he glowered back at her. "Fuck you."

Skye hurled the gun at him. The weapon spun through the air until its barrel froze inches from Jay's temple. Using her telekinesis, she kept him pressed against the wall with a large invisible fist and eased the trigger slowly.

His throat contracted with an audible swallow. Fear radiated from his body and turned his jaw rigid.

Good. She wanted him to be afraid. That was the only way to get the truth out of him.

"Tell me where he is."

He opened his mouth. When only a gurgle bubbled from his mouth, she eased the pressure from his chest and throat.

Jay struggled, kicking his legs, twisting his body against the force that pinned him to the wall. Skye let him struggle until eventually he must have realized how futile his attempts were and he stilled.

"Come on you bastard. Where have you hidden him?"

"Nowhere. I don't have him."

Fury ate into her. "Still the lies. You haven't changed, but I have. This time I know how to get answers." She stepped toward him, keeping the gun trained on his temple with her mind. "We're going to play a little game. Your revolver's perfect for it. It's called Russian Roulette. Ever hear of it?"

"You're crazy."

"Maybe. I left one bullet in the chamber. It's anyone's guess when a bullet will blow your brains across the room." She shoved the gun against his temple, pleased to see a new wave of terror etched across his features. Gone was the dimple, the smile, the charm. No façade, just raw emotion. "Now where is he?"

"I don't know." Eyes wide with terror, he stared at the gun, transfixed.

She eased back the trigger until a click resounded over Jay's frayed breathing.

No bullet.

This time.

Jay slumped and started to slither down the wall until she wrenched him upward. She again inched back the trigger, then dug the muzzle deeper against his flesh. She wasn't about to let the bastard go without a fight.

"Jesus, Skye! Stop it. I'm telling you the truth. I don't know where he is!"

She didn't believe him, but what the hell would it take to get the truth out of him? The trigger clicked again. Skye saw the dark stain appear along the crotch of his pants, but she didn't give a damn.

"That's two now. We've got a total of six. The odds of a bullet in the next one just climbed." Jay may not have ever gotten violent, but the way Skye was feeling right now, she was breathing, craving violence, anything to fill the yawning hole tearing at her insides. "You're a slimy piece of shit. Do you know that? You lie, lie and lie. You wanted him before. It doesn't make sense that you've completely changed your mind. Can you tell me why? Can you?"

She twisted the muzzle against his flesh, enjoying the shiver of fear that visibly shook his body. Slowly the trigger eased, the whisper of metal against well-oiled metal. He squeezed his eyes shut. Tears pooled at the corner of one eye and etched a path down one cheek.

"Because... because he's not mine."

"What?" She edged the trigger back. That made no sense.

"Tyler isn't my kid." He gulped in a ragged breath. "He never was."

"That's impossible."

"They showed me. I saw the DNA test and everything."

Skye shook her head, beyond shock, beyond disbelief. She eased the gun from his brow, but continued to aim the muzzle at his head. "What are you talking about?"

"I'm not Tyler's biological father."

"That's impossible. I've never slept with anyone else while we were married."

"Yeah, right. You had yourself an immaculate conception, did you? If not that, you'll be saying you were abducted by aliens and secretly impregnated."

Skye's gaze narrowed. Even with a gun to his head and having wet his pants, Jay had the gall to be snide. "Then why fight for sole custody of a boy you never fathered? You're the crazy one if you think I'm going to buy that."

Jay must have sensed her patience fray even further, because alarm flared in his eyes. "They paid me. They promised me a whole lot of cash if I got custody of him."

"So you're saying that you intended to sell Tyler?" She stepped back, repugnance crawling across her flesh. To think that she'd been married to this man for years. Had the drugs completely leached his ethics or had he been like this the entire time she'd known him and she'd been a blind fool?

"What the hell did I care? He wasn't mine. You'd lied to me, screwed around behind my back."

She searched his face. Sweat gleamed off his forehead, the stink of urine clung to him, while fear radiated from him in large waves. All the signs revealed Jay might be finally telling her the truth. But this story of his sounded too bizarre.

It was crazy. It was impossible.

But was it?

A man had kidnapped Ty. That same man had died in a car crash where Tyler had miraculously survived the head-on collision. The mystery behind the kidnapper's motives lay buried in the ground with him.

"You mention 'they.' Who are 'they' and why would they want Tyler?"

But she already had one of her answers. They wanted Tyler for his power. His telekinesis was far more sophisticated than her own and David's. With what her son could do, it would allow a person to achieve power, money, any imaginable, twisted dream.

"I didn't want to know who they were," Jay finally said. "And even if I did, they were careful. I never got a name or place. Just cash, and random calls."

She jammed the muzzle against his temple and pulled back the trigger.

"Jesus! Skye don't do it." He squeezed his eyes shut. "For God's sake. I made a mistake. I fucked up. But don't kill me!"

"Give me a name."

She dug the muzzle deeper into his flesh.

"I don't know... I swear—"

Click.

"Shit!" He blinked. Tears clung to his lashes.

"We're down to three now."

"Ferguson. I caught the name Ferguson. And a house. Something to do with a house. That's all I know. I swear. Just don't. Don't kill me. I want to live. I'll change. I swear. I'll get clean."

"House. What do you mean?"

"I overheard talk about a house."

"October house. It that it?"

"Yes. Yes."

Skye eased back on her telekinesis and her hold of him against the wall. Jay slumped to the ground in a quaking mass of wretched humanity and urine. Sweat clung to his brow, his hairline. Mucus dripped from his nose as deep, anguished cries shook his body.

Skye stepped away from Jay, pulling the gun hanging in mid-air into her hand. She'd broken him, a man she thought she'd once loved. A man she believed had fathered her child.

The world tilted. Dizziness assaulted her. She grappled to keep her telekinesis in line. Skye didn't dare panic, didn't dare crumble. Maybe later, but not now, not when her son desperately needed her.

October House. A foster home from her youth. The scrawled writing on the mirror, the kidnappings were all tied to her past. But how?

She stumbled from the apartment, got into the rental car without heaving the contents of her stomach. She tossed the gun in the passenger seat and gripped the steering wheel with a clammy hand. Blankly, she stared through the windshield as the chill of sweat formed on her brow, temple and nape.

She didn't have the energy to drive off. Hell, she didn't even know where to go now. She'd focused so much on Jay, not thinking much of any other possibility. She'd stepped through the threshold of Jay's apartment believing she'd find Tyler, but other than the name of Ferguson, she had nothing other than more questions and a fresh wave of terror. Jay had been tangible, a person she could find, while this Ferguson was a faceless threat.

Her hand tightened around the steering wheel as she peered through the driver's window to Jay's apartment. A street lamp from the parking lot revealed his closed, front door. She didn't think he'd be leaving anytime soon. Not with the way she'd left him. She would have killed him and not cared.

With horror and disgust, she stared at the shadow of the revolver on the passenger seat. The fluid metal lines gleamed through the darkness. She'd stepped over the line, used a violence beyond anything she thought capable of. She'd become one of them, a person she'd always abhorred and taught her son never to emulate. Self-loathing crept across her flesh and tightened around her throat.

Shifting, she reached inside her front jeans pocket and pulled out six bullets and stuffed them in the cup holder.

"What the hell am I becoming?"

She wiped her damp hands across her face, curling into herself. Sobs wracked her body until her stomach muscles cramped with pain. Gasping, she rubbed at her face with her forearm, fumbling for some measure of restraint.

Her son. Oh, God. He needed her.

She thought of the scrawled words on the mirror in Las Vegas. You can't run from your past. You were a bitch then, and you're a bitch now. If these people wanted Tyler so much, why make it so personal? Why scrawl those vicious words on the mirror as if she'd wronged them?

None of it made sense.

Skye ruthlessly pushed down the panic bubbling up her throat. Tyler had to be in Boston. There was no other logical place. It had started here with the kidnapping.

Jay's words leaked into her thoughts. "Next you'll say it was an alien abduction."

A fresh wave of foreboding rolled through her insides. She shivered. Images of the alien from her nightmares, savage incisors, yellow reptilian eyes flashing hatred, bombarded her. No matter how much she wanted, Skye couldn't shake the images from her mind.

She dragged in a long, panicked breath that rattled her entire frame.

What the hell was going on?

CHAPTER 19

ONCE THE ESTATE'S front gates whispered shut, Peter glanced over his shoulder and backed up his car into Ferguson's garage. The lack of banging from inside the trunk didn't worry Peter. He'd pulled one of the seats down in the back, which gave direct access to the trunk and allowed air into the small enclosure. He'd also checked on the kid a couple of hours ago, found his pulse normal and his breathing a bit agitated, but the kid was alive.

After he cut the engine, Peter hit the garage door remote attached to the car's visor and watched the metal panels roll shut. Daylight filtered through garage door cutouts and into the enclosed space, lightening the shadows across denser, darker ones.

He popped the trunk, then shut the driver's door after him. As he walked around to the rear of the car, he snapped on the switch by the door that led into the house, throwing bright, fluorescent light into the garage's interior and chasing away the remaining shadows.

Peter peered inside the trunk. The boy lay curled in much the same position Peter had left him in when he'd checked on his pulse and given him water. Except for two brief and remote stops to take a piss, the kid had been inside the trunk for almost nine hours, ever since Peter had smuggled him out of the last cheap hotel they'd stayed in and into the car.

At nine, thinner than most boys his age, he was far from any threat to an adult male. So why did Ferguson want him so badly? Peter glanced at the immaculate storage cabinets lined on either side and to the Bentley parked against the far wall of the three-car garage. Money didn't seem to be the motivation.

Revenge?

Peter grunted. His eyelid flickered. He blinked and rubbed the skin with the back of his hand. He understood revenge all too well, and because of it, he began to wonder if it was such a good idea to hand the kid over as planned. Yeah, the money was good, but this went beyond financial gain. The idea of killing the boy in front of Skye drummed into his thoughts.

Now that would be perfect. To witness her suffering firsthand. You couldn't get much better than that.

"Hey, kid. I'm about to pull you out. Don't give me an excuse to hurt you. I will if you try something."

In response, the pillowcase over the boy's head quivered and contracted by his mouth with each quick inhalation. Still terrified. Not that Peter could blame him. Getting kidnapped—especially at such a young age—was bound to get someone scared shitless, but hell, that wasn't Peter's problem.

Now Skye. Yeah, that was very much her problem. By now she must be sweating pretty badly. Good. She deserved it. Karma was a bitch.

He grabbed the boy's duct taped wrists and pulled him from his fetal position. Using his other hand, Peter grabbed the waistband at the back the kid's pants and yanked him from the trunk.

The boy twisted, flung a foot into Peter's groin and an elbow into his throat. Gasping, Peter dropped the kid but hooked two fingers around a belt loop before the little shit sprang away. The kid struggled against him, all knees, elbows and hard angles. His frantic movements wrenched the pillowcase from around his face.

"You little shit." Peter squished the kid against his side, hindering more jabs and frantic contortions. Peter thought about snapping the kid's neck and ending the craziness but then reminded himself that Ferguson wanted him alive.

The boy arched against Peter. Sweat glued short spikes of hair against his face. The pillowcase clung to the crown of his head. For the briefest moment the boy's gaze, dark brown, fathomless, weary yet wise, meshed with Peter's before he looked at the car and around the garage.

The sharp cry of the car alarm cut into the enclosed garage, pounding into the air and into Peter's skull. Then the high screech of the house alarm broke over the car's warning system.

What the hell? Tensing, Peter searched the garage for an intruder. No one jumped from the storage units lining the two walls. A freezer and sink rested against another wall. Neither held enough bulk to hide a person.

But there was his car and Ferguson's Bentley. Someone could hide inside or behind either car. Peter might be able to see them approach, but not if they caught him from behind, and he sure as hell wouldn't be able to hear them. With the boy still latched to his side, Peter edged along the perimeter of the garage and peered into what interior he could see of both cars.

"Help!" The boy screamed, his voice drowning beneath the two alarms. "Someone help—"

Tension gnawing through his muscles, Peter slapped a hand over the little bastard's mouth, froze and waited for someone to come at him and attack. A thick and heavy stillness filled the garage's interior, while the high-piercing wail of the two alarms throbbed against car metal and rubber, and cement and drywall.

Ferguson rushed into the garage, slamming the door open and waving a phone at Peter. His thick silver hair shot up from a ruddy, deeply lined face. When his gaze latched onto Peter and the boy, his brown eyes flashed with panic. "What the hell are you doing? Get his head covered. Now!"

"What the fuck do you think I'm doing?" Peter snarled, yanking the pillowcase back down over the boy's face and digging an arm tighter around the kid's ribs to keep him from thrashing around. Peter shifted, looking on either side of him, expecting a bullet or a weapon to his face or body. "There's someone else in here with us."

"Damn it," Ferguson yelled over the sirens. "No one's in here but us. It's the boy you've got to worry about. He's the one that triggered both alarms."

With the boy flailing in his arms, Peter dug into his pants' pocket, found the car's remote and clicked the alarm off. The piercing siren died, but the house continued to scream a high-pitched cry that bombarded his senses as Ferguson punched in a code on the box by the door.

Deafening silence, almost as loud as the alarms had been, permeated the garage. Ferguson dialed a number on his phone and after a pause, said, "I'm sorry for the misunderstanding. There's no need to have anyone come by. I accidentally tripped the alarm. Yes. Okay. Thank you."

He glared at Peter. "I thought I told you to keep his eyes covered at all times. It's imperative that you make sure he doesn't see what's around him, particularly any computerized device. That's our only protection."

"Protection from what?" Just what the hell was it about Skye's son that scared the shit out of Ferguson? And how could a nine-year-old kid turn on alarms without putting a hand on them? If what Ferguson said was true, then that meant this kid was a far bigger fish than Peter suspected.

"I don't pay you to ask questions." Ferguson jerked his head toward the door. "Hurry up. I've got some eye drops for the boy that will keep him momentarily blinded and in line."

Peter's gaze narrowed. All his previous work involved getting the job done and getting out, no questions asked, but this task involved Skye's son and was personal from the very beginning no matter how much he wanted to think differently. This job was about revenge. To hell with the other players, and that included Ferguson and his fucking arrogance.

But along with that revenge, he wanted answers to why this kid was so important. If he set off alarms by his thoughts and was dangerous around computers... The scent of money oozed from the boy's body. If the kid could manipulate a computer, the possibilities were unimaginable.

A fortune.

Far more than he would ever see in his life or longer.

Inching the pillowcase aside while keeping the boy's face concealed, Peter wrapped his fingers around the boy's warm and fragile throat. A pulse point, frantic and uneven, throbbed against his finger. "I can kill him right now. One quick snap, and your golden boy's dead. The power to have him live or die is all up to you. He lives only on the condition I get some answers."

~~*~~

Blinking against the fading but hot July sunlight and the sting of sweat that slipped into one eye, Skye wiped at her brow before hauling herself up the chain link fence. Her jeans caught against the sharp metal ends as she tried to straddle the top. Grumbling with frustration, she yanked at the hem. Fabric tore, sounding like a disembodied cry in the stillness of the afternoon. Skye swore under her breath but managed to get both legs over onto the other side.

She dropped to the ground. The abrupt landing jerked the air from her lungs and forced her to her knees. Grunting, she slapped a palm on the ground, stopping herself from tumbling on her face. Dead, course grass cut into her hand. She rose on unsteady legs and glanced around. No movement on the street from behind or in the yard directly in front of her.

It was a good half-hour since a car had driven past.

Not the most popular place. The closest building around was a barn a good 1000 feet down the road. Skye didn't know whether that was good or bad. She guessed she'd find out soon enough.

As she walked away from the fence, grass brushed across her jean-clad ankles and running shoes, sounding like malevolent whispers filled with secrets and brutality.

Shivering, she paused in the middle of the yard and looked up at the abandoned building, with its boarded up windows, faded, gray roof and three stories of red and battered brick. The picture on the internet of October House had depicted the place's aura of neglect but not its sense of despair.

Before parking on the opposite side of the home, she'd driven into a rural area between the outlying cities. A number of farms still dotted the area, somehow managing to escape the claws of concrete. Once she'd stepped out of the vehicle, she'd crossed a two-lane road with soft shoulders. The property, a good acre Skye guessed, rested on the corner of a four-way stop and was surrounded by a six-foot chain link fence. The house beyond the enclosure had beckoned, hinting of malevolent secrets and past terrors.

For a long moment, she stood and stared with unease at the building now, as dark, fathomless memories scratched below the surface of her consciousness. God, she wanted to remember, but the fear and images of a sick, green face with lizard-like eyes flashing yellow hatred immobilized her.

Jaw tightening, she groped for calm. Tyler was out there, alone, frightened, and in desperate need of her help.

Skye refocused her energy on uncovering the mystery of October House. She might be traveling down a crazy, irrelevant path, but she was frantic. The foster home had to be somehow linked to what was now happening in her life with Tyler. Why else would Jay have heard the name?

Skye ignored the front door. Too visible for anyone who might pass by. Locusts scattered as she walked through the dead grass. One landed on her arm, and she brushed it aside impatiently as she circled the building, looking for a way in.

Turning the corner, she discovered a windowless metal door, the same faded rust color as the brick. She twisted the knob. Locked. Nothing that she didn't expect.

The hum of a vehicle carried through the air and rapidly approached. Tensing, she hunkered down by a bush or weed. Laughter, sharp and at odds with the unease twisting Skye's insides, broke over the sound of tires on asphalt. Frozen, she waited as the growl of the engine strengthened. She edged along the brick wall toward the front yard. On the opposite side of the street her silver, economical rental car still sat on the shoulder. She inched further along the wall until she saw a van roll to a stop at the intersection. Then the vehicle raced off down the road and around a bend, disappearing from view by a layer of trees.

Tension eased from her upper back and shoulders. A couple of people in a van. Nothing more. No killer, kidnapper or psychotic. Just her overactive imagination. Skye rolled her shoulders, calmed her heart, then retraced her steps and searched the back door and the immediate area for any signs of an alarm. Seeing none, she relaxed even further, knowing she could bypass something as unsophisticated as a deadbolt.

Skye focused her mind's energy on the doorknob's lock and the deadbolt. A barely discernible click and snap followed. When she turned the knob this time, the metal gave with a low rumble, making her wonder when the last person had walked through the halls and rooms of this place.

She stepped into the stifling silent hallway and closed the door carefully behind her. Dust and a musty, unused scent assailed her nostrils. With each cautious step, her running shoes whined softly against the wood floor, which coincided with the hard thump of her heart. She walked down a faded, beige hallway where stained rectangles marked the walls from where pictures once hung.

The fear and unease she'd tried to bury resurfaced. Her heartbeat quickened and sweat thickened across her skin, causing her t-shirt to cling tighter against her body. She'd been here before. Skye didn't have to search her memory. She'd lived, breathed inside these four walls as an orphan.

After passing several doorways, Skye stepped into a room to the right. A floorboard creaked beneath her weight. Broken blinds hindered the sunlight from struggling through a large bay window. A couple of desks, decades old sat like large bullfrogs, bulky, brown and weathered. Laughter and tears echoed through the past and into the room, faint but unmistakable memories from Skye's past.

Other children had lived here and died.

She paused, frowned.

A sound, possibly a footstep, resounded from the hall. She backed up against the wall beside the door. Forcing air in and out of her nose, slowly, quietly, she waited and listened.

Silence.

Cautiously, she re-entered the hall and found it empty, dark and ominous. Moving as quietly as possible, she eased back down the hall from where she'd started. By one doorway, 'Office' was stenciled in faded gray across the open door. Sadly, even if there were filing cabinets inside, she didn't think she'd find anything useful inside them. Still...

She slipped inside, past what looked like a waiting room and into an office with three tiers of metal files in the same faded beige as the walls outside. She eased two drawers open and found both empty.

Exactly where would years of records be?

Helplessness gnawed into her stomach. There must be a storage unit somewhere. They couldn't have all been destroyed, could they?

As the drawer scraped shut, the noise almost masked the rustle of clothing. That and the sigh of someone's breath alerted her too late. She gasped. A hand roughly clamped over her mouth, locking the breath in her lungs. Before she had a chance to latch onto the drawer handle, the person jerked her backward. Her fingers clutched at the air.

Focusing past the panic, she forced her mind on the drawer and stared hard at the cabinet. The drawer flew from the cabinet, rushing past and grazing her shoulder but missing her attacker. Damn it. She couldn't get to the person behind her without hitting herself.

Trying to bite at the hand across her mouth, she struggled against the steel-like arm around her stomach. A man. His scent of soap and aftershave filled her senses. Skye stiffened in shock.

David whipped her around and pushed her up against the nearest wall, his hand firmly latched over her mouth. The buckle of his belt dug into her stomach. She shivered as the heat of his body scorched through her clothing and into her skin as fear and a sick sense of excitement rushed through her limbs.

"Shhh," he whispered by her ear, his breath feathering her hair back from her temple. "We're not alone."

CHAPTER 20

TYLER'S BODY DROOPED in Peter's arm as he continued to cup a palm against the boy's neck. Fear must have put the kid into a faint. Good. This way, Peter didn't have to deflect a knee or foot to his body anymore.

"What did you do to him?" Beneath his pin-striped shirt, Ferguson's chest expanded in obvious outrage.

"Not a fucking thing. The kid fainted, but I can make it where he'll never wake up again." Peter wrapped his palm tighter around the boy's slender neck as he stared across the hood of his car at Ferguson.

Peter was lying, but Ferguson didn't need to know that. He had no intention of killing the boy just yet. Now that the moment had come to make the exchange for cash, Peter found he disliked the plan. The idea of taking the kid's life while Skye watched appealed far more with each passing moment. To have her down on her knees, begging him, to be able to witness her life disintegrating right in front of him filled him with growing interest.

But more than revenge kept him from handing over the kid. Peter wondered what it was about Skye's son that sent sweat dripping from Ferguson's brow? If he found the reason, Peter just might be able to use it against Skye in some way.

"Why is this kid so damn important? Give me the answer. The real one, and not some pre-fabricated shit."

At the threat, Ferguson's gaze narrowed and his hand fisted around the phone. For a long moment, he didn't say anything. "That wasn't the deal. It was cash for the boy and nothing more."

"I've changed my mind."

Ferguson's nostril's flared. "I can see that."

"Well?" Peter coolly asked, disliking the arrogant prick.

"How about I just pay you. You leave and I keep the boy. It's simple. Don't make it more complicated."

"Money isn't enough anymore." Peter smiled, seeing the sudden malice flare in the other man's eyes. Ferguson didn't like this new development. The bastard was probably used to having people do exactly what he wanted. Well, not this time. Not with Peter. Ferguson couldn't control him, and Peter suspected the guy was finally figuring that one out.

"Fine, you'll get it, but the garage is hardly the place to have this conversation."

Ferguson opened the door leading to the interior of the house and stepped into a black and chrome colored kitchen. Peter followed, and with an arm around the boy's waist, hefted the kid's limp body higher against his hip. "Where do you want me to put him?"

"This way."

Ferguson walked down a hallway and stopped at a metal door with another alarm system. He punched a code into a keypad, and the green light replaced a flashing red one. The door sighed open beneath Ferguson's hand. He then led Peter down a flight of metal, mesh stairs.

Peter followed at a slower pace. Caution pricked the back of his neck. Even though Ferguson was well in his sixties, overweight and out of shape, Peter wasn't about to underestimate the man.

He'd made that mistake at the library when it came to Bishop's father. Peter had barely managed to get the old man over the rail. He hated loose ends and was frustrated at not finishing him off at the hospital, but he couldn't pass up a perfect opportunity to grab the kid. Skye and Bishop had been too focused on the old man to think of much else.

The stairs led to a large, sterile, rectangular room with three white walls. The fourth consisted of counters and cabinets from the waist down. On the counter were several monitors and computer and other sophisticated equipment. A glass partition, possibly a two-way mirror, separated this room from another deep in shadow.

Ferguson opened a door at the far end of the room and flicked a switch. Light flooded into the other room, revealing a large recliner through the glass, very much like a dentist's chair, except this one had thick metal sleeves by the arm pads and footrests as if waiting for a victim's ankles and wrists.

Shit. The place looked like someone's grotesque, modern-day Frankenstein experiment.

Nostrils pinched, Ferguson opened the door wider. "You can set him on the chair."

Peter walked through the open doorway, passed Ferguson and the animosity and anxiety that radiated from his thick body, and draped the boy across the leather-like chair. That same prickle of awareness raced across his neck, and Peter rolled his shoulders, sensing the threat behind him even though he couldn't see it.

Casually Peter turned back around. The door stood open, while the glass partition proved to be exactly what he'd assumed. A two-way mirror with no sign of Ferguson. He was out there though, waiting to strike. Peter strode toward the doorway and sprang into the other room, tucking his head into his chest, rolling across the cement floor. He kicked out a leg and caught Ferguson's ankle. The other man grunted and landed hard against the ground. A gun flew from Ferguson's hand and skirted across the floor away from the other man's reach and by Peter. The weapon didn't matter. Ferguson didn't have a chance in hell of bypassing Peter to get to it.

Peter bounded to his feet. He watched dispassionately as the other man clawed at the counter with floundering hands and dragged himself up on his knees. Ferguson's mouth wheezed like a fish starved for oxygen. Splotches of red covered his face.

Across his brow and upper lip sweat shimmered beneath the fluorescent light.

Peter kicked the gun into the corner of the room behind him and further away from Ferguson. Then Peter stepped casually toward him. Panic flared in the prick's eyes as he stumbled to his feet. The old man shouldn't have turned on him. Peter rolled his neck back and fourth, hearing and feeling his spine crack several times. He wanted to kill the bastard. The arrogance. The lies. The disappointments. Just like everyone else in his life. Always saying one thing and doing another. Just like his meth addict of a mother.

Ferguson just proved he was no different than all the others, and like all the rest, he'd never disappoint Peter again. Peter wouldn't give him that option, but first, he had to take care of a couple of matters. Like money and answers.

"Did you really think I was going to let you shoot me? I didn't take you for being that stupid." Peter took another step, while Ferguson's hand shook along the counter's edge. The quaking didn't stop there, though. It rushed through his entire body, even rattling his teeth. Peter smiled with pleasure.

"The gun was to keep the boy in line. I swear to God. It was just a safety measure."

Peter laughed without humor. "Really? I didn't think a kid in a dead faint was a threat. At least to my way of thinking. The boy can't weigh much over fifty pounds. Hardly a danger, even at your advanced age and weight."

"It's the truth." Ferguson edged backward, his fingers trailing along the side of the counter. A couple more feet and he would have the wall against his back. He licked his bottom lip and closed his eyes. "You're forgetting the money. I haven't paid you yet."

"The money." Peter felt like his pet boa, George, powerful, deadly and silent as he edged across the cement floor toward Ferguson, enjoying the other man's reaction. The wider Peter's smile, the deeper and more pervasive the fear radiated from Ferguson's face. "I didn't forget. But I'm thinking you owe me a bit more than the fifty we discussed earlier."

Movement flickered at the corner of Peter's vision.

Shit.

The kid. He'd slipped behind Peter. He'd been so focused on Ferguson, he'd let his attention drift from the boy.

Peter leaped forward. He slammed the side of his hand into Ferguson's throat. The boy's footsteps echoed on the metal stairs. He caught a glimpse of the other man clutching at his neck and dropping to his knees before he pivoted and raced after the boy. Duct tape still bound the kid's wrists together, but he must have pulled off the hood from his face.

Shit.

With his vision clear, there was no stopping the kid. Peter dove up the steps, grabbed for the boy's ankle. He missed and clutched at air instead.

Lurching up another three steps, Peter missed again. The kid opened the door and slipped out and onto the main floor. The door clicked shut. The green light on this side of the alarm by the door flashed to red. Peter pulled and twisted the doorknob. He slammed a shoulder, then a foot against the metal.

The door didn't shift a centimeter.

Peter pivoted and looked down to Ferguson struggling across the floor toward the gun yards away. He'd never get to the weapon before Peter. "The code. Give me the code."

Ferguson gasped. Pain flashed across his features. Words tumbled from his lips, none of them intelligible.

"Shit."

Peter leaped down the stairs, grabbed the gun, then Ferguson by the collar of his shirt and half-dragged, half-carried him up the flight to the alarm. He shoved him up against the wall with an arm and checked the safety on the gun before he tucked it into the waistband at the back of his pants. "Punch the numbers in. Hurry!"

Nine. A trembling finger hit another button. Four. Two more wasted seconds. Seven. Peter bit back a curse. Zero.

The flashing light turned green.

He dropped Ferguson, uncaring if the other man tumbled down the stairs and broke his neck. All that mattered was the kid. If Peter lost the little shit, he'd never be able to really pay back Skye for all the humiliation and pain she'd put him through.

After one swift turn of the knob, Peter opened the door. Gun in hands, he rushed down the hall and into the kitchen. A throng of noise swarmed through the house and throbbed through the walls. The high-pitched wailing of the car and house alarms screamed into Peter's head. The clock on the microwave flashed off and on.

The kid was going berserk.

Focused on the most logical escape route, Peter ran from the kitchen and into the living area where music blared from the stereo system and joined the alarms. The front door gaped open.

The little shit had already fled outside.

Peter ran outside, down the entryway and into the front yard. Alarms from neighboring properties screamed their abuse and fought for precedence with the ones coming from Ferguson's property. The garage door to the left rolled to a stop, fully open. Another escape route the boy could have taken.

Then silence. Abrupt. Deafening.

Peter blinked at the sunlight that flooded his eyes. His shirt clung to his sweaty back. He stood unmoving, his hand on the gun tightening as he focused on getting the rapid sawing of his breath under control. The drum of his pulse eased.

It sounded like the whole neighborhood blew a fuse. The kid was scary as shit. He couldn't be human, not the way he'd short-circuited the electricity. Now Peter understood why Ferguson wanted him. The kid was a human weapon, an unbelievable asset to any government or corporation. Given enough years and training the boy would be worth a fortune.

A bird's song filled the air. The rumble of a lawn mower sounded from somewhere in the distance. But no scrape of a shoe or tell-tale noise gave the boy away.

"Come on kid. Tyler. How about you just show yourself and stop wasting both of our time?"

No answer. Not that Peter expected any. If the boy was anything like Skye, he'd inherited her intelligence even though Peter hated to admit a positive trait of any kind from her.

He searched the yard. No one, not even a small, skinny boy, could hide amidst the manicured bushes along the front of the house and adjacent to the driveway.

Peter stood and listened again. A gust of wind swept across his face and sent the leaves slapping at each other from the tree to his right. A few downtrodden leaves raced across the lawn. He stared down the drive to the closed wrought iron gate. There was no possible way the kid could have opened it, slipped outside and have it close behind him that quickly. Peter had been only behind him but minutes.

The eight-foot cement brick fence was impossible to breach by a nine-year-old kid.

But the boy wasn't normal.

Still... Peter rubbed the back of his neck, then rolled his shoulders to get the kinks out. The kid's powers seemed to involve computers and electrical wiring, not leaping over or through metal or brick barriers. He eyed the wrought iron gate with narrowed eyes. The electricity might be down right now, but the city might get it up and running sooner than Peter wanted.

He strode toward the gate and rammed the gun's handle repeatedly against the electronic box attached to the cement wall until the thin metal crumbled and wires pulled from their moorings. After sliding the gun back inside his waistband, he grabbed the sensor protruding from the side of the drive and yanked it back and forth until it hung limply to one side. He tested the wrought iron bar in the center of the fence. One quick push and the metal gave beneath his touch.

The kid could easily slip through and escape.

Swearing under his breath, Peter walked back up the driveway and into the garage. While keeping his gaze on and off the gate, he rummaged through the cabinets until he found a thick metal chain and lock. After grabbing both, he walked back to the fence and wrapped the chain twice around the two center bars, then effectively locked it with a thick padlock. He pocketed the key and stared back up at the house.

He just needed to quickly dismantle the alarm and phone and

he'd have both Ferguson and the boy trapped. There was no way in hell either would get past him and live.

Peter smiled with pleasure. He was back to being in control. Within the hour, he'd have the kid and cash. As to Ferguson... that was a different story.

~~*~~

David cradled Skye against the wall. With her slender body molded to his from breast to thigh and the wild beat of her heart pounding against his chest, a wave of fierce protectiveness surged through him. For the briefest moment, he savored her scent, the warmth of her body, and the texture of her skin as he brushed his lips against her temple. He'd missed her far more than he'd ever thought possible. Knowing that scared the hell out of him.

Somehow he'd let her into his life, his heart, and there wasn't a damn thing he could do about these crazy feelings for her because it was too late. He already cared.

He eased his palm from her lips with a shaking hand. Her rapid breath washed across his throat, and a shiver raced through the complete length of her body.

"Who?" she asked in a trembling whisper.

"I don't know," he replied in an equally quiet voice. "I think there's only one person, but whoever it is, he's on the same floor by the front of the building. There's a car parked not far from here too. I'm going to check the building out, but I want you to stay here."

"The hell I will."

His heart rate kicked up. This furious need to guard her against herself and the scum who had taken her son overwhelmed him. He thanked God he'd found her unhurt, but what if he'd come across a different situation—a scenario where the person stealthily moving through the building had attacked her and left her injured or worse? David didn't even want to wrap his mind around that.

The moment he'd stepped from the airport in Boston, he'd hailed a taxi and given the driver the address to October

House. In full control of his telekinesis, he'd focused on the locks on the front door. The knob, though noisy and rough from disuse, turned easily beneath his hand, and he'd stepped into the building as if he'd belonged. Like sticky cobwebs, memories of the building, the children and employees clung to his mind. Yeah, he'd been here.

Shaking off their fragile strands, David searched the building. He'd started with the basement but found nothing. As he'd climbed to the main floor, he'd heard the fall of footsteps, sounding cautious, furtive but strangely deliberate, as if the person wanted to mask their movements. Then he'd heard the slide of metal and he'd followed that noise on silent feet.

That's when he discovered Skye and someone else was in the building. More important than the person moving in the other part of the building was the need to get Skye safely away.

"I've a taxi outside waiting." He needed to get her out of here and fast. He didn't want to risk her safety even if the other person wasn't dangerous. "I want you to get in that taxi and leave."

"I can't do that. And anyway, I already have my rental across the street. But that doesn't mean anything. I'm not running away."

He swallowed down his frustration. "Please, Skye. I don't know who this is."

"He just might be a janitor or property manager."

"Do you honestly believe that?"

Her chin inched upward. "No. But that doesn't mean anything."

"It means everything. When we get Tyler back, he's going to need his mother fully alert and functional."

"That isn't playing fair," she hissed, her body tensing with obvious anger.

"I don't care. I'm determined to protect you even if you're not willing to do it yourself." Reluctantly, he took a step backward and pulled his arms from around her body. "If you won't leave, promise me you'll stay here and not try anything crazy?"

David waited. Finally when she nodded, he pivoted and forced himself not to look back as he moved carefully from the office and into the main waiting area. From there he eased from the room just as a man stepped into the hall. Dark blond, with shoulder-length hair, tall and strong enough to be a threat, the man turned, and for a brief moment, their gazes locked.

"Hey!" David cried out.

The man stared back for a brief moment. He pivoted away from David and hurried toward the back exit. Ten feet and he'd be at the door and outside.

Jaw tightening, David followed quickly after him, his gaze centered on the knob and the deadbolt. David locked both with his mind. The guy wasn't leaving here without giving him answers. Satisfied that David had him cornered, he slowed, his breath matching the rapid beat of his heart.

"You're not going anywhere," David called out.

At the door, the blond paused and turned, his gazed narrowed. "Watch me."

From the wall to his right, the metal enclosure holding a fire extinguisher snapped open and the red cylinder barreled toward David. Metal slammed into his gut. Air whooshed from his lungs and a black fog edged along his vision as he went down, slamming his knees against the wood flooring as he battled for air. Pain scored down his shins, up his thighs and into the rest of his body.

The extinguisher rolled to rest against the wall. Shock banded around David's throat. The guy was one of them. Had to be the way he'd yanked the cylinder from the wall and thrown it without using his hands.

Gasping, David scrambled to his feet. His stomach muscles contracted in pain. He glanced up. The door stood open. The sky stared back. Empty. Shit. He couldn't let the guy escape. They needed answers, and this man was the only person right now who could give them any.

David rushed onto the landing and outside into the brittle grass. Still no sign of his assailant. He raced around to the side of the yard, the weeds slapping across his ankles, and saw a flash of movement. There. A man. Leaping over the chain link fence to the street beyond.

IDENTITY

A woman's cry ripped through the air behind him. Shock pounded against David's chest. Oh, God. Skye.

CHAPTER 21

DAVID'S ASSAILANT BOUNDED across the street to a white car parked further up the shoulder from what had to be Skye's rental as David swiveled back around toward Skye. Twenty yards behind him, arms outstretched, she crumbled to the grassy yard.

Throat tight with panic, David rushed back across the yard and dropped to the ground on his hands and knees beside her. "Are you alright?"

She pushed off the ground, sat up and flung back her chestnut hair dotted with dirt and grass. With a tentative hand, she touched the abrasion to her chin and winced. "Yeah. I tripped over a stupid tree root or something." Rising, she brushed impatiently at her jean-clad legs. "Forget me. Where did he go?"

He glanced over his shoulder and along the length of the street and intersection. No sign of the white car or the man. David frowned as he scrambled to his feet. There was something about that car. It looked too familiar. "He took off in a car. I swear it's the same one I saw back in Vegas. White and easily forgettable, except it nearly ran me down in a parking lot in Nevada."

"What are you talking about?" She frowned up at him. "The same car? Has someone been following us?"

"I think so. I've never gotten a chance to see the driver."

"Why didn't you tell me?"

"I forgot."

"How could you forget something like that?"

At the antagonism in her tone, he stiffened and struggled to rein in his temper. "Well, let's see. You show up in my life, threaten to ruin my show if I don't let you stay at my house. Then there's—"

"You're right." Her gaze darkened, and she pulled a wayward, chestnut strand behind one ear. "I'm sorry."

He brushed the sweat from his brow with the back of his hand, wanting to wipe the look of guilt from her face. "Don't. You've got nothing to apologize for." David wondered if he'd always act an idiot when it came to Skye. "Tyler. You haven't found—"

"No."

One word, simple but dripping with anguish. She looked down at her running shoes, but not quick enough to hide the sudden sheen of tears in her eyes.

Jesus. He couldn't swallow down the constriction around his throat. He fisted his hands to stop himself from touching her, holding her. In Las Vegas, he'd let her walk away. If he hadn't shown up today—

"What are you doing here?" she asked, glancing from her shoes to the street beyond, her voice thick with hostility. "You should be in Vegas with your dogs and your magic show."

"I've got a neighbor watching the dogs, and my show... I had my publicist take care of everything with the hotel and let them know that I had to back out indefinitely. I guess the Pharaoh decided to temporarily replace me with an acrobatic show."

David stared at her stubborn profile and firm, taut jaw. He deserved her antagonism. Hell, he deserved more than that. He cleared his throat, growing awkward and unsure.

She turned then to face him, her face dramatically softening. "It's not your dad. He's not—"

"No. He's still in a coma. Nothing's changed."

"Then why?"

"I couldn't keep on doing what I've always done. Look the

other way. Pretend I wasn't involved." Shame burned into his face. For far too many years, he'd been a complete ass. He searched in his pockets for his antacid tablets and came up empty. Hell. It was just as well. They really didn't do a damn thing. "I knew it was a long shot, but this is the only place I could think you might show up. Then I get to this property, find you here with a possible kidnapper or murderer in the building—"

"I would have been fine."

"How do you know that?" The skin across his cheeks and jaw tightened with anger and frustration. "You could have been hurt, possibly killed. Do you have any idea how much that would have made me..."

"What?" She hoisted her chin skyward. "And why would you care. You made it pretty obvious how you felt."

"Of course I care!" With two steps, he devoured the distance between them, clutched her upper arms and jerked her up against his chest. He wanted to shake some sense into her, he wanted—

Hell, he wanted to kiss her.

David captured her mouth, wrapping an arm around her waist to drag her more fully against his body. Stiffening, Skye dug her fingers into his biceps, then after a brief moment, softened. Those same fingers slid up along his arms and shoulders to dance across his nape and the stubble of his hair. She moaned against his lips and kissed him back with equal fervor.

Memories of her body, hot, hungry and arching beneath him stormed his mind. God, he'd missed her determination, her self-confidence, even her pig-headedness. How could one woman twist his insides, leave him breathless and wanting more?

David's hand lingered over the smooth silk of her upper arm as he drew away from her mouth with a shaky, reluctant sigh. He looked down to find an unmistakable flush to her face that David liked to believe wasn't from the heat. With dark and turbulent eyes, she stepped away and glanced over to the house.

"I can't seem to keep my hands off you," he muttered with a mixture of dismay and frustration. He followed her gaze to the house. Beyond the brick, unanswered questions and shadowy memories remained. "Let's get out of here. There's nothing here for us but an empty building. I have a taxi waiting down the street."

Lips firming into a grim line, she nodded and straightened her shoulders. "You're right. But let's take my rental. That way, we won't have to worry about being overheard."

After he paid off his driver, David followed Skye down the block to her vehicle and folded himself inside the passenger side of Skye's rental. He leaned his head against the backrest and started to wonder if he'd ever return to his old life. It exhausted him to think of the multitude of lies he'd fed his friends and fans and to realize his childhood was equally strife with layer upon layer of fabrications.

But he'd have to worry about that later. Now he needed to concentrate on Skye and her son. "Have you learned anything while in Boston?"

Skye slid behind the wheel and slammed the door closed. A quick glance his way revealed a gaze filled with sudden anger and determination. "I have a name. Ferguson."

"Have you located him yet?"

She turned on the rental car. A blast of hot air rushed from the vents until the air conditioner kicked in. "I've tried the white pages and went through every Ferguson. At this point, no address and I've found out very little about him."

"There's Miltronics. It's possible he might have worked there."

"He did years ago. He's not on any of the rosters now. Trying to talk to someone at the company about him has been fruitless. It's worse than hitting a brick wall." She pulled onto the street, her hands fastened tightly around the wheel. "But right now, I need to follow up on visiting someone I haven't seen since I left Boston."

"And that is?" Frowning, he glanced over at the delicate curve of her cheek, the straight line of her nose, the smooth, sheen of her chestnut hair. All soft and feminine except for her hard, inflexible jaw.

"I—" A muscle ticked along the ridge of that jaw. "You'll find out soon enough."

Because of her obvious discomfort, David decided not to pursue the topic. Plus, he found out quickly enough. Less than an hour later, she pulled into the parking lot of a two-story building. The moment they stepped through the entrance to the bottom floor, the astringent scents of a dental office battered his senses.

"I don't get it," he muttered as they walked down an empty hallway.

"The building mainly consists of dentist's and doctor's offices. I'm here to see Dr. Schrimager. She's a psychiatrist I was seeing for several months." She sent him a sideways glanced and laughed wryly. "I haven't gone over the bend. Not yet."

"I didn't say a thing."

"You didn't have to." Her voice echoed in the stairwell as she led them up a flight of stairs.

"Okay." He caught her elbow when they stepped into the hallway on the second floor. When she drew to a stop, he dropped his hand to his side. "I need to understand. What has this to do with your son or anything else?"

"My past. That creature showing up in my head whenever I try to delve into my childhood is too bizarre to be normal. I need to find out more, and the only way I can think to do that is through hypnosis. Years before I was forced to be evaluated by the doctor, but now I *need* to see her."

"You're talking about being forced because of your divorce, right?"

~~*~~

Skye met David's fierce expression and folded her arms tightly across her middle. The divorce still filled her with a kaleidoscope of insecurities, and she detested how it left her feeling vulnerable and fragile. So many times she'd told herself she wasn't a failure, but even so, the breakup of her marriage always left her wondering.

She pressed her back against the wall, glanced down both sides of the dark green carpeted hallway. To her right, a door opened, and a boy and woman stepped from one of the offices and walked toward them. Skye nodded at both and silently watched them turn and disappear down the stairwell. When their steps faded and no one else appeared in the hall, she turned back to David and said in a hushed voice. "My divorce was nasty. Jay wanted sole custody, and no amount of pleading or pressure would change his mind. After the kidnapping attempt on Tyler, he told everyone lies that I'd grown paranoid, a danger to my own child. I was forced to have a psychological evaluation because of him. The doctor was also a hypnotist. Through her, I stumbled on sections of my childhood that I had no clue existed, and I continued to see her after the divorce became final."

David shook his head, sympathy softening his brown eyes. "How did you get custody of Tyler? Did your ex change his mind?"

She smiled but couldn't keep the bitterness from her voice. "More like I changed it for him. You see, during the custody battle between us, I found out what I'd suspected for almost an entire year. Jay was skimming off the drug busts and selling on the side. His mistake was that he started using. It made him sloppy." She cupped her throat with one hand and continued to press her other one against her stomach. "I turned him into internal affairs. He lost his job and his friends because of me."

"But it got you Tyler."

A hot tear escaped from her eye. "Until I lost him."

David closed the distance between them, leaned down and kissed the tear that had stilled on her cheek. "We'll find him. Faith. Hold onto it."

"I'm trying. You have no idea, but I wonder..." She inhaled sharply as anguish pounded inside her chest. "You see, this Ferguson—or whoever—wants Tyler really bad. So bad that they paid my ex to fight for custody. Jay planned on selling Tyler to them if he won."

"Jesus, Skye!" He pulled her hand from around her throat and pressed it against his chest, twining his fingers between hers. "He's mad. I can't imagine. I'm sorry."

She closed her eyes as he kissed her brow and continued to

cup her hand with his. David's sympathy and warmth threatened to pull her deeper into a maelstrom of pain. Her fingers tightened around his.

David's undeniable support made Skye realized she didn't have to be completely self-sufficient and suspicious of everyone's motives. She might just be able to trust David, even lean on him if she allowed herself that opportunity. As she stood inches from his tall, athletic frame and stared at the strong column of his throat, she found the idea shocking and a bit frightening. When was the last time she'd counted on someone other than herself?

She didn't know of one.

Taking in a shaking sigh, she met David's gaze and quickly tugged her hand from his and slid along the side of the wall and away from him. She found his gaze both reassuring and disconcerting. She didn't want to admire him or his desire to do the right thing, because then she didn't have to fight her feelings toward him.

"Yes, well..." Skye cleared her throat, forcing her thoughts toward a different topic. "I called earlier to make an appointment but couldn't get hold of anyone, so I thought I'd come by in person. I need to find out if she'll see me today. I'm desperate. I know the key to all this is locked inside my head. When I uncover the past, I'll find Tyler. I just know it."

She pivoted and walked down the hall toward Dr. Schrimager's office and heard David's heavier tread on the carpet following her. When she stopped in front of the doctor's office, Skye frowned. Beside the door, darkness hugged the other side of the smoky, glass paneled window.

"It's not lunch time," David murmured from beside her as he jiggled the knob on the locked door.

"I don't know why she's not here." Skye peered into the window, which didn't make a bit of difference when it came to seeing inside the waiting room. And of course, the tears she blinked back weren't helping her see clearly either. "That's really odd. From what I know of her, she's never been one to miss work."

"A day off?" David tried the door one last time. "It says nine to five, and it's two now."

"No. She works pretty much like everyone else in the building. Monday through Friday."

"Here. I'll ask a neighboring office."

She followed David across the hall and one door down to a dentist's office. An elderly man and middle-aged woman waited in green, metal framed chairs lining one wall. A television in the corner murmured about the historical wonders of Egypt.

From beyond a large rectangular cutout in the wall, a receptionist glanced up from behind a beige speckled counter. The woman, half-glasses precariously balanced on the end of her nose, rolled her chair away from the computer screen and nodded to the clipboard. "Please sign in."

"We don't have an appointment," David said, his hand on the small of Skye's back.

With a smile, the receptionist waited expectantly, her frosted hair gleaming beneath the fluorescent light.

Skye stepped up to the counter. "Do you know why Dr. Schrimager's office is closed? I tried calling yesterday and just got her answering machine. There's usually a receptionist that takes her calls. And today doesn't look any different. The place is closed up."

Something flickered behind the woman's eyes and her smile faltered. "I'm sorry, but were you a patient?"

"Yes."

The woman glanced beyond Skye's shoulder to the other occupants and lowered her voice. "She passed away."

Skye stiffened with shock. "When?"

"Three weeks now."

Sorrow clogged Skye's throat. "I had no idea she was ill. Did she... Was it an accident?"

The receptionist's polite expression tightened, and she shut her mouth into a grim line. After a brief moment, she opened her mouth, then closed it again as if struggling with an appropriate answer.

From behind the receptionist, another woman in her early

twenties with large, blue eyes and a pierced nose, stepped away from the copier and walked up to the counter. She crouched down beside the receptionist and insisted in a harsh whisper, "Tell her."

"Marie, that's enough. We'll get in trouble."

The younger woman shook her head. She stared back at Skye with avid eyes, leaned across the counter and said in a hushed whisper, "They're saying she was murdered."

CHAPTER 22

Dr. Schrimager up and disappeared. Just like that." Face growing as animated as the younger woman, the receptionist must have changed her mind when it came to keeping silent. She snapped her fingers and said in a loud whisper, "Her car is gone, her purse. But everything in her house is the same. I've heard people say she ran off with some guy, but her staff didn't see her with anyone.

"From what I understand the doctor's anal when it comes to schedules and day to day things. So what other conclusion can you reach?" The receptionist inched even closer and lowered her voice. "She's got to have been murdered."

Murdered.

Skye backed away from the counter and the woman's words, nausea swirling in her belly. "You must be mistaken."

Beside the receptionist, the girl with the pierced nose shook her head. "Oh, no. The police were here even asking questions."

Skye didn't want to believe them, but the earnest look stamped across both women's faces was undeniable. She blinked back the sting of tears as David cupped the small of her back.

"There's another psychiatrist on the first floor." The receptionist nodded toward the office's entrance. "He's taking a lot of her old patients."

"No thanks," David answered for Skye. His arm swept around her waist and somehow kept her from collapsing to the floor. "I think we'll pass."

David led her quickly from the office. Once in the hall, Skye sank back against the wall a few feet away from the dentist's entrance, battling another wave of nausea that bubbled up her throat.

"We need to get you out of here," David insisted in a voice thick with concern as he swept a tendril of hair from her brow. The warmth of his hand penetrated her clammy skin.

"Not yet." She pressed her arms against her stomach and grappled for calm. Other than her ex-husband, Dr. Schrimager was the only other person who knew about the attempted kidnappings on Tyler. The woman had delved into Skye's past—a past somehow entwined with the present. She knew the woman would be alive now if Skye had avoided the doctor after the initial custody evaluation. "I killed her."

"Skye, don't even think that way." David's voice sharpened. "You're jumping to conclusions. They haven't found a body. There could be any number of other reasons why she hasn't shown up, so don't start blaming yourself."

"Don't worry." She grabbed David's upper arm and didn't know whether to push him away or bury herself in his arms. The sympathy and kindness in his brown eyes threatened to crush the last of her control she so desperately desired. "I'm not going to add more guilt to what I already have."

"You don't know if her disappearance had anything to do with you. If for some reason the woman does turn up murdered, it could be a completely random act," David insisted as he searched her face with dark, solemn eyes.

"It's too much of a coincidence, David. You know it. I know it." Her grip tightened on his arm. "They must be frightened of what I might have told her. I know she recorded our conversations."

"Say that you're right—what could you possibly have told her that was worth killing for? And how could that be tied to Tyler?"

"I don't know!" She released David's arm and ground the

heel of her hand into her temple as tears of frustration spilled over her lashes. Helplessness gnawed through her insides.

Tyler.

Skye's control splintered even more. Her child was out there with some sick pig. Just to feel his small arms around her neck, the soft, supple touch of his cheek against hers, to see those big, brown eyes sparkle with mischief.

God, without her son, she felt like a husk, empty, brittle, lifeless.

A woman stepped from the dentist's office. The door snapped closed after her as she passed the two of them. Skye wiped at the tears tracking down her cheeks, hating how she was falling apart in full view of David and complete strangers.

Abruptly, she pushed off the wall. "I need to use the restroom."

She fled the hall and David and turned left into a small alcove. The pain squeezing around her chest threatened to cut off her breath as she scrubbed her damp cheeks with the back of one hand. The door to the woman's bathroom stood open, and Skye stepped around a yellow plastic triangle propped up in the middle of the entrance warning of a wet floor.

Overhead lights glared off the wall of mirrors, which revealed white walls and two empty stalls in dull, ugly gray. After Skye quickly used one of the toilets, she stepped up beside an elderly woman with silver hair and faded skin brushing her teeth.

As Skye washed her hands, the scent of the woman's toothpaste assailed her senses. Peppermint.

The smell drove a wave of anxiety through her body. Peppermint. That smell. She hated it, couldn't rid herself of the odor as it clung to her nose. She forced the air in and out of her lungs, struggling to appear normal as the woman slipped the toothpaste in her purse and stepped from the room. Once the woman's footsteps faded to silence, Skye grabbed onto the black and white speckled counter as her vision fogged around the edges. The cloying scent stung her lungs.

The image of the lizard snapped into her thoughts. Oh, God. Not that. She clutched the counter tighter, floundering under vicious, yellow eyes. Incisors. Huge. White. Razor-sharp. Mentally, she lurched past the image into memories she thought deeply secreted inside her head.

A picture flared in her mind's eye. Her hands gripped the arms of a chair from her past. Metal clamps kept her wrists tied to the leather. A person stood to her right and along her peripheral vision.

She didn't dare look. She couldn't. Because if she did... No. Their presence filled her with terror. But it didn't matter. She couldn't stop the person's silhouette from edging closer. A man in a white lab coat stepped from the shadows. His face appeared as he leaned over with a needle in one hand. His teeth flashed, and his breath washed over her.

Peppermint.

Brown hair mixed with gray. His face, elongated nose and sharp, brown eyes sent shivers of dread crawling across her spine. He was from her childhood nightmares. The man in shadows.

Then the needle slipped into her skin as she lay tied to the chair. A hospital gown covered her body, but her legs lay naked, exposed and in stirrups. A diamond glittered beneath the light from her finger. An engagement ring hugged her wedding band.

She didn't understand. It didn't make sense. She wasn't a child but a woman, married to Jay.

Skye's breath hitched against her throat as she twisted her arms, vainly jerking her wrists against the metal clamps. Whimpering, she turned her head to the side as her childhood nightmare placed the syringe on a metal table beside her and picked up what looked like a turkey baster.

Oh, God, what did it mean? The stirrups. The man. Oh, God. No.

Vision darkening, Skye dropped to her knees. Then nothing.

~~*~~

Two hours later, after disabling the house's main alarm system and phone and retrieving Ferguson's cell phone, Peter hadn't yet found the little fuck, but he wasn't giving up, only taking a break to get some answers from Ferguson. The kid was somewhere on the property or inside the house, holed up and silent. If the boy had pissed his pants in fear, Peter hadn't been able to smell the stench in any of the rooms.

With the electricity back on and the air conditioning humming, Peter now stood over Ferguson. When he'd discovered the bastard passed out on the top of the stairs to the kitchen earlier, Peter had dragged him into the two-way mirrored room and tied him in the dentist-like chair. Just as Peter taped the bastard's mouth shut with the roll of silver duct tape he'd used on the kid, Ferguson came to.

Blinking, the other man turned his head against the backrest and looked around. Then realization and panic flared in the other man's eyes as he twisted beneath the metal bands clamped around his wrists and ankles. The tape muffled the words spewing from Ferguson's mouth. The old man probably never thought he'd end up being the experiment, but life was ironic. Always had been.

As much as Peter would love to keep Ferguson's mouth shut, he knew he wouldn't get any intelligible answers. With a sigh of resignation, Peter dug a finger beneath a corner of the duct tape and ripped it off.

A cry sprang past the man's lips. Peter suspected he'd hear more of the same in the next half hour.

"Okay, Ferguson, now that you're back in the living, you can tell me what's with the boy and why he's so different. No bullshit this time. I want the truth." Peter smiled down at his victim. "But before you get into a long-winded discussion, I want the cash."

"I'm not crazy," Ferguson said through gritted teeth, his gaze wary. "The minute I tell you, you'll kill me."

"I don't think you understand." Peter forced his lips into a smile. The prick wasn't cooperating, but Peter had been known to be very persuasive when it came to changing a person's mind. "If you don't tell me, you'll be begging me to kill you at the end."

Below the metal cuffs, Ferguson's fingers gripped the armrests until the skin around his knuckles thinned to fragile parchment. At his stubborn silence, Peter's patience, already worn by mishandling the kid, frayed further.

This bastard wasn't going to get in the way of Peter's ultimate goal of getting revenge against Skye. But he also deserved the cash. Peter hadn't grabbed the kid and brought him here for free. Yeah, maybe he'd first just wanted to steal him from under Skye's nose, but now Peter wanted it all. The cash, the perfect payback. He deserved both with how she'd ruined his life.

Absolutely no one was going to screw with Peter's plans.

Without warning, he grabbed Ferguson's middle finger and yanked it back. Bone snapped. Gasping, Ferguson arched over the chair, wrenching his arms and legs against the constraints. The metal held, locking him into the chair. With the entire length of his body quivering in reaction, Ferguson slumped against the leather cushions.

"Oh, sorry, I seem to have broken something." Casually Peter leaned a hip against the side of the chair and peered down into the other man's face. Sweat soaked the collar of his once pristine, crisp, dry-cleaned shirt. He didn't look so immaculate. In fact, he looked a little wilted.

Peter lifted a brow. "You know, putting up a brave front isn't going to help you."

Peter had only so much patience. He needed to find the kid. That or set a trap to get him out in the open. But he couldn't do either until he'd taken care of the old man.

This time Peter grabbed a thumb, ignored Ferguson's quick, indrawn breath, and with one savage twist, dislocated the joint.

"Jesus!" Tears gleamed in Ferguson's eyes and spilled down the sides of his face. "Are you crazy!"

"Possibly. I've been told on occasion that I am." Peter mused aloud. "Now have we decided to tell me the location of the money you owe me? It's all up to you whether or not you want me to go through each finger. I can also move on to your toes."

He met Ferguson's gaze and waited. After a brief silence, he reached over for another finger.

"Okay, okay! I'll tell you." Ferguson's breath rattled inside his chest. "It's in my closet. In the bedroom. A paper bag on one of the shelves."

Peter caressed the other man's forearm with an index finger, slipped lower over the thick metal cuff and tapped the back of Ferguson's hand. "Are you sure?"

"Yes. Yes. Just stop! Stop!"

"If you insist," Peter murmured, believing Ferguson as he inched away from the chair.

Ferguson expelled a large breath of air in relief.

At the scent of peppermint and stale breath, Peter wrinkled his nose. The prick was far too weak-willed to be lying. Two more minutes with him and Peter knew Ferguson would be selling his soul, his mother and anyone else he could screw. He'd met his kind before too many times not to recognize the ink.

He patted Ferguson's broken and twisted fingers. "I'll be right back. Don't go anywhere."

Peter suspected his humor was lost on the other man, but he didn't much care. Fifty-thousand sounded pretty good about now. But he wasn't a fool. He needed to make sure the money was there before he finished up with Ferguson

Peter left the two-way mirrored room, then trotted up the stairs to the main section of the house. After easing the metal door open, Peter crept through the kitchen and around the pots and pans that littered the black tile floor on silent feet, his gaze alert to any movement. Earlier, he'd pulled open the cabinet doors in search of the boy. Every one of them gaped back almost as if mocking him at his inability to find the skinny runt.

Hell, Peter'd find him. He just had to think like the kid. And while he did that, the little shit could sweat it out.

After he found the bag in the closet, checked the amount of cash inside, and stuffed the bundle under an arm, Peter swept a hand through the clothing across the two L-shaped tiers and double-checked for a small body squeezed against the wall. Nothing but an empty shelf.

Still confident Tyler was shaking, scared and crammed in some impossibly tight corner hiding, Peter returned to the basement. Ferguson, of course, hadn't moved, but the sweat stains around his neck had widened and new ones had crept beneath his arms.

Peter peered down at Ferguson's damp face, the color of

day-old dough. "You not only promised the cash but information on the boy."

"There's nothing to tell about the boy."

"Really?" He grabbed another of Ferguson's fingers, yanked, and ignored the man's brief, sharp scream. "I'm thinking differently. This kid is beyond normal. He looks and acts human, but he short-circuits electrical wires and manipulates computers with his mind. Hell, I've never seen that done by anyone."

"He's nothing," Ferguson said between a deep wheezing breath. "Just an experiment."

With narrowed eyes, Peter searched Ferguson's sweat-coated features, then met the other man's eyes and stared. For several silent seconds, Peter stilled.

Those eyes.

Realization slammed into Peter with the strength of a punch to the chest. Peter now understood what he'd failed to notice for months. Ferguson's eyes, the same shape, the same shade... He sucked in a mouthful of air, then expelled the breath in one long rush. After a moment, he recovered his voice. "You're one crazy fuck, you know that? I thought I was bad, but I'd never experiment on my own kid."

CHAPTER 23

ON THE SECOND floor of the dental and medical building, David paced across the dark green carpet, eyeing the doorway to the women's restroom where Skye had disappeared into several minutes before. Pausing, he frowned and glanced along the drab, beige walls for a clock, but didn't find anything. The silence in the empty hallway thickened with David's growing concern.

Skye was taking too long. An elderly woman had exited a good five minutes before, but he hadn't seen anyone else slip in or out since.

He hadn't liked Skye running off like that. Not when she'd been so upset. Not with a kidnapper out there with Tyler. Not when her doctor might have been murdered. Hell, someone might be intending to kill Skye next.

To hell with it. David didn't care about embarrassing himself or Skye. Jaw clenched, he strode toward the entrance, sidestepped the wet floor sign and stepped into the bathroom.

Skye lay sprawled across the floor on her back with her hands flung out on either side of her head and her hair a dark chestnut stain on the white tile.

He sucked in a mouthful of air. "Skye!"

She didn't move, didn't open her eyes.

He dropped to his knees. With a shaking hand, he brushed

her hair from her neck. The silken strands clung to his fingers. Panic sent talons of tension into the muscles of his back and shoulders and threatened to shatter his thoughts and leave him floundering on what to do.

Damn it. He didn't understand. She'd been fine minutes before. Upset but still okay.

Had she fainted? Had someone attacked her?

David glanced to the right and the two visible stalls. All empty. He didn't see a window where someone could escape, and no one had stepped from this room other than the elderly woman.

When her breath whispered across his wrist, and he saw the low rise and fall of her chest, tension across his muscles eased only fractionally, but he couldn't shake off the alarm still burrowing into his body.

"Skye? Please wake up. You've got to wake up." He crouched over her, his fingers now brushing the hair from her temple. His thumb glided over the dusting of freckles across the curve of one cheek. The overhead lights magnified her pallor and revealed skin free of bruising or scrapes. With shaking fingers, he probed through the thick waves of her hair and across the back of her skull.

She was so fragile, her wrists and neck easily crushed in the wrong hands, but at the same time, he'd never met a woman more fierce than Skye when it came to her son and her beliefs. A complete contradiction, but damn it, she was his contradiction.

He found nothing. No head injury. No broken skin or blood. But that hardly made him relax.

Seeing the tear tracks from the corner of her closed eyes twisted at his insides. What the hell had happened to cause them? The death of the doctor or something more?

"Come on, Skye," he coaxed, his voice thick and unsteady. "Talk to me."

Her lips parted to reveal the even line of her teeth. Movement flickered briefly beneath her eyelids, and a jean-clad leg shifted on the cool tile.

"That's it." He inched closer on his knees, cupping her

shoulder with his other hand as he continued to glide his thumb across her cheek. "Wake up for me, Skye."

He was never going to let her out of his sight again. He'd come to Boston to help her, and he hadn't done a damn thing right to protect her yet.

Skye opened her eyes and stared directly up at him. Confusion drew a fine line between her brows and marred the perfect matte of her skin. "What happened?" Bewilderment seeped from her face. "Oh, God."

Her expression of horror hit him in the chest. "What's wrong? Did someone do this?"

He cupped her elbow, but as she scrambled to her knees, she hit her head against the sinks' counter. Wincing, she grabbed her skull and pushed away his attempt to help her to her feet. "Don't. I..."

She caught the counter with a clumsy hand, pulled herself up and hung over the sink as if she were going to heave her guts out. The lights amplified the sheen of sweat across her brow, cheeks and upper lip. He stood up beside her and waited, curling his hands into fists to keep from touching her as he watched her struggle from some invisible place inside her head.

"I passed out," Skye finally said as she splashed water on her face, then stared at the mirror, her features a pale reproduction of her former self. She clutched the counter's edge and leaned further across the sink toward her reflection. She seemed to be looking beyond the mirror to an unimaginable place.

A chill snaked down his spine. He didn't like her stillness. Beyond her blank expression, he sensed a charged emotion boiling near the surface, one that was going to rip from Skye's carefully controlled demeanor. "Here. We need to get you out of here."

This time when he cupped her elbow and drew her away from the sink and counter, she didn't push him away as he curled an arm around her waist. David's lips firmed. Skye might be able to disguise her feelings behind an empty mask, but she couldn't hide the tremors racing through her limbs as she sank against his side.

He half carried, half led her out of the building and into the passenger side of the vehicle without doing damage to either one of them. Once inside the rental, she glanced across the console and for the briefest moments her façade fractured, and he glimpsed into her soul.

Anguish.

Stark. Painful. Undeniable.

~~*~~

Skye sat in the passenger seat and plucked at the seat belt strap between her breasts. Elongated shadows clung to the ground from passing cars and buildings. Street lamps fled by, their light a beacon for the coming night, while darkness hovered, smothering the last of the sun's rays clinging to the horizon.

When David guided the car onto the freeway entrance and melded into traffic, Skye frowned. "Where are we going?"

"I'm going to check us into a hotel room."

"I don't have time for sleep."

"Jesus, Skye. You need to rest. You've just had another blow with the possibility of your doctor being murdered. With a couple hours of sleep, you'll be able to focus and regroup."

Skye opened her mouth but snapped it shut and slumped against her seat. She couldn't find the words to argue. Shock still left her feeling numb and shivering as if her mind had been scraped raw. She wanted to be oblivious. She wanted to pretend she didn't remember the office, the doctor, the horror, but images from the past were as vivid and bright as daylight as they slipped back inside her head. Her legs splayed, a man's dry cold hand touching her. His rabid, knowing smile as he held what looked like a meat baster in one hand and eased it between her legs.

Squeezing her thighs together, she folded her arms against her stomach. She hadn't believed Jay. She'd thought her ex completely crazy, spewing lies about Tyler not being his son. Jay hadn't been lying. Not this time.

When though? When had it happened? And how could she not know she'd been impregnated by a crazy man? Skye frantically searched in the hollows of her mind for past opportunities. She dug her forearms against her stomach. Then a memory seeped from the past. A stranger knocking into her. Waking up in her car. A memory loss of eight hours.

Oh, God. She'd been so wrong thinking Jay as the kidnapper. She'd been wrong about everything. And Tyler's biological father? What if he was the kidnapper? And if that were the case, what in God's name did he want with her son? She wasn't naive to think love had anything to do with it.

But why? She knew if she understood the answer, she'd find Tyler. And that's all that mattered—finding her son. Because he was out there in the city somewhere. Another night approached with empty leads and no sign of Tyler.

Skye's throat constricted with panic, threatening to cut off the air to her lungs. She crossed her ankles in an attempt to stop the shaking, but she couldn't keep her heart from racing or her thoughts from churning. God, where was her strength, the composure she'd always prided herself on? She bit down hard on her lower lip.

David's knuckles whitened as he twisted a hand around the steering wheel again and again. He threw her a dark, solemn glance. "I'm sorry about the doctor's disappearance."

"This isn't about Dr. Schrimager," she whispered. The moisture building in her eyes blurred the freeway and rental's console. A shiver crawled across her skin. She felt dirty, used.

"Then what?" A car horn blasted moments before David hit the brakes. "Stop being so damn strong, Skye. Tell me what's going on. How can I help when you're holding back on me?"

She blinked away the tears. The slowing traffic in front of them came into focus. Thick, green oak trees passed them to the right along with the dark, velvety lawn of a neighborhood park. No desert brush or arid landscape in sight. Strange how much she'd missed the smells of exhaust, wet grass and dirt. But she'd gladly leave Boston forever if it meant having her son.

She glanced over at David's profile, all hard angles and stubborn lines. He caught her gaze and she quickly turned away from the intensity in his expression and stared at the black Volvo directly ahead. To keep her nausea at bay, she dug her arms against her stomach.

"When I confronted Jay about kidnapping Tyler, he told me Tyler wasn't his son. I didn't believe him. I actually thought he was crazy for even saying it. He was the only man I was sleeping with. For God's sake, I was married to him!" She pressed her arms harder against her middle. "I also thought he was just saying that to get back at me and using it as an excuse for his sick behavior of selling his son, but I remember flashes of being in a room."

Skye swallowed down the taste of bile. The images from her past weren't dreams or fears from her subconscious. She squeezed her eyes shut. They were far too real, too overwhelming to be false.

"Go on," David urged, his hand on the steering wheel stilled.

"Remember how we've talked about that lizard? The one that always shows up when we try to remember certain things from our past?"

"Yeah."

"Well, somehow I managed to get past that image. I think it was the scent of peppermint that triggered this memory." She opened her eyes and blinked away the tears as she plucked again at her seatbelt, searching for the right words and struggling to vocalize them aloud. "Dr. Schrimanger dug up points in my past when it came to my childhood. None of it had anything to do with being an adult until today. This memory though, this scene I remember is when I was married to Jay. The horrifying part is that I was in a doctor's office beside this man. The same man from my childhood. What made me remember him was his breath. The scent of peppermint."

David swore softly. "I've always hated the smell."

Skye frowned as she suddenly thought of Gordon. "Your father. I don't know exactly when, but I remember him smelling of peppermint. Does he chew gum?"

"No. Not that I know of." His voice grew guarded. "Why? What are you saying?"

"I don't know." She sighed in frustration. "He's not a doctor, not capable of doing what this man…"

Almost a full minute passed in silence until David asked softly, "What did this man do?"

"I—"

David exited the freeway and turned north. He pulled into the driveway of a hotel and parked in a slot by the main entrance. "If this is too painful for you, Skye, I'll understand if you don't—"

"No. I need to say this out loud to get everything out in the open. Otherwise, it'll just fester and get worse." Grabbing the seatbelt and tugging the suffocating strap from the side of her neck, she twisted at the waist until she met David's gaze. Darkness had since fallen, but the yellow artificial light from the parking lot lights and the hotel's logo illuminated his stark features. "This man—I believe he was a doctor, the same one from my childhood. I think he's also more than a gynecologist. I can't prove anything yet, but I'm pretty positive he impregnated me through artificial insemination."

"My God, Skye. I—I don't know how to respond to something like that." He dragged in a rattling breath. "So you're saying Jay was telling the truth. That he isn't Tyler's father? But then if he isn't—"

"Then I have no clue who the father is."

CHAPTER 24

ESUS." DAVID REACHED across the console between the front seats, and with a shaky hand, cupped her jaw and caressed a thumb over a tear that had slipped onto her cheek. "I'm so sorry, Skye. All you've been through and now this. I just don't understand how. Was the memory wiped out like our childhood ones?"

"Yes. But looking back, I know now when it happened. I had been at a mall parking lot. I'd just closed the door, I think. My memory's a bit fussy here, but I ran into someone by the car and almost fell. The man—I wouldn't remember what he looked like now if my life depended on it—helped me up and that's all I remember until I woke up in my car eight hours later. I saw a doctor that same week, thinking something was wrong with me, but the tests they took turned up normal."

David kissed her, a tender whisper of lips against her brow. "All this time you thought your ex was the father—"

"But it doesn't change a thing." She pressed her face against his palm, weakening beneath his compassionate look and touch. Longing mushroomed with the urge to share her fears, her uncertainties with this man. "Tyler is still my son. Always will be. I'm going to find him, and I don't care how I do it."

He slipped his hand from her cheek only to capture her own

and twine his fingers between hers. He lifted their bound fist and kissed the back of her hand. The softness in his face shifted and hardened. Outrage simmered in the depths of David's eyes. "I'll kill the bastard who did this to you."

Before her resolve to stay strong completely shattered, she hurriedly tugged her hand from his grasp, unsnapped her seatbelt and slipped from the car.

In the lobby, when he asked for one room Skye glanced sharply at him. He explained when they stepped from the lobby with two card keys. "I want you near me. I can't be of any help if something happens and you're somewhere else."

"And here I thought it was my stellar personality," Skye joked, using humor to mask the sudden awkwardness engulfing her at the idea of sharing a room.

"I have no complaints," David responded in a dark, smoky voice. "Far from it. I wish to hell we'd have met years before, during a different time."

His unexpected honesty sent warmth rushing into her cheeks. Awareness danced across her senses as he led the way up a flight of stairs to the second floor and down the hallway to the right. The lift of his strong jaw, the sure, smooth stride of his walk, the erect line of his carriage spoke of a natural confidence Skye always wanted but never attained.

The memory of the last time they'd been together in his bedroom stormed into her thoughts. David had been fierce, tender, hungry. He'd made her feel incredibly sexy, and—

Skye didn't dare go there. She needed her wits and uncompromising control over her emotions, and right now she was feeling far too raw. One look or touch from David and she was liable to turn into a needy, incoherent mess. She was still reeling at the idea of some strange, unidentified man being Tyler's father. The thought sickened her no matter how much she told herself it didn't matter.

Lies. For years now. All this time she'd thought Jay the father of her child, but no longer.

Why had this doctor picked her? Had he known of her powers, and had he conspired with Tyler's biological father? Or were they the same man? Either way, this had been a deep secret until now. Why the change?

"Why what?" David asked.

Skye stiffened. "I hadn't realized I was talking out loud."

David's gaze narrowed, but he let her comment pass as he unlocked and opened their door. After flipping on the switch, he led the way into a sterile, functional hotel room with royal blue drapes bracketing the sliding glass door and matching comforters covering two queen beds. The room smelled stale and neglected even with the air-conditioner's circulation.

"I'm going to get something for us to drink and eat. Why don't you get a bit of rest in the meantime? When I get back, we can come up with a plan."

Tension rippled across Skye's spine. The room yawned back at her, empty and intimidating. She'd be alone with her thoughts, with only the television and two empty, lifeless beds as company. She didn't want that time to think, to react, to—

"Don't," she protested in a panicked voice as she turned and clutched David's wrist.

"What's wrong?"

With her hand still latched to his arm, she looked up and met the sharp intelligence of his brown eyes. She couldn't handle being alone. Fear coated her mouth. She struggled for the right words, the ones that wouldn't reveal just how vulnerable she felt. "I—I don't... I want—"

Skye needed him to ease the pain, the fear and uncertainty bombarding her. With shaking fingers, she released his wrist and swept a hand past his elbow to grip his upper arm. She took one step toward him until she felt the heat of his body and the whisper of his chest against her breast.

"Say the words, Skye. I'm not going to touch you unless you say the words." A dark flush stained the prominent line of his cheeks, while his eyes darkened to mahogany. Between the two beds, the lamp on the coffee table flickered. "Your pain. I want nothing more than to ease your hurt, but I don't want you doing anything you'll hate the next day. I don't want regrets. Not when it comes to us."

"Dammit, David. You're not making this easy for me." She couldn't look away from the intense heat in his eyes. Then she realized exposing her weaknesses in front of David didn't much matter. Not at this point. He'd seen her at her worse far too many times, and right now with her life in shambles, pride seemed a wasted emotion.

"All right. When you—" She cleared her throat. "It hurt when I left and you stayed in Vegas. More than I like to admit. And to have you with me again scares me, because it makes me realize I need you. I've let you into my heart more than any other man in a long while. You can make me forget everything but the moment, and I need you to let me forget just for a little while again. Please make the memories go away"

"Shit, how the hell can I say no to you?" David slipped an arm around her waist and slowly, relentlessly urged her against him. From breast to knee, every hard, male and unyielding inch of him molded over her body. The intensity in his face, the tension radiating from his body sent her heart drumming erratically inside her chest and the breath hissing loudly between her teeth.

As a wave of desire scored through her limbs, she arched her hips even closer.

David lowered his head. His lips whispered across her mouth, hinting at unimaginable pleasure, seduction and fierce tenderness. Within his arms, Skye knew he would make her forget everything but the gentle stroke of his touch and she gladly succumbed to temptation. With a soft sigh of anticipation, she swept her hands up the corded muscles of his arms and across the taut slope of his shoulders to pause along the nape of his neck, sliding her fingers over his crew cut.

The lamp flickered again. From the hunger burgeoning throughout her body, Skye suspected she caused it this time. With David, she lost control, her pride and judgment and the ability to rationalize. Which was fine. She'd live with that and this moment without remorse as she dipped her fingers beneath the collar of his shirt to caress the warm, supple flesh of his neck. Then she cupped his jaw with both hands and opened her lips against his mouth to touch her tongue to his.

A groan rumbled in David's throat, and he caught her up tighter against his body, kissing her with an exquisite hunger that sent another wave of longing raging through her body. The way his hands shook in her hair, the rapid pounding of his heart and the quick intake of his breath thrilled her. To have this man undone with the simple touch of her mouth and hands excited Skye that much more.

With immense tenderness, David drew away from her lips and her body. A harsh hum swelled into the room, then a distinct click. She couldn't control the surge of telekinesis from her mind as the bedside light flashed and extinguished abruptly, casting the room into abrupt darkness. Slowly, moonlight filtered into the room and glowed through the sheers draped across the large sliding glass door.

David stared down at her. The light from outside softened the harsh line of his cheekbones and jaw but masked the expression beneath the shadow of his brows. Still, Skye sensed his tension, need and taut control. "You're beautiful," he whispered into the hushed silence. "Fierce, passionate—"

"Don't talk." Kicking off her shoes, she unbuttoned her blouse and shrugged out from the sleeves. She discarded the garment by her feet. "Don't say a word."

His quick intake of breath sent her heartbeat racing. His obvious excitement magnified the longing that pooled between her legs as she caught David's hand and placed his palm against her left breast. At his sudden stillness, Skye shivered. Then David swore under his breath and stroked a thumb over the material of her bra to caress her nipple. She arched into his hand and groaned, relishing the warmth of his fingers on her body.

"Take your clothes off," she whispered as she fumbled with the buttons of his shirt.

After quickly toeing out of his shoes, he shrugged out of his shirt and pulled off his pants and underwear. Skye watched with a mouth gone dry. Moonlight caressed the breadth of his chest, the corded strength of his arms, the taut muscles of his stomach and lower... At the thought of him inside her, her legs trembled and her insides twisted with anticipation. She latched onto his arms and edged toward him until his hard, silken length branded her belly.

With clumsy yet gentle hands, he helped her out of her jeans and underwear. The light shimmering through the sheers caressed David's body and turned muscle and sinew into silver. But there was nothing cool about his flesh. Heat radiated from his body and burned into her own as he compelled her backward over the carpet. Her thighs hit the edge of the mattress before she tumbled onto her back with David quickly following. His elbows bracketed both her arms as he devoured her mouth in a deep, hungry kiss. He took, demanded a response, and Skye answered him back with her lips, tongue and hands.

Skye shifted impatiently. Her hands turned urgent, even desperate as they trailed up and down his back. Then she dragged his head down. The warmth of his breath danced across her skin before his mouth brushed across her own, once, twice, tentative at first, then confident, even forceful with passion.

Her body warmed, turned liquid beneath David's touch, while the room around her dissipated and she drowned in wave after wave of sensation. She craved everything about him. His body, his mind, what made him distinct from any other man who had touched her life.

Love. A four letter word she thought she'd never feel for another man again, but with David, she couldn't help falling in love.

With a deep groan, David surged into her body, the hard, length of him filling, stretching, turning her limbs into molten heat as hunger, yearning and desire melded and pulled her deeper into an ocean of pulsing need. He kissed her jaw, shoulder and neck, his breath quickening, growing erratic as his mouth pressed against her temple. As she jerked her hips to meet him thrust for thrust, he swept an arm beneath her body and clutched her bottom as he ground into her after each powerful plunge of his hips.

She cried out. Ecstasy raced through every nerve of her body, shattered every thought of the past or the future. Just the moment, every glorious second bound her in pleasure.

David gasped, shivered, then stiffened, every rigid inch of him pulsing inside of her. He pulled her deeper into his arms and rolled to the side, taking her with him and easing his weight from her body.

"Jesus. I—" David brushed his lips over her brow, trailed a thumb over her lower lip, then kissed the spot his finger once touched. "I'm never going to let you walk out on me again. Here on out, you're mine."

Skye closed her eyes and smiled into the darkness. She should be appalled at his chauvinistic comment, but his possessiveness thrilled and melted her insides.

Sighing, she nestled deeper into his arms and let the room's hushed darkness and David's slow, sure breath and protective arms pull her into the oblivion of sleep.

~~*~~

Skye jerked awake. For a moment she lay on her back and stared at the ceiling. The light from the bathroom clung to the ceiling in faded yellow. She must have slept only briefly because a fine mist from the bathroom's shower swirled from the doorway.

For the briefest of seconds, she forgot and stretched beneath the cotton sheet, delighting in the soreness of her limbs and the heavy languor of her body, but unbidden memories cut into her thoughts and she bunched the sheets in one hand as she took in a shuddering breath.

Skye licked suddenly dry lips. Thirst and anxiety propelled her from the bed. She scrambled into her jeans and wrinkled blouse, then wedged her feet into a pair of running shoes, not bothering with the ties.

"I'll be right back," she called to David in the bathroom, before grabbing the ice bucket and hotel key off the desk, and stuffed the card into the back pocket of her jeans.

She slipped into an empty hallway, the door clicking closed from behind. Her step even though muffled against the thin, maroon carpet echoed against the long corridor. No one stepped from the elevator or any of the other rooms lining the hallway. After turning right, she walked toward the ice and vending machine room.

They'd find Ty. With the help of David, nothing or no one would stand in her way. She didn't have any other option, because if she didn't find her son alive, didn't hear his voice or feel his arms around her neck again, life—

No. She clamped her jaw into a rigid vice. Thinking that way would never give her what she wanted. She needed to be positive and strong. Tyler depended on her intelligence, stubbornness and resourcefulness.

Skye glanced down both sides of the hall to check for anyone suspicious. After finding the hallway empty, she stepped into the small room where the ice and vending machine butted up against the left wall. Sticking the bucket inside the pocket, she pressed it against the plastic pad and watched ice rattle into the container. She flinched at the loud, jarring noise.

As she released the button and pulled out the plastic container from inside the machine, movement flashed in her peripheral vision. Stiffening, she pivoted. The ice bucket in her hand swung wide, spraying ice against the machine, wall and floor.

The door leading into the hallway and her only escape route from inside slammed shut.

CHAPTER 25

FROM INSIDE THE windowless room, Skye stared at the closed door. Cautiously she set the ice bucket on a low-lying table against the wall, stepped forward and jiggled the knob. The door wouldn't open. For several long, drawn-out moments she listened.

Silence from the hallway.

Maybe the door had a self-closing hinge she hadn't realized. The knob itself didn't have an inside lock release, but it looked like management used a key to lock up the room. Great. She'd locked herself inside inadvertently. Unless...someone wanted her trapped inside, which didn't make a bit of sense. She didn't see a possible threat inside the small room.

Still...

Frowning, she withdrew her hand and centered all her power with her mind on the knob until she heard a soft click. Just as she started to turn the handle, the lock snapped back. She jerked away from the door and flipped the mechanism mentally back to open. Again the metal shifted and locked her inside.

Tension snapped up her spine. "Who's there?"

A heartbeat of silence. "Let's just say someone from your past."

Skye skidded backward, slipping on an ice cube. She caught

the wall with a hand and steadied herself. "What the hell is that supposed to mean?"

Tension bound her muscles like barbed wire as she edged closer and slipped her fingers around the doorknob, ready to use her powers if the person decided to shove his way into the room and attack her.

"I don't have much time." Even with the wood separating them, his voice came out smooth and calm.

Skye tensed, expecting the worse.

"This guy you're with. David. Don't trust him."

She blinked. Her breath hitched, and she shook her head. He was talking about David. Her David. That didn't make sense. David was the only person she *could* trust.

"His father is connected with a slimeball named Ferguson."

Her grip on the doorknob tightened. My, God. What was he talking about? "How do I know you're not lying? You could be the one that kidnapped my son." She pressed a cheek against the wood panel, unable to keep the desperation from her voice. "Are you? Do you have Tyler?"

Skye squeezed her eyes shut and waited into the silence.

"No."

"Then how do you know Ferguson?"

"I don't. Not personally, but I've been inside his house."

"Why?"

At the lengthening silence, she wondered if she'd pushed too far with even that simple question.

"I needed information on the October House. I thought he had a complete list of the children who lived at the home when that explosion at Miltronics hit in the early nineties."

"What's so important about the orphanage?" She jiggled the doorknob again, desperate for answers and the identity of the person in the hallway. "This is crazy talking like this. Unlock the door so I can see you."

What sounded like a laugh filtered into the small room. "I'm not crazy. I know what you're capable of."

"What do you mean?" she hedged, not liking how he knew everything about her and she had nothing on him.

"You know exactly what I mean." What sounded like amusement lightened the dark, smoky texture of the man's voice. "You're not the only one with powers. There are others out there like you, me, David."

With her cheek still pressed against the door, Skye closed her eyes, wanting to believe him but still terribly afraid to hope there were others. "And the lock?"

"A simple trick I learned before I was nine."

After opening her eyes, she stared hard at the wood barrier. So many mixed emotions, so many uncertainties. "Why are you here? Why come to me? And you never answered my question. What's so important about the orphanage?"

"I want to find my sister. Like me, she lived there for a time as a child until we were separated. I thought you might be her. So much so, I followed you to Vegas. Do you remember a blond-haired boy with freckles?"

Frowning, Skye searched her memories, but panic churned and threatened to take hold. She sensed the creature from her nightmares about to erupt into her conscious mind. "I can't remember much."

"None of us can. Ferguson intentionally implanted a false memory into our head to keep us from digging into our past. I swear the bastard got his idea from the movie Alien. I'm sure you've got some similar lizard-like monster running around inside your head."

"Yeah. How did you—"

"It doesn't matter." Impatience edged his voice. "What about the boy? The name would be Logan. Anything?"

"No."

"And what of a girl? Freckles also. Red hair. Do you have any memory? She would have been close to seven."

"No."

"Do you have any memories of a deck of cards? The jack of hearts?"

"I don't know what cards—"

"Just answer. Please."

"I'm sorry. No."

"Shit."

Skye stared at the door and splayed her right hand across the smooth wood. Even though she heard the rawness in his voice, she didn't dare soften. "If you thought I was your sister, why are you coming to me now and not before?"

"Hell. One, I don't trust you. Two, Gordon's son is glued to your side, which makes it damn difficult to get near you. Third, I felt I had to do something now because you're getting in way over your head." Frustration thickened his voice. "I tried earlier at the October House to talk to you, but he showed up before I had a chance. And remember the roulette wheel? And how the ball hit a different number than either one of you planned?" He didn't wait for her answer. "That was me feeling you both out to see what either one of you were capable of."

Skye frowned, distrust and unease pricking the back of her neck. "I don't know you, and you won't even show your face. Tell me why I should believe you and not David?"

"No real reason other than a healthy dose of caution. Plus, David's father and Ferguson were inseparable for a couple of years. Gordon saved Ferguson's life back when David's father was a cop. You'll find the story in the archives of the local paper if you look hard enough. Then soon after Gordon ends up with a son. All very strange. Actually, more than strange when you find out that Ferguson's ties are linked with the October House. What's a little adoption without papers between friends, right?" A sigh whispered along the edges of the door as if the man had brushed against the wood. "Seems to me Ferguson decided to return the favor after Gordon saved his life."

His voice faded as if he'd stepped away from the door and was about to leave.

"No! Don't go. Tell me about Ferguson! Where can I find him?" She grabbed the doorknob, rattled the metal between her fingers, then waited, desperate for an answer and fearing he'd already left.

"I can't tell you that. He's dangerous. He experimented on all of us from October House. At least the ones that didn't die from contaminated groundwater. He didn't care how much pain he inflicted, how much sorrow. It was all about finding out what made us tick."

"He has my son. Tyler. I have to find him. Please. He's just a child. He means everything to me."

Silence. Oh, God. He'd left without answering her. Closing her eyes, she slumped against the wall beside the door. She should have threatened him, cajoled, done anything to get him to tell her.

Now she had nothing but empty hope.

"He's over on Elm Street and 40th."

Awareness snapped open her eyes and hurdled across the bones of her spine. "And?"

"It's the second house from the corner. The gate's like many of the others, but there's a lion's head on the wrought iron entrance. Just watch your back. He might not appear dangerous, but he's got all the right people around him. As for David. Don't trust him. The tie between his father and Ferguson might get you killed, and I sure the hell don't want another death on my hands."

She dragged in a shuddering breath. "Thank you."

Her heart crashed against her ribs. Finally. A lead. One that would guide her to Tyler.

I'm almost there, sweetie.

Relief, giddiness, almost hysterical in intensity swept through her body. Then just as quickly ugly reality and doubt perforated Skye's thoughts.

The stranger on the other side of the door could easily be lying, leading her to a trap, a complete rouse to keep her away from Tyler. She needed to confront him face to face, read the truth in his eyes.

Skye stared at the lock and reined in her scattered thoughts. A pulse point later, the latch unlocked. With an unsteady hand, she wrenched open the door, ready to confront the person on the other side but already suspecting what she would find.

No one.

She stumbled outside. Both sides of the hall lay empty. A whisper of sound to the left propelled her down the corridor and toward the intersecting hallway.

She ran past several closed doors, then slammed a hand against the wall directly in front to stop herself from colliding against the drywall as she reached the next hallway. She looked on either side of her.

Empty save for a startled man in slippers and silver hair.

Dry, stale air rasped loudly in and out of her lungs as she rested both hands on her hips and grappled with getting her breath under control. Damn it. The stranger was more elusive than a shadow during a moonless night.

"You okay," the man asked, his gaze wary as he shuffled past.

"Yeah."

A lie. She wasn't okay, but she imagined if she told him the exact truth, he'd scurry away that much faster. She pulled her hair away from her face with cold, trembling hands and turned back to her room. After a quick, fumbling sweep of her key card, Skye stumbled into the hotel room.

"Where have you been? I was just about to go out after you. What the hell—" David paused from buttoning his low-slung jeans as he stood in the middle of the room. He must have stepped from the shower seconds before. The soft glow of the room's bedside lamp revealed the sheen of moisture clinging to his upper torso. He rushed over, caught her wrist and tugged her over to the bright glare of the bathroom light. With a deep, penetrating gaze, he searched her face. "What happened? Are you okay?"

Skye stared up into his concerned face. The man from the hall and his accusations about David's father sent doubts swirling. Could Ferguson and Gordon have some sinister past that David knew about? All this time, was David hiding it from her and deliberately sabotaging her pursuit of her son? Worse yet, could he, in fact, be somehow involved with Tyler's kidnapping?

Did she dare trust him? Could his every action and word be a carefully disguised act?

David's fingers twined with hers. "Skye, did you see someone or something?"

Skye searched the sincerity in his face and felt the tension and concern animating from his large body. Only moments before she'd been in his arms, surrendering her heart to the possibilities of something more than passion.

Then Skye realized she not only needed David, she needed to trust him. For too many years, she'd lost the ability to believe in herself and the people around her. Fear had kept her from reaching out for help, and she'd had a reason, but there came a time when she had to take that leap.

Skye decided to tell him everything she'd just learned. She just hoped to God she made the right decision. "I know where Ty is."

~~*~~

Pillowcase in one hand, Peter walked down the hall on the second floor of Ferguson's estate. So far, no car alarms, microwaves, radios or other electronic devices had acted up. At least he'd dismantled the house alarm. The kid was probably hiding out, huddled in some corner and exhausted. He'd escaped five hours ago, but Peter wasn't worried, not with the gate locked and an eight-foot block fence surrounding the perimeter.

But time was up. With no more distractions, Peter wanted to quickly capture and disarm the boy. He'd struggled with a way to do that without the kid sending the electrical wiring into a frenzy until Ferguson supplied the perfect solution. A solution that would crush Skye and have her feel the type of hell she'd put him through.

Hard to believe he'd lowered himself to chasing after a nine-year-old kid. But he could thank Skye for that. He'd once had the respect of his other co-workers in the police department. Respect not garnered by fear like he had now. He'd been damn good at what he did on the force. Hell, yeah he'd taken bribes, done some stuff on the side, but he hadn't been the only one. But Internal Affairs had thought differently, all because of Skye, the stinking bitch.

He ground his teeth together. The second Internal Investigations had started nosing in on him, he'd been treated like a leper from his co-workers, the same ones who were just as dirty as him.

Again, he could thank Skye for that. Hand tightening around the pillowcase, Peter slipped into one of the guest bedrooms and turned on a floor lamp by a recliner in the corner of the room. Pain throbbed along the side of one temple. He yanked open the closet door and swore silently. Other than a few boxes on the top shelf, empty.

Come on, you little shit.

"Hey, Tyler," he called, injecting warmth into his voice. He'd find the kid soon, because he didn't plan on playing this hide and seek game much longer. "It's safe to come out. Seriously. That old man made me bring you here. But now he's gone and you don't have to worry."

Peter moved out in the hall then into another bedroom, his step muffled against the thick carpet as he snapped on the switch by the door. Light flooded the room, revealing bedding and walls in muted shades of green and tan. "Seriously, kid. You're safe. I promise."

No answer other than the hum of the air conditioner. Peter's nostrils flared. The little shit was going to be difficult.

So far, Peter had gone through each room on the main floor a second time, checking cupboards beneath bathroom sinks and kitchen countertops. Finding nothing, he'd moved on to the second floor.

In the bedroom, he paused by a low slung window with a bench seat and peered outside. Night had since descended across the city. The light from a neighboring street lamp filtered through an old, elm tree. A breeze kicked up, slapping at the leaves. Branches scraped across the window, sounding strangely like Ferguson's last cry.

From beside the queen-sized bed, Peter dropped down on his knees, whipped back the bed skirt and peered along the floor. Only the scent of dust greeted him. Peter smothered a savage oath and rocked back on his heels. For a second, he'd thought—

A hollow, metallic sound carried into the room.

Stiffening, Peter thrust the bedding away and rose silently to his feet. Careful not to make noise, he edged around the bed and glanced to the doorway that led into an adjoining bathroom.

Agitated breathing. Unmistakable.

Peter smiled. On silent feet and still carrying the pillowcase in one hand, he moved closer to where the lamp threw light across the bathroom's beige marble floor. His athletic shoes whispered across the tile until he stopped in front of the bathroom vanity with its raised sink. He flung open both ornate cabinet doors.

The kid sprang through his legs.

"Fuck!"

Peter whirled, then lunged. He grabbed the kid's ankle as the bathroom light flashed on then off. Any second the alarm would go off, and he didn't have Ferguson to convince the security company they were dealing with a malfunctioning system.

Peter yanked the kid backward. He didn't care about inflicting any bruising, broken legs or superficial wounds. He just wanted Skye's son alive long enough for her to see him one last time.

The boy kicked out, twisted his ankle from Peter's grasp and started to scramble on hands and knees across the floor. An alarm clock went off in the bedroom.

"You little bastard."

Peter maybe had one more second and all hell would break loose when it came to the kid setting off the electrical wiring everywhere. He leaped and landed on Tyler. Ignoring the boy's grunt, he used a knee against his back for leverage and two fingers across the vulnerable section of his neck.

The boy slumped. The squirming stopped.

CHAPTER 26

BEYOND THE STREET lamp's artificial glow, Skye stood tensely beside David as the scent of leaves and grass clung to the night air. Light pooled over the driveway leading to Ferguson's house and a wrought iron gate with a lion's head soldered to the bars. A thick chain and padlock bound the two sides of the fence, effectively preventing anyone from coming in or out of the property.

They'd parked several blocks away, hopefully, inconspicuous enough to keep neighbors from growing suspicious. Even so, Skye didn't get a good feeling about the situation. She wasn't a fool. A trap waited beyond the fence.

"Wouldn't Tyler be able to unlock the chain from the gate and get out by using his powers?" David asked softly beside her.

"No," she answered just as quietly, mindful of the silence around them and how easily their voices carried through the night. "He can't move objects like us. He's able to manipulate electrical currents, but not with any great control yet. At least not like he does when it comes to accessing computer programs. Several years back, he managed to do that. Problem was he got caught. What's so strange is that the newspapers reported him as a brilliant kid but still nothing more than a hacker. If only they knew exactly how he got inside the company's computer system..."

"Exactly when did he make the newspaper? Was the kidnapping soon after his name turned up in the news?" David peered down at her, the hard angles of his face inscrutable from the shadows.

Skye sucked in a breath. She'd been so blind. All this time she'd missed the clues, blatant and unmistakable now. "A couple months after. Ferguson must have guessed his talents. I never suspected that anyone knew of Tyler's unique abilities with computers when the story hit the newspapers."

"Ferguson must have had people waiting in the shadows, wanting to get their hands on your son. To get into a computer by remote access and manipulate the system without being detected all through telekinesis? Any military faction or corporation would be ruthless in acquiring that ability. Tapping into the international, financial sector would involve billions. And the power. It would be unimaginable."

"No wonder they want my son," Skye whispered, unable to shake off feelings of stupidity.

"Who wouldn't?" Disgust thickening David's voice. "Especially when it would be so easy to manipulate and frighten a boy into submission."

At his words, Skye's stomach rolled but she shoved her fear aside and forced her shoulders back with fierce determination. She glared at the chain wrapped around Ferguson's fence. The lock clicked into the night, sounding like an engine backfiring much to Skye's dismay.

David walked up to the gate and carefully unwrapped the chain. The black of his shirt and dark jeans melded against the shadows of a large oak tree. He eased the chain onto the grass to the side of the driveway, unable to completely mask the sound of metal against metal.

After David eased open the wrought iron gate, they both slipped inside and moved along the perimeter, their feet muffled from the lawn. Skye glanced between two, large, maple trees and saw the house forty yards away. The white siding glowed gray against the black windows. "Ferguson's in there waiting for us."

"Or he might be out for the evening."

Even she heard the doubt in David's voice. "Or he's got a diabolical trap set and ready to go." Skye stopped and searched the yard for any movement. "And even if that's the case, it's not going stop me. Not tonight. Not any night. If Tyler's behind that front door, I'll find him."

"Holding off until morning might be more of an advantage. What with not knowing the floor plan."

"I can't." Just the idea of waiting a minute longer tore at her insides.

David cupped her shoulder with a large hand. "I'm with you. Whatever you want to do."

The gentle, reassuring pressure of his touch brought a well of emotion rolling up her throat. She swallowed and took in a lungful of air. Right now, any sign of compassion threatened to weaken what strength she'd garnered.

"Let's try the back of the house," David whispered. "There's probably several windows and possibly more than one back door."

"I'll try the front."

He slid his hand from her shoulder and caught her wrist to tug her closer. "We need to keep together."

"No." She wasn't going to be told what to do, not when it came to her son. "We've more of a chance if we go separately. What if we both run into a trap at once? Then what? Who's going to get us out of the situation?"

With a firm grasp still on her wrist, David grunted, his warm breath fanning her temple as he leaned closer. "I don't like it."

"I don't care."

She didn't wait for him to try to change her mind but wrenched her arm from his grasp, hunched down into a crouch and raced across the yard and driveway toward the front of the house. David's muffled curse followed her but not the sound of his footsteps. When she glanced over her shoulder to double check, she found his figure had disappeared into the other shadows. He must have moved toward the rear of the property.

Heart racing, breath ragged from fear and exertion, Skye slowed and eased around the corner of the house. She reached the front door on silent feet and placed a hand on the metal doorknob.

The handle turned easily. Unlocked.

Biting down hard on her lower lip, she let go of the knob without opening the door and eased back a step. She suspected Ferguson waited inside with a full-blown trap. He had to be. What else could she think? No one left their front doors unlocked anymore.

It didn't matter. Nothing or no one was going to stop her tonight.

After inching toward the right of the entrance, she rested a shoulder against the wood siding and focused, centering her mind's energy on the doorknob. The handle turned without much pressure, and the door opened. A black well of nothingness yawned back at her, defiant, fearless, as if mocking her. Neither object or person flew out of the house to attack her. Still, Skye was far from relieved.

Taking in a fortifying breath, Skye moved forward along the wall and slipped into the mouth of the house.

~~*~~

David watched Skye disappear toward the front of the house. He wanted to race after her, shake her until she realized running off on her own was a terrible idea. Knowing how foolhardy that would be, he instead moved stealthily toward the back of the property. The cloying, almost suffocating scent of grass and roses permeated the air as a warm breeze kicked up, scraped across his buzz cut and flicked at the leaves above.

He hated the idea of Skye out there alone. Damn it. His chest tightened. If anything happened to her...

He'd never cared for another woman before, but now... everything had changed. With Skye... Having blown away all his preconceived ideas of love and relationships into fragmented lies, she'd tunneled a path into his mind and heart. Hell. His life had been so damn shallow.

He couldn't fail. He needed to save Tyler. David was too close to achieving unimaginable happiness. Way too close.

Fear for Skye's safety urged him through the shadows and closer to the back of the house. From behind the thick trunk of a tree, David drew to a stop twenty yards away from the sliding glass doors on the ground floor. He waited five minutes, giving Skye enough time for her to get inside.

Squaring his shoulders, he inched closer to the house and centered his mind and telekinetic powers on the back entrance. The door opened. Silence carried across the distance. No alarm sounded, unless Ferguson had one wired to a local security company.

Over a minute passed.

David hunkered low to the ground and moved stealthily through the shadows toward the door. As he slipped inside a master bedroom, a cloud drifted across the sky to reveal the moon. Light shot through the slats of the window's blinds. He caught sight of his reflection in the dresser's mirror as he moved past a king-sized bed with a massive wood frame. Even though no one appeared from the corners of the room, unease rippled across David's back.

The room was too silent, too still as if waiting for him to make one stupid, thoughtless mistake. He left the Arcadia door open behind him as he crept deeper into the room. The air conditioner kicked on, thrusting cold air against David's exposed skin and shoving his heart deeper into his chest.

From the hallway, he walked into the main part of the house, his step muted by the carpet. At a sound, faint and indistinguishable, David pressed his back against the wall, brushing up against a picture. The frame scraped against the wall. His pulse kicked up into a crazy rhythm and drummed into his temples.

David waited, suspecting he'd given himself away. He listened for Skye or for someone far more dangerous, his senses attuned beyond his loud and erratic breathing.

Then he heard a noise he couldn't decipher. Frowning, he inched down the hall, his hands fisted at his sides, his gaze able to form the shadows into solid objects. The sound intensified and clarified into a faint, but distinct voice.

Ferguson? Tyler? The voice sounded more like an adult male

than a boy. Did Skye also hear it? Was she cautiously moving toward the same sound in another part of the house? He needed to confront this person first. He wasn't about to let Skye get in the line of a kidnapper and possible killer.

But what if he found Tyler dead? What then? He wouldn't be able to ease Skye's anguish. It would be too much. The agony of having a father near death in the hospital would be incomparable to the loss of a child.

Hell. David couldn't go down that route. He'd find a way to fix things. For Skye's sake.

Tyler might not even be here. He could be somewhere completely safe. Frightened, uncertain maybe, but still unharmed. Skye's son had to be safe. She'd been through too much as it was. She didn't deserve what these assholes had put her through. And there had to be more than one. The way Tyler had been snatched this time and those previous times had to involve more than one person. And if for some reason only one person was involved, then they were just as deadly as they were intelligent, which—

Sudden silence.

David froze.

A good ten seconds passed. Then the male voice sounded again. David crept closer, and paused by the doorway leading into the kitchen. He searched the room, not liking the open cabinets and how the pots and pans littered the floor. Some type of struggle? For a wild second, he thought of Skye. But no. He would have heard a fight between her and an assailant in here.

The air vibrated with latent anger as David carefully sidestepped the metal pans flung across the room, hating how his shoes against the ceramic tile echoed into the stillness.

A man's voice grew louder and more distinguishable as he crossed the kitchen. Moonlight spilled from the window over the sink and cut a path along the floor to edge past a doorway where steps lead into a black void.

"You must move the ball into the numbered slot. Twenty-two. Focus only on that number and the ball. Push the ball into twenty-two," the husky baritone drifted up the stairs and into the kitchen. "If the white ball goes into any other numbered slot, I will hurt you. You won't want me to hurt you, now do you? We don't want you screaming like a little pig, now do we?"

As the man's voice drifted into silence, tension cut a vicious swath across David's shoulders. Those words. The tone, the cadence, the cool, detached voice crawled across his flesh. David had heard those words before. And with them came the pain. Always excruciating pain. The chill of sweat clung to his brow. Memories like slivers of cut glass scraped his mind.

Shit. Gaze narrowing, David edged toward the stairs and peered into the darkness, but a wall of impenetrable black blocked him from seeing further than a foot away.

"Never." The voice turned dark and baleful and echoed from the basement to slide across David's skin like a snake's tongue. "Do you understand? If you even attempt to remember, you will be savagely attacked by a lizard-like alien. Its teeth will rip at your flesh, cut your throat until your life drains from your body."

The air caught inside David's lungs. He recognized that voice now. Jesus. Its insidious tone filled his nightmares and had the power to torment him. Along with the images of a lizard with yellow hate-filled eyes and a rabid mouth.

All this time, his fiendish dreams hadn't been based in reality or fears from his childhood but false memories carefully and systematically drummed into his head.

Too many nights he'd lain awake as a teenager, wondering if his horrific nightmares were frighteningly...real.

The meaning behind his fascination with the roulette wheel and the number twenty-two David now understood. He'd been forced to play some telekinetic game, but unlike any childhood board game, if he lost, he would be punished. Unlike the phantom monster from his past, the pain had been all too horrifyingly real. He remembered the screaming. His screaming.

With the back of his hand, David wiped the sweat from his brow, but he still couldn't rid himself from the fear. He inched onto the first step and pressed his back against the stairwell's wall. He didn't try to find a light switch, knowing if he did, he'd quickly expose his presence and possibly get himself killed.

David had no idea if the person attached to that voice carried a weapon or how he had his victim restrained.

Was Tyler that victim? Was the boy drugged, tied up and being forced to submit to these unholy, hypnotic suggestions? David didn't dare wait and find out what this freak intended to do next and he sure as hell wasn't about to let Skye take the risk of finding out the situation beyond the stairs. He could easily be walking into a trap or into a wall, but it didn't matter. He hadn't come across the country to do nothing.

The need to do something—anything—propelled David from the kitchen. With his back still against the wall, he descended onto the first riser, then the next and the next as the voice gnawed at his concentration.

A red light cast a bloody glow through the thick, black stillness. He slipped down to another stair as confusion pulled his brows together. The voice sounded unnatural, almost tinny even. As if...

Four more steps and David reached the floor without incident. Black now faded to several patches of deep charcoal. Still, he was unable to make anything out other than what looked like a counter, blocking his ability to move closer to the red beam. Then he realized a window above the counter separated him from the pinprick of light. With a hand against the counter's edge, he moved parallel to its length, forcing his breath to remain slow, quiet and controlled. But he felt far from controlled.

As he reached a doorway leading into another room, David finally understood that strange tinny quality to the man's voice. A recording. Not a live person after all.

"October House is a foster home. Nothing more than a place you stayed as a child seeking refuge after the death of your mother. If you even attempt to delve into anything to do with the foster home, you will experience a certain death. Your life inside the home has always been normal. So normal you can't remember anything of consequence."

Again, those words. Bile rose in David's throat. He'd also heard them before. All those years ago he'd been brainwashed to believe something else. A vise-like pressure squeezed around his.

He stepped into the room, but something pressed against his thighs, halting any movement forward. Tensing, David searched the area in front of him. His fingers grazed something soft and cool. Then his touch grew bolder. He jerked his hand back.

Flesh.

An arm.

Blinding light shot into the room. David blinked, focused. His gaze snagged on a man sprawled across the length of a dentist's chair in front of him. With skin tinted to match the gray of his hair, the man's eyes stared back at David, sightless, dead.

"Jesus," David swore under his breath.

The man from his childhood past and the creator of his nightmares.

A noise grazed the air behind him. Pivoting, David caught a glimpse of movement in his peripheral vision. Something hit him across the neck.

Then a black wave crashed in on him.

CHAPTER 27

"David?" Skye whispered. "Ty?"

Her words sounded like an explosion in the silence of Ferguson's house. She paused at the head of the stairs on the second floor. Again. Another noise. The same as seconds earlier. A muffled whisper. Somewhere on the first floor.

As she peered over the side of the balcony to the living area below, she gripped the handle of the wood railing with taut fingers. Dark rectangular and square shapes melded with the other shadows. No movement. No sound. Only the wild beat of her heart against her ribs.

She knew she wasn't alone. Unease trickled down her nape. Swiveling, she glanced behind her toward the hall she'd just left.

Empty. Like every room on the second floor. She'd searched beneath the beds, inside the bathroom cabinets and bedroom closets. She hadn't found Tyler, and she hadn't found anyone else. But that wasn't going to make her start acting rash by rushing through the house and yelling for Tyler or David.

A noise yet again. From downstairs. David or someone else? It sounded different than a person's sigh. Almost like rustling clothing.

She pressed up against the balcony and peered to the right to try to make out the other section of the house. Swallowing her frustration, she started to creep down the stairs of the carpeted U-shaped stairs. Walls bracketed her. They blinded her to the rest of the house and anyone who might rush up the first section of stairs.

A cry ripped through the rooms. Loud, high-pitched, short. As if abruptly cut off.

Her breath grew agitated. She stole down the remaining stairs to the landing between the two flights of stairs, mindful to keep her step silent.

More rustling. It had to be David. Because if it wasn't...

"Mom!"

Skye stumbled, almost fell on the landing. She caught the side of the wall with the flat of her hand. "Ty!"

"Mom! Help!"

Fear and joy exploded inside her chest. Tyler. He was here. Alive. His cry for help came from the ground floor and what she suspected was the dining room or kitchen. She turned around the landing and surged down the remaining stairs and out into the living area. She peered through an archway and recognized the faint gleam of a chrome refrigerator. She pivoted around a sofa and rushed toward the kitchen. Ferguson must have also heard her son's cry. She needed to get to Tyler first.

Body trembling with anticipation, she stepped into the kitchen.

There. She saw his shadowy form.

Wonder and excitement bubbled up her throat. "Oh, Sweetie, I'm here."

Odd. He sat in a kitchen chair in the middle of the room and not by the table off to the side. He didn't get up to rush toward her, didn't even move. Unease prickled across her flesh.

And David hadn't appeared. He must have heard Tyler. He would have come running if he were capable, if he were okay...

For a wild moment, she thought the child was someone other than Tyler as she moved deeper into the room. But no. She recognized his slender frame, his short dark hair and his eyes... The whites around his irises gleamed against the moonlight that speared between the slats of the kitchen blinds. Tape bound him to the wrought iron back and legs. As his body shivered against his bindings, terror glittered in Tyler's eyes.

Dread crawled down her spine.

From behind, someone grabbed her throat and dug a finger and thumb into the tender muscle of her neck.

Only one thought tumbled into Skye's consciousness as her body gave out. She'd failed her son.

~~*~~

David woke up. With his cheek pressed against the cold floor, he lay sprawled on his stomach. A headache pounded against the back of his neck and skull and stabbed at the sides of his head and temples.

Darkness wrapped around him. David realized he was on the floor of the basement. He hadn't gotten far. He'd been attacked. Or had he? He didn't remember anything beyond the flaring light and the dead body. A dead body still probably draped across a dental chair. At the idea, nausea threatened to rise up his throat.

Question was, was it Ferguson? David wasn't sure. He'd managed to glimpse translucent skin and the gray hair of an old man. But he'd seen enough to recognize the man of his childhood nightmares. Years before he'd been a man in his prime, a man with a cold smile, passionless eyes and a white lab coat. He'd administered needles and terror. Memories of being strapped in a chair, of being forced to play game after game of roulette, of being wheeled down corridors of sterile halls and into hopeless rooms bombarded his head. David hadn't been the only one. They'd been others. He'd heard their cries as they were also experimented on, witnessed the fear in their eyes before David was briskly led into another room.

He didn't want to remember. He didn't like these memories, but the present was worse. A man lay dead in the same room with him. David hadn't seen any visible wounds that revealed how he'd died. At least none that David managed to see. The man's death was no accident. Of that he was positive. He'd had been killed deliberately.

Murdered.

Within the four walls of a house that Skye searched. And would she find her son just as David had found this man? Dead?

Panicked, David placed both palms against the tile and lifted off the floor. It felt like a sledgehammer slammed into his skull. "Shit."

Groaning, he dropped back down to his stomach. He needed to move, to get out of wherever the hell he was and find Skye.

Unlike the man in here with him, David's attacker had let him live. Why? It didn't make sense. Unless the killer had a crazy motive that David could only attempt to guess at? Or was he playing a twisted game? One where David somehow was one of the pawns?

David bit back an oath as he shoved off the ground and into a sitting position. Ignoring the pressure that cut into his head, he wiped at his face. His hand came away wet. He rubbed his damp fingers beneath his nose and smelled the metallic scent of his own blood. When he fell, he must have hit his head.

He searched the room. Impenetrable blackness surrounded him. Not one discernible item. Not even the glow of red light from before. How easy it must have been to lure him into this room. He'd been stupid and fallen for the rouse, blinded by feelings evoked by that damn tape. The words, tone, and everything about that voice had left him raw, exposed and feeling like the child he'd been years before.

Light flashed on from the door to the kitchen and illuminated the empty staircase. David's eyes narrowed. The games were beginning.

A muffled scream carried down into the basement.

Oh, God. Skye.

~~*~~

Skye opened her eyes, winced at the searing light and closed them. Shifting in what felt like a straight-backed chair, she moved her hands in her lap and stilled in shock. Her wrists were bound together. Oh, God. Her legs too. Rope or tape fastened her ankles to the legs of the chair.

She tried reopening her eyes. The bright glare in her face

forced her lids closed. She couldn't look beyond the light. She wanted to see her captor, to see Tyler and ensure his safety.

The whisper of a footstep sounded from somewhere in front of her and to the right. Stiffening, she angled her ear in that direction. She shifted and squinted into the light. Pain throbbed against the back of her eyes. At the fierce glare, tears crested over her lashes. Panic welled in her throat.

Something was wrong with her eyes. Terribly wrong. What had this person done to her? Fear kept her from asking aloud, because once she acknowledged she wasn't alone, her situation would be real.

She yanked at her wrists. The binding—duct tape if she could go by the sticky flexibility—didn't loosen but only pulled at her skin. The air by her face moved. She froze. Breathing. Close by. The person was watching her. She stopped herself from biting her lip, but the urge to cry out from fear threatened to rush past her lips.

An object fell to the floor to her left. Skye flinched. She didn't know if she'd caused it from her telekinesis or someone else had.

Jaw clenched, she grasped for a way to calm down. Counting. She started counting but after ten, the suspense and terror of not knowing about her son's welfare wrenched the words from her lips. "Ty? Are you there?"

"He's in the room with you."

At her captor's deep, male voice, Skye jerked back against her seat. Glass shattered. Possibly a plate or drinking glass. This time she knew she'd been the cause.

"What the..." A man's voice tinged with disbelief carried across the room. A footstep crunched against the floor.

If only she could use her telekinesis to aim a weapon at Tyler's kidnapper. She yanked hard on her bindings. The tape only tightened around her skin. At the lengthening silence, she cocked her head to the side and listened.

There. More breathing. In front and to the right. Quick and agitated.

Tyler. So close, but with so many insurmountable obstacles keeping him from her.

"What have you done with my son? Why hasn't he said anything?"

"It's called tape. I don't want to hear a bunch of screaming. Not yet anyway."

Rage and impotence banded around her throat. "If you've hurt Tyler, I swear to God I'll—"

"What? Hurt me?" Humor laced his words but didn't ease the dark, edgy tone of his voice. "Relax. He's okay...for now."

She opened her eyes and looked toward where she suspected Tyler's kidnapper stood. Blinding light cut into her vision. It kept her from seeing anything but a brief shadow. The glare from a lamp or overhead light forced her lids closed again. The condition of her eyes hadn't changed. They seemed even worse.

Skye swallowed her panic, but it rushed back up. He'd blinded her. Oh, God. How could she possibly use her telekinesis to save Tyler when she couldn't even see?

"My eyes," she managed, unable to keep the fear from her voice.

"I dilated them. Nothing permanent, but it's far more effective. You can't dislodge drops like a blindfold." The man's voice drew closer. "I wish you could see me." He stroked her face from her brow to her jaw.

Skye jerked to the side, sending her hair across one cheek. For a wild second, she thought he'd touched her with a metal weapon—possibly a gun or knife. But no. He'd used his finger, warm and encased in some type of material that smelled of rubber.

"Why are you doing this? I have no money. And my son. He's just a child. Completely innocent." She turned her face toward the left where she believed her attacker had moved. By keeping her blinded, she hoped it was a sign that he didn't intend to kill her. But then she sadly realized, she'd hunted him down in his own home. He wasn't about to let her go with a slap to her wrist. "We've done nothing to deserve this."

"Deserve?" The man's voice shifted into a tone where rage scratched at the surface. "That's where you're wrong. You deserve far more than this."

Skye's spine stiffened. She remembered the letters on the mirror back in Las Vegas. Dread burrowed into her stomach. For a while, she'd forgotten about those hate-filled words and assumed these last twenty-four hours Ferguson wanted Tyler's powers. Now she started to wonder if she'd been completely wrong. The oddness of the situation hit her.

"Don't you think you deserve more?" he whispered by her ear, his hot breath shifting through the strands of her hair to crawl across her skin.

She bit down on her inner lip to cut off her cry of surprise. Her heart crashed against her ribs. "You tell me."

"Oh, no. That would make it too easy for you." He touched her. A quick, caress along the vulnerable slope of her neck.

She flinched. She couldn't help it. He was playing some type of mind game. He had to be. If he'd just wanted her son, he would have killed her off immediately. He also didn't appear to want money or a trade. Did he have another plan then? Torture?

"What do you want?" Skye asked. She hated the tremble in her voice.

The light suddenly dimmed. She opened her eyes and found a spotlight pointed away from her body. But from above, the kitchen's fluorescent light made any images impossible to identify. A man's face appeared a foot in front of her. Skye snapped back against her chair. Shaggy brown hair, lean face, sunken cheeks and violent blue eyes inflicted their gaze at her with unmasked hatred.

She pressed deeper into her chair, too stunned to think to react as the light returned to her face. She blinked, tears welled, then she squeezed shut her lids.

"That's it?" he asked. "You have nothing to say?"

The casual tone of his voice didn't hide the suppressed rage shimmering near the surface. Skye shifted in her chair in growing alarm. She didn't understand. This man couldn't be Ferguson. He was too young to have been experimenting on children decades before. He looked to be only a couple years older than herself.

Biting down on her lower lip, she searched for a plausible

answer, one where the words might diminish his rage. She feared if she said anything wrong, it might push him down an irreversible and deadly path. She couldn't allow that. She needed time. Time to think. To formulate. To plan. To pray. This wasn't just her life in jeopardy. There was Ty. And David.

Oh, God. What of David? Was he dead? Murdered by this lunatic? David's body could be in this very room, and she wouldn't know it. She couldn't ask. Because if she asked—

Skye mentally shook off her rising panic and realized their kidnapper might see through any platitudes. "I don't know what you expect me to say."

"Don't you recognize me?"

Dread squeezed and twisted her stomach. What had she done to this man? His rage skimmed the surface, but she knew a second later with the wrong reply, that same fury might erupt and he would act on it.

"You don't even remember me, do you?"

"I—"

"Don't lie." He grabbed her face and dug his thumb and finger on either side of her mouth. His breath fanned across her nose and lips. "What about Weaver? Peter Weaver. Now do you get it?"

She sensed him bare inches from her face. Oh, God. He'd just revealed his identity. He had no intention of keeping them alive. A deep, shiver wracked her body. The chill of terror clung to her pores.

Tyler's whimper and quick intake of breath pierced across the distance of the room and compounded her fear.

Think. She needed to think. But panic scattered her thoughts, blew them into tiny particles that she couldn't collect into anything meaningful.

Weaver. Weaver. That name. Peter. Yes, Peter Weaver. Memories from another year, one she'd tried so hard to forget crushed any hope of absolution. Peter, a co-worker of Jay's. Her ex-husband and Peter had worked in the same precinct. Dealing coke and dirty money.

After her ex sued for custody, pushed her into a corner, she'd searched for a way out and stumbled on Jay's sideline of dealing drugs behind the shield of his badge. She'd turned him in and started a chain reaction that touched more than their lives. Internal Affairs had implicated three police officers, including Peter. None had been arrested, but because of her actions, they'd lost their jobs and their credibility.

"I remember you," Skye whispered.

"And what? Don't you have anything to say?"

He dug his fingers deeper into her cheeks until the pressure bit into her gums, bruising the flesh and ripping a cry from her lips. She knew if she didn't answer, he would inflict more pain. "You want revenge."

"Ah, revenge. Why shouldn't I ask for it?" His voice thickened with disgust as he released her face with a quick jerk. "Can you give me one reason why I shouldn't retaliate?"

"It won't get your job back. You'll be worse off, wanted by the police, on the run. Your life won't get any better."

"Ah, we have a damn philosopher. Well, you know what?" he asked, an odd, dangerous note thickening his voice as he wrapped his hand gently around her neck. His thumb caressed the pulse point beneath her left ear. "I don't care."

Skye didn't move, didn't swallow. Why give him that satisfaction? But she couldn't hide the wild thump of her pulse or the tension snapping into the major muscles of her body. She waited for the pressure to increase around her throat as he continued to caress the skin below her ear. How could she hope to save herself and Ty? She bit back the urge to retaliate with words. Flinging insults would only guarantee their death.

He released his hand from her throat and a shudder of relief rolled through her entire being. A reprieve. But for how long?

She needed to keep him talking. That's what they did in the movies. But this was real. This person had an agenda. He wasn't some actor who conveniently spewed his guts to give the victim time to save themselves.

Skye searched for sounds from Tyler. There. Still breathing. Nothing more. But it was enough. Enough to keep hope from turning to bitter ash as she frantically searched for a way out of this crazy situation. "What of Ferguson? I don't understand the tie between you and him."

"You don't need to understand. You're not here to understand. You're here because I want you here." He moved back and forth in front of her, the whisper of air creeping across the distance between them as his shoes scraped against the tile. "Ferguson wanted you dead. He wanted your son for his ability to manipulate computers and hired me to get him and take care of any loose ends. He didn't want you alive. He hated you as much as me, always digging into things that didn't concern you. You haven't changed a bit."

"And the doctor?"

"A loose end. Ferguson knew you'd been talking to her, spewing your guts on stuff he didn't want out there. He paid me well." A footfall sounded directly in front of her, and his voice turned nasty. "Tell me? How's it feel to have some nutcase impregnate you? Did you like being his little white, lab rat? The egomaniac wanted to see if his sperm and your powers could get himself a wonder kid. Maybe after a little bit of dissecting and experimenting with your brat, he hoped to raise a little army and sell them to the highest bidder. Who knows. The guy was a whack job."

Skye cringed, hating Tyler being a witness to Weaver's hateful words. "How could you know that when—"

"It's amazing how he started blubbering after dislocating a couple of his fingers." He laughed. "God, it feels good knowing how much of your life must have been a lie. Jay. What an idiot. He was clueless for the longest time."

Envisioning Peter's gloating smile, she turned her cheek to the side, avoiding the heat of his breath and the stench of hatred to hit her head on.

"I see you don't like hearing that. Well, that's too bad. It won't matter anyway, because in a little bit you're going to be dead. You—" Peter crushed a palm across her mouth. She wrenched backward and struggled in her chair, her cry smothered by his latex-covered hand. Once again, he squeezed his fingers into her cheeks. This time though, he dug the tips of his fingers from his other hand into the tender spot of her inner arm inches below her armpit. A wave of pain shot up into her shoulder and down into her fingers. She gasped against his palm, unable to get air, fearing she might faint.

With pain inundating Skye's every pore and thought, he finally relaxed the pressure to her arm. She slumped against the chair and hated her weakness, her inability to fight back.

A moment later, she understood why Peter wanted her quiet.

CHAPTER 28

BLOOD DRIPPED INTO David's eye from a wound to his brow. Blinking rapidly against the sting of blood, he tried to peer up the stairwell to the kitchen from the basement. He listened for sounds above. Nothing other than his own breathing and the drumming of his heart filled the nearly black room. He'd heard Skye's muffled cry. Had she been attacked by his assailant? But if he called out, he'd give away his position and possibly Skye's.

He rubbed the back of his hand against his eyes to clear his vision. He couldn't focus. At the oddness of the light, he frowned and crept up the stairs, mindful of the sound of his shoes on each riser.

He squinted toward the kitchen. The light's intensity forced him to look to the side. Damn it. What the hell was wrong with his eyes? Had the blow to his head impaired his vision? If he couldn't see, he couldn't use his telekinesis.

David paused near the top of the stairwell, remaining hidden in the basement's shadows. With his back and shoulders pressed against the wall, he listened. Silence. But that didn't mean a damn thing. Beyond the blinding light, someone might be waiting, ready to attack or kill him. Still, David had to act. He had no other option. Skye was out there, ferocious when it came to protecting her own, but all too vulnerable.

Her muffled cry had haunted him and launched a collage of horrifying images of her fate in his head—dead, her throat slit. Or her body, broken, abused and sprawled across the floor upstairs.

Dread crawled across his flesh. He glanced back up at the light. The chill of sweat clung to the back of his neck. His heart thundered inside his chest. Still silence. Then a shadow appeared in the doorway into the kitchen and launched itself in his direction. David lurched to the other side of the stairs. He deflected a blow to his midsection, which instead glanced off his temple as he ducked and sprang up the last few stairs and into the kitchen.

"Tyler?" Skye asked from somewhere nearby, her voice thick with anxiety. "David?"

He turned at Skye's voice just as his attacker tackled him from behind. The force sent David forward. His chin hit the floor, rattling his teeth. He grunted as he twisted around and rammed an elbow into a man. The bastard caught him in the neck. He wrapped his fingers around David's throat. The pressure against his neck intensified until his world turned black.

David came to. His head throbbed. He didn't know how long he'd passed out for, but the light was worse. It glared into his right eye with needle-like intensity. His other eye was damaged, swollen shut he suspected.

"Well, what do we have here?" a man asked, his voice filled with delight. "Your boyfriend's coming to."

Beyond the amusement, David heard a darker tone, threaded with malevolence and rage. Lying on the floor, he grew conscious of his wrists bound behind him, his legs tied at the ankles. The heat of a lamp touched his face and neck. He squinted to get his bearings. Pain knotted the muscles around his injured eye while the light's beam cut into his other. Jaw rigid, he closed his eyes. He didn't dare let fear immobilize his thoughts.

"Why did you have to hurt him like that?" Skye this time. Her voice, strong but shaky, carried directly across the room—he guessed a distance of several yards.

She sounded okay, considering. Thank God.

"I could have killed him, but he's more useful to me at the moment." Footsteps moved across the floor and stopped in front of David's face.

David waited tensely, determined to keep his expression blank of emotion.

A shoe nudged his chin.

David jerked back. A growl of impotence and frustration rumbled from his chest.

"Pretty convenient how he managed to walk right up here without me lugging his sorry ass up here, don't you think?" David's attacker mused aloud. "He appeared right on schedule as planned."

At his blatant arrogance, David's jaw tensed. Much to his shame, he'd fallen victim to the bastard's plan. But their attacker's arrogance could turn out to be his weakness.

"Let him and Tyler go," Skye pleaded. "You've got me. Isn't that enough?"

David twisted his wrists behind him. The binding didn't give. "Where's Tyler? Is he here?"

"Of course. Blinded with eye drops, hogtied and waiting for slaughter. Like you." Smugness thickened the man's words.

David listened, trying to decipher if he'd heard that voice from somewhere in his past. Nothing. Not in the man's tone or cadence. But he did hear frantic and erratic breathing to David's left. Tyler. Had to be, because Skye was more in the center of the room and in front of him.

"Amazing how a couple of eye drops can leave all of you useless, isn't it?" his attacker asked but didn't appear to care for an answer. "I'll have to thank Ferguson for that."

David stilled. "What are you talking about?"

"Ferguson hired him to kidnap Tyler," Skye whispered. "His name's Peter Weaver. Like Jay, he thinks I ruined his life. But unlike my ex, he's willing to kill to get his little piece of revenge. Just another dirty cop who thinks he's above the law."

Their chances of coming out of this place alive plummeted. All the money and talking wasn't likely to change someone's mind when it came to wanting to settle a score.

"If you're trying to get me angry," Weaver's tone softened dangerously. "It's working."

"Let her and the boy go," David demanded.

"I don't think so," Weaver replied, a razor-like edge sharpening his voice. "And who are you to make demands? Hell, you're on the floor tied up like a fucking pig. I didn't come all this way to walk away without spilling blood. I want someone dead."

"Why?" David asked. Panic and frustration shredded his fragile restraint and made him lash out. "What could they have ever down to you? We're talking about a woman and a boy for God's sake. Only a coward would go after them."

Footsteps scoured the tile. Then Weaver's sharp-edged toe rammed into David's hip. Pain pummeled David's side, extracting a ragged groan from his lips. Lifting his neck from the floor, he looked around but the room's blinding light forced his eyes shut.

"Stop it!" Skye cried out. "Don't hurt him. David has nothing to do with me and you. Let him go."

"Hell no," Weaver spewed as the sound of his footsteps retreated. "Shut up, or I'll pull the hair from your skull."

Skye's cry broke over David's labored breathing. Oh, God. Weaver was hurting her because he'd goaded the other man. Her whimper sliced at David's heart and tore at his insides.

"Take me instead." David gasped through the pain, twisting his wrists back and forth behind him to pry off his binding but the tape didn't loosen. What sounded like a glass shattered to David's left. Grappling for some fraction of calm, he ground his teeth together. He needed to reign in his telekinesis. If he let his control slip, he could inadvertently hurt Skye or Tyler. "If you want your revenge, let them go and use me."

"Just who the hell are you?" Disgust thickened Weaver's voice as he moved back across the room, his step brushing to a stop approximately a foot in front of David's face. "You're just as strange as the kid, but with you, it's breaking things."

David tensed. He waited for a kick to his head or gut and smothered the urge to curl his legs into his chest.

"Do you think your powers are going to save you, Skye or the boy?" Weaver's voice drew nearer, as if he'd hunched down in front of David. "Are you hoping to be her hero?"

David blinked into the room's light. Not even a discerning shadow to latch onto. Weaver must have strategically planted the lights in a way to keep them all victims. And the crazy bastard was enjoying how they were flying around like fish in the desert sun. If David could just use his telekinesis on some object, any object to use as a weapon, he could turn this around.

"Answer me, damn it!"

David ground his jaw. He'd learned all too well that verbally lashing out would only hurt Skye again and ruin her and Tyler's chances. He slumped against the floor. Right now, he didn't see an immediate way out of this alive. "Hero? No. I'm just someone who cares."

"Someone who cares," Weaver said, his sarcasm grating across David's nerves. "How touching. Obviously, you haven't learned caring doesn't get you anywhere. But you'll find that out soon enough, and Skye, here, will be the one to show you. Isn't that right, Skye?"

David didn't like the change in Weaver's voice. His snide tone now held too much confidence, too much arrogance. Almost as if he was gloating over a secret joke.

"I don't know what you're talking about." Skye's words heavy with anxiety carried across the room.

"Then how about I explain it to you in simple terms, hmm?" A short pause of silence, pregnant with menace followed.

The bastard enjoyed enacting this unholy parody in front of a captive audience. But if David had a say, this play wasn't going into the next act. From behind his back, David dug under his taped wrists. He worked a thumb between his skin and the binding's sticky underside but stilled at Weaver's next words.

"I want you to choose," the other man ordered, his words laced with unmistakable pleasure. "Who lives and who dies. Your son or...lover. Their life is in your hands."

"You're crazy," Skye replied in a strangled voice. "I can't do that."

"You're going to have to," Weaver returned. "Otherwise I'll choose for you."

"Leave her alone!" David bucked against the floor, hitting the back of his head against a bottom cabinet. He twisted harder at his bindings. His ties didn't give, didn't even slacken. Helplessness clawed at his insides. "You're insane."

The lights. If he could just break a bulb.

"So who is it going to be?"

Weaver's question slammed into David. He couldn't let Skye chose. The guilt would kill her. He didn't care about dying, not when living would ruin her life and that of her son. He loved her. She had such determination, fierce loyalty to her son. He'd never met anyone like her, and he wouldn't again. He knew that.

"Take me," David growled. "Kill me."

"No," Skye whispered. "Don't, David. How do we know he's telling the truth? Please..." She took in a rattling breath.

"I don't see any other choice," David insisted. Tyler was a boy with a full life ahead of him. Just a kid, with years of learning, of discovery, of being. David would never recover if he knew his life depended on the death of not just another person, but Skye's innocent son.

"Don't do this," Skye insisted, unmistakable panic rising in her voice.

"I'm not asking you," Weaver said, a rabid edge to his voice. "I'm telling you. If you don't choose and soon, I'll choose for you."

"Me. Kill me." David dug his thumb deeper between his wrist and the tape binding his wrists together. The binding didn't give. A snarl slipped past his gritted teeth. Next, he twisted and turned his hands, chaffing his flesh until moisture—probably his own blood—clung to his skin. He swung his bound legs out in front of him and then backward in the hope of connecting with a floor lamp, but his feet hit nothing but space. "Damn it. You're crazy."

The sharp edge of a shoe rammed into David's stomach. He gasped as another cutting kick from Weaver drove into David's gut. Pain knifed into David's muscles and beyond. Groaning, he tucked his legs toward his chest. Jesus. Struggling to regain his breath, David fought from blacking out as fog clouded his thoughts. He took in a slow, deep lungful of air and managed to clear his head.

"Shut up. I'm tired of your mouth." Weaver took a step back from David, his heel scraping lightly across the tile floor. "Another word and the kid gets it."

David bit down on his lip to stop the words of outrage from spilling into the room. There had to be a way to stop Weaver.

"Decide now, Skye," Weaver demanded.

Silence. Then crying. Skye.

The sound of a cough resounded within the kitchen.

David flinched. His fingers stilled along the tape around his wrists. At the odd noise, dread squeezed the breath from his lungs.

"Did you hear that?" His step quick and as if with purpose, Weaver crossed the kitchen floor to the left of the room and where David's suspected he had Tyler tied. "That's a gun with a silencer."

Another cough. David jerked, stunned, wildly wondering who'd been hit as he opened his good eye. The light, as savage as any knife piercing into his brain, forced his lid shut. Air sawed loudly from David's lungs. He flipped onto his back. When he didn't feel a new fissure of pain, he realized if he wasn't shot... then that would mean—

"Tyler? David?" Skye asked in a hesitant whisper.

Pressure squeezed David's throat, making the words come out as if strangled. "I'm okay."

"You bastard!" Skye yelled. "Tyler? Are you there?"

A smothered response to the left of the room, but a response none-the-less. Still, David didn't relax. The boy could be bleeding. Jesus.

Weaver laughed. "Skye you should see your friends face here. What a hero. He doesn't look like much—other than terrified." His voice thickened with amusement. "You're not shot yet. Either is the kid. At least not yet."

David fought back his rage, knowing he needed a clear head,

because he had to do something. Now. Panic propelled him off the floor and onto his knees.

"What the hell do you think you're doing?" Weaver asked, his voice rising in disbelief. "Are you that stupid?"

He was to David's left. If he could just launch himself at the man and take him down. But if David made a mistake, then they were headed to the morgue. Still, he had to act.

Metal slammed into David's face. The force flung his head to the side. He reeled backward, almost lost his balance from the blow but some miracle kept him on his knees.

David opened his good eye, saw a shadow. Weaver. Right in front of him.

It was enough.

David launched himself at the other man. His shoulder rammed into flesh and bone.

It wasn't enough.

The gun went off again. This time the bullet didn't hit the air. There was no mistake this time. The bullet entered flesh. His flesh.

CHAPTER 29

SKYE HEARD THE cough of the gun. A sigh, then groan. Her pulse drummed against her temples. Bile rose in her throat as she opened her eyes. The light had faded. Discernible shadows. Two forms. One standing, the other on their knees. Then another shadow off to the side. A smaller form. Ty. Oh, God. It had to be her son bound in a chair.

Hurt? Alive?

When she heard a soft whimper from her son to the left of the men, Skye struggled with renewed vigor. If David could keep Weaver occupied for just a bit longer... From beneath her, the chair tipped, hit the leg of the kitchen table to her left, but righted itself. The light around her wavered, then flared. A lamp. There had to be one on the table. Squinting, she made out what looked like the base of a lamp on top of a large, round table. Jaw clamped with raw determination, she twisted in her chair and jerked all her weight to her left in hopes of overbalancing the lamp and breaking the bulb. Once, twice. Light bounced. Again—this time with more weight behind her—she collided harder against the table. Metal clanged against wood. A blinding flash. The sound of shattered glass rained across the table's top.

The shrill ring of a telephone broke into the room and over the noise of both men struggling. Skye jumped, her gaze skating off the table as the sound of a siren's cry broke through the night and into the fractured chaos of the kitchen. A man towered over another as he swung back a hand. The drops still distorted her vision and masked his identity.

The phone stopped ringing, but the blare of the siren strengthened.

Skye struggled to move her ankles. The tape dug into her jeans and kept her legs firmly bound to the chair. Frustration gnawed at her insides as she gritted her teeth. Help was still too far away. Someone would be dead before the police arrived.

Flesh connected against flesh. A grunt erupted into the room. A shoe scraped across the floor.

"David?" she called out, despair thickening her voice. "David?"

No answer. Tears slipped down her cheeks. The phone started to ring again. If she could just find the blasted thing and distinguish it from the other shapes, she could use her telekinesis to answer it.

Skye glanced back to the table. The sharp glare from the kitchen's one remaining light from the ceiling bounced off three knives and slashed across her vision. All neatly lined up to torture and maim. Shivering from the sweat coating her nape and underarms, she blinked, squinted. A butcher's block, inches beyond the knives on the table.

She whipped her gaze back to the two shadows. One standing. Thinner with shaggy hair. He had to be Weaver. Ignoring the urge to hesitate, she zeroed in the butcher's block and willed all her mental energy on the knives' holder. She latched onto the block with her mind and flung it physically through the air. The sickening sound of wood against flesh carried across the room.

A cry. The man standing went down. The phone stopped ringing. The siren died. Complete silence.

Oh, God. They were both on the ground. Maybe she'd hit David by accident. Frantic, she fastened her gaze on the knives, pulled one from the table with her telekinesis. She used her power to saw through the bindings above her hands with the blade, nicking her flesh in her hurry. She broke her wrists apart and yanked the tape's remains from her body. She caught the knife in mid-air with one hand and sliced through the bindings around her ankles. Still holding the weapon, she sprang from the chair toward Tyler. When she reached her son, she crashed to her knees, quickly cut through the tape binding him to the chair and dropped the blade. With hands like frenzied hummingbirds, she searched her son's body.

"Are you okay?" No wounds. But he still might have internal injuries.

At his nod, a new wave of trembling rolled through her body, keeping her knees locked to the ground. The relief was mind-numbing. She shivered and struggled to peel the corner of tape covering Tyler's mouth but failed.

Okay. She needed control. Now. Jaw tensing, she focused and managed to calm the quaking in her fingers long enough to ease the tape from Tyler's mouth. When he dove against her chest and his arms, thin, fragile and young, wrapped around her neck, she shuddered in relief. She slipped a palm over the soft cap of his head. His silken strands teased her fingers.

"Oh, Mom..." He snuggled deeper in her arms and hiccupped twice. "He said you were dead. He made me think—"

"Shhh...it's okay. Everything's okay now." Skye squeezed her eyes shut. But they'd never be the same again.

"Is he dead?" Tyler snuffled by her ear.

Tension clamped across the muscles of her back. She shifted on knees and stared at Peter sprawled across the tile on his back. Motionless. Eyes shut to the world. But was he dead? The effects of the drops in her eyes lingered, making it still difficult to see clearly.

Then she saw David's prone body to the left of Peter. Oh, God. He lay on his side and to the left of Tyler's kidnapper. Tape bound his wrists and ankles together.

"Let me see if he's okay. Just stay here," she urged, but Tyler's arms wrapped tighter around her neck. "I'm not leaving the room. You'll be fine, but I've got to check on David. Peter doesn't look he's going to hurt anyone for a long time."

She stared at Tyler's large brown eyes, waited a moment, then unwound his thin arms from her body. When he didn't latch onto her again, she grabbed the knife by her knee and crawled toward David's body, while watching Weaver's motionless form.

When she reached David's side, she wanted to cry again. His face. His dear, beautiful face. Congealed blood clung to a wound at his temple. Oh, God. His left eye was swollen shut with the surrounding skin bruised and scraped. A cut scored a path along the corner of his mouth. She bit down hard on her lip and blinked several times. Tears weren't going to help David. She glided a hand over his jaw, the prickle of beard scraping across her palm.

David jerked back. His good eye flashed open. He winced. For a moment, he stared at her as if unsure of her or his surroundings. Then he blinked a couple of times, glanced over at Peter to his right and appeared to relax. "What the hell happened?"

She followed David's gaze. Peter's chest rose and fell. Uneasiness scraped across her senses. Tyler's kidnapper still remained a threat. "I hit him with a butcher's block."

He smiled and winced again. "I always knew you were resourceful." He leaned away from the cabinets and nudged his thigh against her knees. "Here. Cut me out of this before he comes to."

Skye sliced through the bindings at his ankles, but when he twisted around so she could get at his wrists, she sucked in her breath. Sweat and blood coated the gray duct tape and clung to the creases and the skin on each side of his bindings. He'd rubbed his flesh raw. This time, she cut through the tape with gentle strokes until the strips gave.

She sank back on her heels and noticed his dark gray polo shirt for the first time. A stain ate into the fabric by his waist. In a loud hiss, air rushed into her lungs. Nausea curdled inside her stomach. "You've been shot."

He glanced down to his side and eased the shirt up over his waist, exposing a wound to his left side. The bullet had grazed his skin. Several inches inward and it might have hit a vital organ.

David touched the edge of the wound. "He just nicked me. I'll be okay. Believe me, I'd be dead if he'd wanted me that way."

Skye's lips firmed. He didn't look okay. His bruised face, wrists rubbed raw and torn skin at his waist spoke of pain, and sacrifice.

"Don't look at me like that," David insisted in a fervent whisper. "I'm not going anywhere. I'll be damned if a couple of scratches are going to keep me away from you."

David caught her upper arm and tugged her toward him until her lips whispered across his own. She closed her eyes and took in his scent. Earthy, male, and pure David. She dragged in a ragged breath. With a distinct tremor in his fingers, he cupped her chin and touched his lips to hers in a soft, tender kiss. A kiss that left her shattered as she eased back on her heels.

He stared at her with intense brown eyes. "I thought I'd lost you. I swear to God. I don't know what I would have done without you or Tyler—"

"It's okay." She kissed his mouth, lingering on the full sweep of his bottom lip. God, how she loved him. Because of her, David might have ended up dead by risking his life to save Tyler.

Pounding against the front door resounded into the kitchen. "Police. Open the door. Now."

Skye wrapped an arm around Tyler who had shifted up behind her as the lights from a squad car flashed through the sides of the closed kitchen blinds that Tyler's kidnapper must have closed previously. With eyes almost restored to normal, she stared at Peter lying on the floor. His breathing carried across the distance. He was alive. And soon in police custody. She glanced back at David. "See? It is okay. Everything's going to be okay."

But the next couple of hours didn't feel 'okay.' She'd avoided the kitchen and moved into what looked like a game room to shield Tyler. They hadn't watched the police handcuff and take away Peter or wheel Ferguson out in a body bag. Tyler didn't need additional trauma. He'd been through too much for a boy of nine, and Skye honestly couldn't stomach facing Peter or a dead body right now.

David stepped into the room. A uniformed policeman with a wave of thick gray hair and jowls rivaling a boxer's followed him.

The bruising and swelling around David's left eye were more pronounced than ever, magnifying their ordeal of only hours before. Paramedics had already looked at his wounds, and the gunshot to his side had actually turned out to be superficial like David had insisted. Thank God.

"Can we leave now?" Skye asked the officer as she sat on a low, slung leather sofa with Tyler snuggled up against her. A lamp on the end table to her right cast the room in muted light. Still, her eyes had adjusted, the drops having lost their effects a good thirty minutes earlier.

"Yes. We'll contact you if we have any further questions." The police officer stepped further into the room and smiled down at Tyler. "You're some amazing boy."

Frowning, Tyler wrapped both arms around his drawn up knees. "No, I'm not."

"That's where you're wrong. You survived. Not many kids your age, never mind adults would be alive right now." The man shook his head, his thick jowls quivering. "You were up against a brutal killer and won."

"He tried winning. He really did. He acted as if we were best friends. But he lied about my mom being dead. I knew my mom was alive. I just knew it." Tyler glanced up at Skye with large, solemn brown eyes before resting his chin on one raised knee.

"Well, you're a brave kid. Your mother must be really proud of you." The officer waved a hand and turned back toward the doorway.

"Words don't even come close." Skye wrapped an arm around Tyler's thin shoulders and closed her eyes, undone by the fierce love in Tyler's voice. Tonight she could have lost it all.

They'd managed to survive. The police would have been too late if she hadn't managed to knock out Peter with the butcher's block. Strange how the police had somehow known they'd been in trouble. Skye frowned. Too odd. None of them had dialed 911, and her son wouldn't have been able to with his vision disabled. How could the police possibly know they were fighting for their lives? Peter had used a silencer, muffling any gunshots that might alert the neighbors.

"Officer," Skye called out before he disappeared from the room.

The man turned and raised a thick, gray brow.

"How did you know that we were in trouble? Neither one of us called the police."

David sat down on the arm of the sofa beside her and placed a comforting hand over her shoulder. "You're right. How did you know anything was going on?"

"Some guy called it in."

"Some guy?" Skye asked. "Do you know who?"

"I think it was Logan. He said something about knowing you when you were kids."

Skye nodded, too stunned to reply with any sane or logical answer as she watched the officer slip from the room. The man from the hotel. The one that had locked her inside the vending room and shown up at October House.

Though David didn't say a word, she sensed his gaze on her profile, his curiosity, his silent strength.

Finally, she shook herself mentally and glanced up to David with wonder and uncertainty. "Logan thought I might be his sister. He made out that there were others just like us. Could it be possible?"

"Anything's possible. I've found that out because of you." Gently, David squeezed her shoulder. "As a foster home, the October House had more secrets than either one of us imagined."

"It all started there, all those years ago. And here I thought I was alone."

David withdrew his hand from her shoulder and slipped a wisp of hair from her brow. "I want you to know that even though I might not have been there for you in your childhood, I'm right here with you now and in the future, hell or high water. You can count on it. You'll never be alone again."

The tenderness of his touch, the heat of his eyes dissolved the horror of the previous hours. Her chest expanded with wonder and excitement. All these years she'd relied on no one else but herself, and now she realized she didn't have to. Not anymore. She could always depend on David. He'd proven that these last twenty-four hours.

She loved this dynamic, private man. This man who expected nothing of her but to be herself. If she'd stopped hoping, she would never have reached this pinnacle of joy with David on one side and her son on the other.

Life. Until this moment, she'd never realized just how wonderful it could be.

EPILOGUE

AN OVERCAST SKY pressed against the wall of windows to the right and clouded the waiting room even with the overhead fluorescent lighting. Two people seated in the corner of the waiting room sat huddled, whispering in earnest, frightened tones. The dark mood of the room hung heavy against his shoulders and magnified the dread in the pit of his stomach.

"How about I join you in a bit?" Skye murmured. She twined her fingers with his and nodded toward Gordon's hospital room. "He needs just you. The both of you have a lot to talk about, and right now I'll just get in the way. There'll be time enough. Ty's in school until 3:30."

David glanced toward the closed double doors but still hesitated. He'd been in to see his father previously, but on both occasions, he had been asleep or disoriented. Today though, the nurses insisted his father was lucid. The swelling inside his skull had subsided, and he'd pulled out of the chemically induced coma with all his faculties.

He couldn't delay seeing his father. When the hospital staff had put his dad into a coma, the idea of never having another opportunity to talk to him had torn at David's guts, but now that it was time for a face-to-face meeting, David hesitated. He'd always believed in his father, expected him to tell the truth, to have a code of conduct to look up to. The lies of David's childhood left him floundering, though, and questioning everything he'd ever believed of his dad.

Skye tugged at his hand, nodded encouragement, then gave him a quick, hard kiss. "Go."

Lips firming, David nodded, squeezed her hand briefly, then turned and opened the door with a cautious hand. Rain peppered the window as he stepped into the private room, and weak light filtered through the open blinds. A television in the corner of the room glowed against the bedding. His father lay propped against a pillow and raised bed with bright, crisp sheets folded over his lap. David was glad to see more color in his cheeks today.

His dad didn't acknowledge David. Instead, he lifted a remote control in one hand and flipped channels until he reached a football game.

"You're doing better today," David ventured as he stepped deeper into the room. He grabbed a plastic chair. Metal legs scraped against the linoleum as he pulled it to the head of the bed. He sat down on the cushioned bottom.

"Yes well, no thanks to the staff," he muttered over the roar of the fans as he glared at the television where a player slammed a football to the ground in the end zone. "I swear if they stick me with another needle, I'll sue them for abuse."

"You almost died, you know."

"That's what I've heard." His father's gray brows dipped, and he waved the remote in no particular direction. "Did you go after her?"

David blinked. "Skye?"

"Well, who else am I going to mean?"

David's lips tightened, struggling for patience as he folded his arms across his chest. His father never had been the best patient. "Why are you asking me this? And why are you so upset?"

His father glared at the television. "Because even though I knew you had to help Skye out, I never wanted you to go back..."

"To Boston," David finished for him. "You were afraid of what I'd find."

The skin around his knuckles tightened as he gripped the remote and continued to glare at the television. "Are she and the boy okay?"

David wasn't going to be dissuaded or ignored. They'd been dodging David's past for too many years. "Why didn't you tell me about October House, Miltronics and everything else? And turn off the television. I can't have a conversation with it blaring like that."

The muscles across his father's neck visibly constricted as he swallowed. He hit the off button of the remote, dousing the room into sudden silence. He then raised his chin and turned to face David. His eyes widened. "What the hell happened to your face?"

David shrugged a shoulder. "Long story. I'll tell you after you tell me about October House."

His father opened his mouth as if to argue, but then he sighed and appeared to sink deeper into the pillow and mattress. "Because I was afraid. Afraid of your reaction. Afraid that you'd walk away and never talk to me again."

David shook his head, unable to mistake the moisture in his father's eyes for anything other than tears. Now he finally understood. Fear had kept his father silent. "Dad. I'd never turn my back on you. You might not say it, but I've always known how much you care, and how you've tried to be the best father you could be."

Gordon grunted, looking as if he really wanted to believe David.

"Why are there no adoption papers? I think it's about time I deserve the answers from you, the real truth and not some fabricated story from someone who wasn't there."

His father ground his index finger and thumb against his brow and took in a ragged breath. After a moment, his hand fluttered to his lap. "There was a robbery at a local restaurant, and the thug had a gun to this man's head. I was off duty at the time, and I did what any cop would have done. I disabled the punk, and the victim—Ferguson was his name—felt he needed to repay me. We'd kept in touch since then. He worked as a scientist."

"Where at?"

"A pharmaceutical company called Miltronics, but he had connections to people at a foster home nearby called the October House. I don't know how or why for sure—but I always assumed it was because the company he worked for gave them thousands in donations. Hell, I wasn't going to ask questions to make waves. He'd learned I'd always wanted a child, you see, and crap, he felt he owed me after I saved his life. He wanted to return the favor."

"So he offered me up as that favor," David whispered, unable to keep the shock from his voice. Ferguson had given him away like a commodity. David couldn't understand how that could happen in the United States.

"Yeah, and don't judge me because—"

"I'm not. I couldn't." David wasn't going to tell him about the groundwater or the experiments or how he suspected that same water had affected many of the children's genetics, including himself. Maybe in time, but right now, he hated the idea of adding more guilt to his father's shoulders.

His father's lip trembled. "He offered me this dream after we'd given up on trying to have a biological child. I couldn't refuse. It was wrong. I knew that, but I didn't care. My God, do you have any idea how much I dreamed about having a son? The minute I saw you, I wanted you."

"But Mother? Did she want me?" David watched as a pulse throbbed along the side of his father's jaw. He waited but already knew the answer. The strange part was he didn't care anymore. Skye had shown him what real love entailed between a mother and son, unlike his own mother who would never be able to fathom that connection.

A tear tumbled from the corner of his father's eye. "I never wanted to disappoint you. You had it tough there with the divorce, your mom leaving, and I always felt that you blamed her." He cleared his throat, and he crumpled the bed sheet between his fingers. "But I was just as wrong when it came to our marriage and what I did to her. I expected more from her than she was willing to give. She didn't want to be hemmed in, tied down with a family. I pushed that on her and more. I made her keep quiet as to how we got you. She wanted none of that."

David shoved his chair closer and clasped his father's frail hand gently with both of his. "You're the best father I could have ever hoped for."

His father shook his head as if overcome with emotion.

"Don't doubt your ability, Dad. You did what you could with what you had. Hell, I couldn't have done better." David realized he'd almost missed his chance to tell his father how he felt. He'd been so damn stupid. You didn't take people for granted. "I love you, got that?"

"So you forgive me?"

David met the uncertainty in his father's eyes and realized for all the bravado his dad portrayed over the years, the man masked a soft, sensitive side and was just as fallible as David and anyone else. "Jesus, Dad. There's nothing to forgive. Everyone makes mistakes. God knows, I've done too many to count. Nothing's changed. I want you around for when I have my own family."

"Family? Since when do you start talking about family?" His father shook his head and relaxed against the pillow, his eyes growing rueful. "Oh, I get it now. It's this Skye. She's going to be part of this family along with the boy. Am I right?"

"Yeah."

"Like I've told you before, she's trouble."

"I know."

"And she'll twist you all up in knots. But it'll be worth it."

"I know."

His father arched a brow. "Are you up to that? Because right now I wouldn't think it with the way your face looks. Jesus, did someone hit you with a baseball bat?"

"No." Still holding his father's hand, David sank back in his chair, unable to stop the silly grin from spreading across his face even though the action tugged at his wounds. "And I'm up to anything with Skye. That is, if she'll have me."

"She will," Skye said softly from behind him. "She most definitely will."

Swiveling, David let go of his father's hand. At Skye's

unexpected arrival, he rose to his feet and met her gaze. Her eyes shimmered with unmistakable love. For him. Hell, he felt moved, humbled and for the briefest of moments terrified that he'd never live up to what she expected of him. Then he realized she'd taken him just the way he was.

Two steps and he reached her side, wrapping an arm around her waist, tugging her toward him. He dipped down and brushed his mouth over her uplifted lips. She tasted better than before. A tremor rolled through his body.

Gordon grunted. "How about you guys take that outside?"

David's chest expanded as he looked down at Skye's upturned face. "I'll do more than that."

Her gaze darkened. "Is that a promise?"

"Oh, yeah." His voice thickened and deepened with raw emotion. "You've made me change, made me want to be the man I thought I never could be. I promise you, here on out, I will be that man."

THANK YOU!

THANK YOU FOR reading all six episodes of *Identity* I hope you enjoyed it, and if you did, don't forget to leave a review.

For news on latest releases, contests and other news, you can sign up for my newsletter (http://eepurl.com/xmxQD). Also, if you feel like contacting me, you can always catch me on Facebook (https://www.facebook.com/authorhdthomson).

COMPLETE LIST OF TITLES

ROMANTIC SUSPENSE

SMOKE & MIRRORS SERIES

ANXIETY #1
DUPLICITY #2
IDENTITY #3

PARANORMAL ROMANCE

ONYX SERIES

A KISS BEFORE DYING

SHADES SERIES

DEADLY SHADES #1
SHADES OF HOLLY #2
KILLER SHADES #3
SHADE SERIES BOX SET #1-3

CONTEMPORARY ROMANCE

THE LONG ROAD HOME
PROTECTING KATIE

ABOUT THE AUTHOR

H. D. Thomson moved from Ontario, Canada as a teenager to the heat of Arizona where she graduated from the University of Arizona with a B.S. in Business Administration with a major in accounting. After working in the corporate world as an accountant, H. D. changed her focus to one of her passions-books. She owned and operated an online bookstore for several years and then started the company, Bella Media Management. The company specializes in web sites, video trailers, ebook conversion and promotional resources for authors and small businesses. When she is not heading her company, she is following her first love-writing. You can read more about her and her books at HDThomson.com.

What they're saying about H. D. Thomson's books:

"My applause to the author on an entertaining read."
— *Romance Novel Junkies*
"Author H.D. Thomson does a great job of keeping the reader guessing."
— *Paranormal Romance Party*
"Bravo H. D. Thomson!"
— *Writer's and Reader's of Distinct Fiction's Top Read.*
"Thomson's writing is spot on…"
— *Confessions of a Bibliophile.*